The point was, as much as she'd tried to resist his charms, she'd fallen for him, too. Glancing over at her, he wondered why. Not that he considered himself repulsive, but what was it that drew two people together? In the past, he'd written numerous columns about the principle of attraction and could discuss the role of pheromones, dopamine, and biological instincts, but none of this came close to explaining the way he felt about Lexie. Or presumably the way she felt about him. Nor could he explain it. All he knew was that they fit somehow and that he felt as if he'd spent most of his life traveling a path that led inexorably to her.

It was a romantic vision, even poetic, and Jeremy had never been prone to poetic thoughts. Maybe that was another reason he knew she was the one. Because she'd opened his heart and mind to new feelings and ideas. But whatever the reason, as he rode in the car with his lovely bride-to-be, he was content with whatever might happen to them in the future.

He reached for her hand.

Did it really matter, after all, that he was abandoning his home in New York City and putting his future career plans on hold to move to the middle of nowhere? Or that he was about to embark on a year in which he had to plan a wedding, set up their household, and prepare for a baby?

How hard could it be?

Nicholas
SPARKS

At First Sight

sphere

SPHERE

First published in the United States of America in 2005 by
Warner Books
First published in Great Britain in 2005 by
Time Warner Books
This paperback edition published in 2006 by
Time Warner Books
This edition published by Sphere in 2006

A CIP catalogue record for this book
is available from the British Library

ISBN-13: 978-0-7515-3657-7
ISBN-10: 0-7515-3657-1

Typeset in Sabon by Palimpsest Book Production Limited,
Polmont, Stirlingshire

Printed and bound in Great Britain by Clays Ltd, St Ives plc

Sphere
An imprint of
Little, Brown Book Group
Brettenham House
Lancaster Place
London WC2E 7EN

A Member of the Hachette Livre Group of Companies

www.littlebrown.co.uk

*This novel is dedicated to
Miles, Ryan, Landon, Lexie,
and Savannah*

Acknowledgments

·····❖·····

For this novel in particular, I have to thank my wife, Cathy. Not only was she the inspiration for Lexie's character, but she showed amazing patience while I was writing the novel. I wake every day knowing that I'm lucky to have married her.

My kids—Miles, Ryan, Landon, Lexie, and Savannah—who never let me forget that even though I'm an author, I'm first and foremost a father.

Theresa Park, my agent, deserves my thanks for letting me bend her ear whenever the mood strikes. But more than that, she always knows exactly what to say when the going gets tough. I'm fortunate to work with her.

Jamie Raab, my editor, has once again earned my undying gratitude. She's not only insightful, but charming, and I couldn't have written this book without her.

Larry Kirshbaum, the illustrious head of Time Warner Book Group, is heading to different pastures, but I can't let him leave without a final word of praise. I know it was a tough decision, but I'm sure you know what's best for you. It's been my honor and privilege to work with you, and I'd like to wish you the best of luck in whatever future awaits.

Maureen Egen, another "biggie" at Time Warner Book Group, has always been a delight. She's as sharp as they come, and I've loved every minute we've spent together.

Denise Di Novi, my patron saint in the world of Hollywood, is, and always has been, a blessing in my life.

Howie Sanders and Dave Park, my agents at UTA, always look out for me, and I'm thankful to work with them.

Jennifer Romanello and Edna Farley, my publicists, are both fabulous and gifted. They are treasures, and it's because of them that I'm still able to get out and meet my readers.

Lynn Harris and Mark Johnson, responsible for *The Notebook*, are, and always will be, my friends.

Scott Schwimer, my attorney, has not only a kind heart, but an extraordinary ability to make sure every contract is just as it should be.

Flag, who does my covers; Harvey-Jane Kowal, who handles some of the editing; and Shannon O'Keefe, Sharon Krassney, and Julie Barer also deserve my gratitude.

I'd like to thank a few more people. First, Dr. Rob Patterson, who talked to me about amniotic band syndrome. If I got anything right, it's because of him; attribute all errors to me. And to Todd Edwards, who salvaged this novel from the hard drive when my computer crashed, all I can say is that I'm grateful that he was around.

Finally, I'd like to thank Dave Simpson, Philemon Gray, Slade Trabucco, and the track athletes at New Bern High School and TRACK EC (the Junior Olympic program) whom I've had the pleasure to meet and coach. Thanks for giving me your best.

Prologue

···· ❖ ····

Is love at first sight truly possible?

Sitting in his living room, he turned the question over in his mind for what seemed to be the hundredth time. Outside, the winter sun had long since set. A grayish sheen of fog was visible through the window, and aside from the gentle tap of a branch against the glass, all was quiet. Yet he wasn't alone, and he pulled himself up from his spot on the couch and walked down the hall to peek in on her. As he stared, he thought about lying beside her, if only to have an excuse to shut his eyes. He could use the rest, but he didn't want to risk falling asleep just yet. Instead he watched as she shifted slightly, his mind drifting to the past. He thought again about the path that had brought them together. Who was he then? And who was he now? On the surface, those questions seemed easy. His name was Jeremy; he was forty-two years old, the son of an Irish father and Italian mother; and he wrote magazine articles for a living. Those were answers he would offer when asked. Though they were true, he

1

sometimes wondered whether he should add something more. Should he mention, for instance, that he'd traveled to North Carolina five years ago to investigate a mystery? That he fell in love there, not once but twice that year? Or that the beauty of those memories was intertwined with sadness and that even now he questioned which memories would endure?

He turned away from the bedroom doorway and returned to the living room. Though he didn't dwell on those events from long ago, he didn't avoid thinking about them, either. He could no more erase that chapter of his life than he could change his birthday. While there were times when he wished he could roll back the clock and erase all the sadness, he had a hunch that if he did so, the joy would be diminished as well. And that was something he couldn't contemplate.

It was in the darkest hours of the night that he most often found himself remembering his night with Lexie in the cemetery, the night he'd seen the ghostly lights that he'd come down from New York to investigate. It was then, however, that he'd realized for the first time how much Lexie meant to him. As they had waited in the blackness of the cemetery, Lexie had told him a story about herself. She'd been orphaned as a young child, she explained. Jeremy had already known that, but what he didn't know was that she'd begun having nightmares a few years after the deaths of her parents. Terrible, recurring nightmares in which she witnessed the death of her parents. Her grandmother Doris, not knowing what else to do, finally brought her to the cemetery to see the mysterious lights. To a young child, the lights were miraculous, heavenly, and Lexie instantly recognized them as the ghosts of her parents. It was, somehow, what she'd needed to believe, and those nightmares never plagued her again.

Jeremy had been touched by her story, moved by her loss and the power of innocent beliefs. But later that night, after he too had seen the lights, he'd asked Lexie what she thought they really were. She'd leaned forward then and whispered, "It was my parents. They probably wanted to meet you."

It was then that he knew he wanted to take her in his arms. He'd long since pinpointed that as the moment he first fell in love with her, and he'd never stopped loving her.

Outside, the February wind picked up again. Beyond the murky darkness, he could see nothing, and he lay down on the couch with a weary sigh, feeling the pull of that year draw him backward in time. He could have forced the images away, but as he stared at the ceiling, he let them come. He always let them come.

This, he remembered, is what happened next.

One

···· ❖ ····

"See, it's simple," Alvin said. "First, you meet a nice girl, and then you date for a while to make sure you share the same values. See if you two are compatible in the big, 'this is our life and we're in it together' decisions. You know, talk about which family you're going to visit on the holidays, whether you want to live in a house or an apartment, whether to get a dog or a cat, who gets to use the shower first in the morning, while there's still plenty of hot water. If you two are still pretty much in agreement, *then* you get married. Are you following me here?"

"I'm following you," Jeremy said.

Jeremy Marsh and Alvin Bernstein were standing in Jeremy's Upper West Side apartment on a cool Saturday afternoon in February. They'd been packing for hours, and boxes were strewn everywhere. Some of the boxes were already filled and had been stacked near the door, ready for the moving van; others were in various stages of completion. All in all, it looked as if a Tasmanian devil had burst through the door, had himself a party, then left once there was nothing else to be destroyed. Jeremy couldn't believe how much junk he'd accumulated over the years, a fact that his fiancée, Lexie Darnell, had been pointing out all morning. Twenty minutes ago, after throwing up her hands in frustration, Lexie had gone to have lunch with Jeremy's mother, leaving Jeremy and Alvin alone for the first time.

"So what on earth do you think you're doing?" Alvin prodded.

"Just what you said."

"No, you're not. You're messing up the order. You're going straight to the big 'I do' before you even figured out whether you two are right for each other. You barely know Lexie."

Jeremy shoved another drawer's worth of clothing into a box, wishing Alvin would change the subject. "I know her."

Alvin began shuffling through a few papers on Jeremy's desk, then shoved the stack into the same box Jeremy was loading. As Jeremy's best friend, he felt free to speak his mind.

"I'm just trying to be honest here, and you should know that I'm saying what everyone else in your family has been thinking in the past few weeks. The point is, you don't know her well enough to move down there, let alone marry her. You only spent a week with her. This isn't like you and Maria," he added, referring to Jeremy's ex. "Remember, I knew Maria, too, a whole lot better than you know Lexie, but I still never felt as if I knew her well enough to marry her."

Jeremy removed the pages and put them back

6

on his desk, recalling that Alvin had known Maria even before he had and still remained friends with her. "So?"

"So? What if I was doing this? What if I came to you and said I met this great lady, so I'm giving up my career, abandoning my friends and family, and moving down south so I can marry her? Like that gal . . . what's her name . . . Rachel?"

Rachel worked at Lexie's grandmother's restaurant, and Alvin had hit on her during his short visit to Boone Creek, going so far as to invite her to New York.

"I'd say that I was happy for you."

"Puh-lease. Don't you remember what you said when I was thinking about marrying Eva?"

"I remember. But this is different."

"Oh yeah, I get it. Because you're more mature than me."

"That and the fact that Eva wasn't exactly the marrying type."

This was true, Alvin admitted. While Lexie was a small-town librarian in the rural South, someone hoping to settle down, Eva was a tattoo artist in Jersey City. She was the woman who'd done most of the tattoos on Alvin's arms, in addition to most of the piercings in Alvin's ears, making Alvin look as if he'd just been released from prison. None of which had bothered Alvin; it was the live-in boyfriend that she'd neglected to tell him about that finally doomed their relationship.

"Even Maria thinks this is crazy."

"You told her?"

"Of course I told her. We talk about everything."

"I'm glad you're so close to my ex-wife. But it's none of her business. Or yours."

"I'm just trying to talk some sense into you. This is happening too fast. You don't know Lexie."

"Why do you keep saying that?"

"I'm going to keep saying it until you finally admit that you two are basically strangers."

Alvin, like Jeremy's five older brothers, had never learned how to drop a subject. The man was like a dog with a bone, Jeremy decided.

"She's not a stranger."

"No? Then what's her middle name?"

"What?"

"You heard me. Tell me Lexie's middle name."

Jeremy blinked. "What's that got to do with anything?"

"Nothing. But if you're going to marry her, don't you think you should be able to answer the question?"

Jeremy opened his mouth to answer, then realized he didn't know. Lexie had never told him, nor had he ever asked. Alvin, as if sensing that he was finally getting through to his delusional friend, pressed on.

"Okay, how about these basics? What was her major in college? Who were her friends in college? What's her favorite color? Does she like white or whole-wheat bread? What's her favorite movie or television show? Who's her favorite author? Do you even know how old she is?"

"She's in her thirties," Jeremy offered.

"In her thirties? I could have told you that."

"I'm pretty sure she's thirty-one."

"You're 'pretty sure'? Can you even hear how

8

ridiculous you sound? You can't marry someone if you don't even know how old she is."

Jeremy opened another drawer and emptied it into another box, knowing that Alvin had a point but not wanting to admit it. Instead, he drew a long breath.

"I thought you were happy I finally found someone," he said.

"I am happy for you. But I didn't think you were actually going to move from New York and decide to marry her. I thought you were kidding about that. You know I think she's a great lady. She really is, and if you're still this serious about her in a year or two, I'll drag you down the aisle myself. You're just rushing things, and there's no reason to."

Jeremy turned toward the window; beyond the glass he saw gray, soot-covered bricks framing the functional, rectangular windows of a neighboring building. Shadowed images swept past: a lady talking on the phone; a man wrapped in a towel headed for the bathroom; another woman ironing as she watched television. In all the time he'd lived here, he'd never said so much as hello to any of them.

"She's pregnant," he finally said.

For a moment, Alvin thought he hadn't heard correctly. It was only when he saw the expression on his friend's face that he realized Jeremy wasn't kidding.

"She's pregnant?"

"It's a girl."

Alvin plopped down on the bed as if his legs had suddenly given out. "Why didn't you tell me?"

Jeremy shrugged. "She asked me not to tell anyone yet. So keep it a secret, will you?"

"Yeah," Alvin said, sounding dazed. "Sure."

"And one more thing."

Alvin looked up.

Jeremy reached for his shoulder. "I'd like you to be my best man."

How had it happened?

Strolling with Lexie as she explored FAO Schwarz the next day, he still had trouble answering that question. Not the pregnancy part; that was a night he'd probably remember forever. Despite the brave front he'd put on for Alvin, it sometimes felt as if he were about to play a part in a crowd-pleasing romantic comedy, one in which anything was possible and nothing was certain until the final credits rolled.

What happened to him, after all, didn't usually happen. In fact, it almost never happened. Who travels to a small town to write an article for *Scientific American*, meets a small-town librarian, and falls head over heels in just a few days? Who decides to leave behind a chance at morning television and life in New York City to move to Boone Creek, North Carolina, a town that was nothing more than a hiccup on the map?

So many questions these days.

Not that he was second-guessing himself about what he was about to do. In fact, as he watched Lexie sorting through stacks of GI Joes and Barbies—she wanted to surprise his many nieces and nephews with gifts in the hope of making a good impression—he felt more certain than ever about his decision. He smiled, already visualizing the kind of life he was about to settle into. Quiet dinners, romantic walks, giggling and cuddling in front of the television. Good stuff, stuff that made life worthwhile. He wasn't naive enough to believe they'd never have an argument or struggle, but he had no doubt they would navigate those rough waters successfully, realizing in the end that they were perfectly matched. In the big picture, life would be wonderful.

But as Lexie nudged past him, lost in concentration, Jeremy found himself staring at another couple standing by a pile of stuffed animals. Actually, the couple was impossible not to notice. They were in their early thirties and sharply dressed; he had the air of an investment banker or an attorney, while his wife came across like someone who spent every afternoon at Bloomingdale's. They were loaded with half a dozen bags from half a dozen different stores. The diamond on her finger was the size of a marble—far larger than the engagement ring he'd just purchased for Lexie. As Jeremy watched, he had no doubt that they usually brought along a nanny on an outing like this, simply because they seemed completely bewildered as to what they were supposed to do.

The baby in the stroller was screaming, the kind of piercing wail that peeled wallpaper and made others in the store stop in their tracks. At exactly the same time, her older brother—maybe four or so—was screaming even more loudly and suddenly threw himself down on the floor. The parents wore the panicked, shell-shocked expressions of soldiers under fire, and it was impossible not to notice the bags under their eyes and the translucent pallor of their faces. Despite the impeccable facade, they were plainly at the end of their rope. The mother finally worked the baby free from the stroller and held the infant against her as the husband leaned toward her, patting the baby's back.

"Don't you think I'm trying to quiet her down?" she barked. "Deal with Elliot!"

Chastised, the man bent down toward his son, who was kicking and pounding the floor, throwing the mother of all temper tantrums.

"Stop that screaming right now!" the husband said sternly, shaking his finger.

Oh yeah, Jeremy thought. Like that's going to do it.

Elliot, meanwhile, was turning purple as he writhed on the floor.

By that point, even Lexie had stopped browsing and turned her attention to the couple. It was, Jeremy thought, sort of like staring at a woman who mowed her lawn in her bikini, the kind of spectacle impossible to ignore. The baby screamed, Elliot screamed, the wife screamed at the father to do something, the father screamed back that he was trying.

A crowd had gathered, ringing the happy family. The women seemed to be watching them with a mixture of thankfulness and pity: thankful that it wasn't happening to them, but knowing—most likely from experience—exactly what the young couple was going through. The men, on the other hand, seemed to want nothing more than to get as far away from the noise as possible.

Elliot banged his head on the floor and began to scream even louder.

"Let's just go!" the mother finally snapped.

"Don't you think that's what I'm trying to do?" the father barked.

"Pick him up."

"I'm trying!" he shouted in exasperation.

Elliot wanted no part of his father. As his father finally grabbed him, Elliot wiggled like an angry snake. His head flailed from side to side, and his legs never stopped moving. Beads of sweat began to form on his father's forehead, and he was grimacing with the effort. Elliot, on the other hand, seemed to be getting larger, a mini Hulk expanding with rage.

Somehow the parents were able to get moving, weighed down with shopping bags, pushing the stroller, and managing to keep hold of both children. The crowd parted as if Moses were approaching the Red Sea, and the family finally vanished from sight, the slowly fading wails the only evidence they'd ever been there.

The crowd began to disperse. Jeremy and Lexie, however, stood frozen in place.

"Those poor people," said Jeremy, suddenly wondering if this was what his life would be like in a couple of years.

"You're telling me," Lexie agreed, as if fearful of the same thing.

Jeremy continued to stare, listening as the wailing finally ceased. The family must have left the store.

"Our child will never throw a tantrum like that," Jeremy announced.

"Never." Consciously or subconsciously, Lexie had placed her hand on her belly. "That definitely wasn't normal."

"And the parents didn't seem to have any idea what they were doing," Jeremy said. "Did you see him trying to talk to his son? Like he was in the boardroom?"

"Ridiculous." Lexie nodded. "And the way they were snapping at each other? Kids can sense the tension. No wonder the parents couldn't control them."

"It's like they had no idea what to do."

"I don't think they did."

"How could they not?"

"Maybe they're just too caught up in their own lives to take enough time with their children."

Jeremy, still frozen in place, watched the last of the crowd vanish. "It definitely wasn't normal," he offered again.

"That's exactly what I was thinking."

Okay, so they were deluding themselves. Deep down, Jeremy knew it, Lexie knew it, but it was easier to pretend that they would never be confronted with a situation like the one they'd just witnessed. Because they were going to be more prepared. More dedicated. Kinder and more patient. More loving.

And the child . . . well, she would thrive in the environment he and Lexie would create. There was no doubt about that. As an infant, she'd sleep through the night; as a toddler, she would delight with her early vocabulary and above average motor skills. She would maneuver the minefields of adolescence with aplomb, stay away from drugs, and frown on R-rated movies. By the time she left home, she would be polite and well mannered, she would have received high enough grades to be accepted to Harvard, become an all-American in swimming, and still would have found enough time during the summers to volunteer for Habitat for Humanity.

Jeremy clung to the fantasy until his shoulders slumped. Despite having zero experience in the parenting department, he knew it couldn't be that easy. Besides, he was getting way ahead of himself.

An hour later, they were sitting in the back of a cab, stuck in traffic, on the way to Queens. Lexie was thumbing through a recently purchased copy of *What to Expect When You're Expecting* as Jeremy watched the world beyond the windows. It was their last night in New York—he'd brought Lexie up to meet his family—and his parents were planning a small get-together at their home in Queens. Small, of course, was a relative term; with five brothers and their wives and nineteen nieces and nephews, the house would be packed, as it often was. Even though Jeremy was looking forward to it, he couldn't quite get his mind off the couple they'd just seen. They'd seemed so . . . normal. Aside from the exhaustion, that is. He wondered whether he and Lexie would end up that way or whether they'd somehow be spared.

Maybe Alvin had been right. Partially, anyway. Though he adored Lexie—and he was sure he did, or he wouldn't have proposed—he couldn't claim to really know her. They simply hadn't had time for that, and the more he thought about it, the more he believed that it would have been nice for him and Lexie to have had a chance to be a regular couple for a while. He'd been married before, and he knew it took time to learn how to live with another person. To get used to the quirks, so to speak. Everyone had them, but until you really knew someone, they tended to be hidden. He wondered what Lexie's were. For instance, what if she slept with one of those green masks that were supposed to keep wrinkles at bay? Would he really be happy waking up and seeing that every morning?

"What are you thinking about?" Lexie asked.

"Huh?"

"I asked what you're thinking about. You have a funny expression on your face."

"It's nothing."

She stared at him. "Big nothing, or nothing-nothing?"

He turned to face her, frowning. "What's your middle name?"

Over the next few minutes, Jeremy went through the series of questions Alvin had proposed and learned the following: Her middle name was Marin; she had majored in English; her best friend in college was named Susan; purple was her favorite color; she preferred whole wheat; she liked watching *Trading Spaces*; she thought Jane Austen was fabulous; and she would, in fact, turn thirty-two on September 13.

So there.

He leaned back in his seat, satisfied, as Lexie

continued to thumb through the book. She wasn't actually reading it, he figured, just skimming passages here and there in hopes of getting some sort of head start. He wondered if she had done something similar whenever she had to study in college.

As Alvin had implied, there really was a lot about her that he didn't know. But at the same time, there was a great deal he did know. An only child, she'd been raised in Boone Creek, North Carolina. Her parents had been killed in an automobile accident when she was young, and she had been raised by her maternal grandparents, Doris and . . . and . . . He decided he'd have to ask about that. Anyway, she'd gone to college at the University of North Carolina in Chapel Hill, been in love with a guy named Avery, and had actually lived in New York City for a year, where she'd interned at the NYU library. Avery ended up cheating on her, and she went back home and became the head librarian in Boone Creek, as her mother had been before she'd passed away. Some time later, she'd fallen for someone she referred to vaguely as Mr. Renaissance, but he'd left town without looking back. Since then she'd led a quiet life, dating the local deputy sheriff now and then, until Jeremy came along. And oh yeah: Doris—who owned a restaurant in Boone Creek—also claimed to have psychic powers, including the ability to predict the sex of babies, which was how Lexie knew their baby would be a girl.

All of which, he admitted, everyone in Boone Creek also knew. But did they also know that she tucked her hair behind her ears whenever she got nervous? Or that she was a wonderful cook? Or that when she needed a break, she liked to retreat to a cottage near the Cape Hatteras Lighthouse, where her parents had been married? Or that in addition to being both intelligent and beautiful, with violet eyes, a slightly exotic, oval face, and dark hair, she had seen right through his ham-fisted attempts to charm her into the bedroom? He liked the fact that Lexie didn't let him get away with anything, spoke her mind, and stood up to him when she thought he was in error. Somehow, she was able to do those things while still projecting a charm and femininity that was underscored by a sultry southern accent. Add in the fact that she was downright stunning in tight jeans, and Jeremy had fallen head over heels.

And as for him? What could she say she knew about Jeremy? Most of the basics, he thought. That he'd grown up in Queens as the youngest of six in an Irish-Italian family and that he'd once intended to become a professor of mathematics but realized he had a knack for writing and ended up becoming a columnist for *Scientific American*, where he often debunked the allegedly supernatural. That he'd been married years earlier to a woman named Maria, who eventually left him after they'd made numerous trips to a fertility clinic and were finally told by a doctor that Jeremy was medically unable to father a child. That he'd spent too many years afterward trolling the bars and dating countless women, trying to avoid serious relationships, as if subconsciously knowing he couldn't be a good husband. That at the age of thirty-seven, he'd gone

18

to Boone Creek to investigate the regular appearance of ghostly lights in the town cemetery in the hope of landing a guest commentator gig on *Good Morning America* but found that he spent most of his time thinking about Lexie. They'd spent four enchanting days together followed by a heated argument, and though he'd headed back to New York, he'd realized that he couldn't imagine a life without her and had returned to prove it to her. In exchange, she had placed his hand on her belly, and he finally became a true believer—at least when it came to the miracle of pregnancy and a chance at fatherhood, something he'd never considered possible.

He smiled, thinking it was a pretty good story. Maybe even good enough for a novel.

The point was, as much as she'd tried to resist his charms, she'd fallen for him, too. Glancing over at her, he wondered why. Not that he considered himself repulsive, but what was it that drew two people together? In the past, he'd written numerous columns about the principle of attraction and could discuss the role of pheromones, dopamine, and biological instincts, but none of this came close to explaining the way he felt about Lexie. Or presumably the way she felt about him. Nor could he explain it. All he knew was that they fit somehow and that he felt as if he'd spent most of his life traveling a path that led inexorably to her.

It was a romantic vision, even poetic, and Jeremy had never been prone to poetic thoughts. Maybe that was another reason he knew she was the one. Because she'd opened his heart and mind to new feelings and ideas. But whatever the reason, as he rode in the car with his lovely bride-to-be, he was content with whatever might happen to them in the future.

He reached for her hand.

Did it really matter, after all, that he was abandoning his home in New York City and putting his future career plans on hold to move to the middle of nowhere? Or that he was about to embark on a year in which he had to plan a wedding, set up their household, and prepare for a baby?

How hard could it be?

Two

..... ❖ .....

He'd proposed at the top of the Empire State Building on Valentine's Day.

He knew it was a cliché, but weren't all proposals something of a cliché? There were, after all, only so many ways he could do it. He could do it sitting, standing, kneeling, or lying down. He could be either eating or not eating, at home or someplace else, with or without candles, wine, sunrises, sunsets, or anything that might strike someone as vaguely romantic. Somewhere, sometime, Jeremy knew that some guy had already done it all, so there wasn't much sense in worrying whether she would be disappointed. He knew, of course, that some men went all out—skywriting, billboards, the ring found during a romantic scavenger hunt. But he was pretty sure that Lexie wasn't the type to require total originality. Besides, the view of Manhattan was breathtaking, and as long as he remembered to hit the highlights—why he wanted to spend the rest of his life with her, the presentation of the ring, popping the question— Jeremy figured he had it pretty much covered.

21

It wasn't as if it were a total surprise, after all. They hadn't specifically talked about it beforehand, but the fact that he was moving to Boone Creek, coupled with various bits of *we*-type conversation in the last few weeks, had left no doubt that it was coming. As in, *We* should go shopping for a bassinet to put by our bed, or *We* should visit your parents. Since Jeremy hadn't contradicted those statements, a case could be made that Lexie had already sort of proposed to him.

Still, even if it hadn't come as a complete surprise, Lexie was obviously thrilled. Her first instinct, after wrapping her arms around him and kissing him, was to call Doris to let her know the news, a conversation that lasted twenty minutes. He supposed he should have expected that, not that he minded. Despite his outer calm, the fact that she'd actually agreed to spend the rest of her life with him was overwhelming.

Now, nearly a week later, they were in a cab on the way to his parents' house, and he noted the ring on her finger. Being engaged, as opposed to dating, was the *Next Big Step*, one that most men, Jeremy included, rather enjoyed. He could, for instance, do certain things with Lexie that were pretty much off-limits to anyone else in the world. Like kissing. For example, he could lean across the backseat right now and kiss her. More than likely she wouldn't be offended. She'd probably even be pleased. Try that with a stranger and see how far it got you, Jeremy thought. The whole concept left him feeling rather good about what he'd done.

Lexie, on the other hand, was glancing out the window and appeared troubled.

"What's wrong?" he asked.

"What if they don't like me?"

"They're going to love you. What's not to love? And besides, you had a good lunch with my mom, right? You said you two really hit it off."

"I know," she said, sounding unconvinced.

"Then what's the problem?"

"What if they think I'm taking you away?" she asked. "What if your mom was just being nice, but deep down she feels resentment?"

"She doesn't," he said. "And I'm telling you not to worry so much. For one thing, you're not taking me away. I'm leaving New York because I'd rather be with you, and they know that. Trust me, they're happy about this. My mom's been hounding me to get remarried for years."

She pursed her lips, thinking about it. "Okay," she said. "But I still don't want them to know I'm pregnant yet."

"Why not?"

"They'll get the wrong impression."

"You know they're going to find out anyway."

"I know, but it doesn't have to be tonight, does it? Let them get to know me first. Give them a chance to come to grips with the fact that we're getting married. That's enough shock for one night. We'll deal with the rest of it later."

"Sure," he said. "Whatever you want." He leaned back in the seat. "But just so you know, even if it does slip out, you won't have to worry."

She blinked. "How would it slip out? Don't tell me that you've already told them."

Jeremy shook his head. "No, of course not. I might have mentioned it to Alvin."

"You told Alvin?" she asked, her face paling.

"Sorry. It just slipped out. But don't worry, he won't tell anyone."

She hesitated before finally nodding. "Okay."

"It won't happen again," Jeremy said, reaching for her hand. "And there's no reason to be nervous."

She forced a smile. "Easy for you to say."

Lexie turned toward the window again. As if she hadn't already been nervous enough, now she had to deal with this, too. Was it really that hard to keep a secret?

She knew Jeremy didn't mean any harm, and that Alvin would be discreet, but that wasn't the point. The point was that Jeremy didn't quite understand how his family might view this sort of news. She was sure they were very reasonable people—his mother seemed nice enough—and she doubted that they would accuse her of being a harlot, but still, just the fact that they were getting married so quickly was going to raise eyebrows. Of that, she had no doubt. All she had to do was see it from their perspective. Six weeks ago, she and Jeremy had never even met, and—after the whirlwind of all whirlwinds—they were now officially engaged. That was shocking enough.

But if they found out she was pregnant?

Well, now they'd *understand*. They'd make the assumption that Jeremy was marrying her simply for that reason. Instead of believing Jeremy when he said that he loved her, they'd simply nod and say, "That's nice." But as soon as Jeremy and Lexie left, you could bet they'd huddle to discuss the matter. They were family, a close, old-fashioned family that got together a couple of times a month. Hadn't he been telling her that? She wasn't naive. And what did family talk about? Family! Joys, tragedies, disappointments, successes . . . close families shared all of it. But if Jeremy slipped again, she knew what would happen. Instead of the engagement, they would talk about her pregnancy, if only to wonder aloud whether Jeremy really knew what he was doing. Or worse, that maybe she'd trapped him somehow.

She could be wrong, of course. Maybe they'd all be delighted. Maybe they'd find the whole situation completely reasonable. Maybe they'd believe the engagement and the pregnancy had nothing to do with each other, because that was the truth. And maybe she'd just flap her arms and fly all the way home.

She didn't want in-law problems. Granted, as a general rule there was nothing you could do about them, but she wasn't eager to get off on the wrong foot.

Besides, as much as she didn't want to admit it, if she were Jeremy's family, she'd be skeptical, too. Marriage was a big step for any couple, let alone a couple that barely knew each other. Though Jeremy's mother hadn't put her on the hot seat, Lexie could feel her sizing her up as they got to know each other, as any good mother would do. Lexie had been on her best behavior, and at the end, his mother had hugged and kissed her good-bye.

A good sign, Lexie admitted. Or a good start,

anyway. It would take time for the family to fully accept her into the clan. Unlike the rest of the daughters-in-law, Lexie wouldn't be around on the weekends, and she'd probably be on a probation of sorts, until time showed Jeremy hadn't made a mistake. Probably at least a year or two, maybe more. She supposed she could speed up the process with regular letters and phone calls . . .

Note to self, she thought. *Buy stationery.*

If she was completely honest, though, even she was a little shocked at how fast things were moving. Was he really in love? Was she? She'd asked herself those questions a dozen times a day over the last couple of weeks and always came up with the same answers. Yes, she was pregnant, and yes, it was his child, but she wouldn't have agreed to marry him unless she believed they would be happy together.

And they would be happy. Wouldn't they?

She wondered whether Jeremy ever questioned how fast this all seemed to be happening. Probably, she decided. It was impossible not to. But he seemed so much more relaxed about it than she did, and she wondered why. Maybe it was because he'd been married once before, or maybe it was because he'd been the pursuer during his week in Boone Creek. But whatever the reason, he'd always seemed more certain about their relationship than she was, which was odd, since he was the one who called himself a skeptic.

She glanced at him, noting the dark hair and dimple, liking what she saw. Remembering that she'd found him attractive the first time she'd ever seen him. What had Doris said about him after meeting

26

him the first time? *He's not what you think he is.*

Well, she thought, she was going to find out, wasn't she?

They were the last to arrive at the house. Lexie was still nervous as she approached the door and stopped on the front steps.

"They're going to love you," he reassured her. "Trust me."

"Stay close, okay?"

"Where else would I be?"

It wasn't nearly as bad as Lexie had feared it would be. In fact, she seemed to be more than holding her own, so despite his earlier promise to stay close, Jeremy found himself standing on the back porch instead, bouncing from one foot to the other with arms crossed in an attempt to ward off the chill in the air, watching his father hover over the barbecue. The man loved to barbecue; the weather outside never entered his thinking. As a child, Jeremy had actually seen him shovel snow off the barbecue and disappear into a blizzard, only to reappear inside half an hour later with a platter of steaks and a layer of ice where his eyebrows were supposed to be.

Though Jeremy would rather have been inside, his mother had told him to keep his father company, which was her way of telling him to make sure his father was doing okay. He'd had a heart attack a couple of years ago, and though he swore he never got cold, she worried about him. She would have done it herself, but with thirty-five people wedged into a small brownstone, the place was a madhouse. She had four pots going on the stove, his brothers took up every seat in the living room, and the nephews and nieces were continually being shooed from the living room back to the basement. Glancing through the window, he made sure his fiancée was still doing fine.

Fiancée. There was something odd about that word, he decided. Not that it was odd to think of having one, but rather how it sounded coming from the lips of various sisters-in-law, since they must have said the word at least a hundred times already. Immediately upon entering, before Lexie had even removed her jacket, Sophia and Anna had come rushing toward them, peppering practically every statement with the word.

"It's about time we get to finally meet your *fiancée*!"

"So what have you and your *fiancée* been doing?"

"Don't you think you should get your *fiancée* something to drink?"'

His brothers, on the other hand, hung back and avoided the word completely.

"So you and Lexie, huh?"

"Has Lexie enjoyed her trip so far?"

"Fill me in on how you and Lexie met."

It must be a woman thing, Jeremy decided, since he, like his brothers, had yet to use the word. He wondered whether he could do a column about it, before deciding his editor would probably pass, claiming that it wasn't quite serious enough for *Scientific American*. This from a guy who loved articles about UFOs and Bigfoot. Even though he'd agreed to allow Jeremy to continue writing

28

his columns for the magazine from Boone Creek, Jeremy wouldn't miss him.

Jeremy rubbed his arms as his father flipped one of the steaks. His nose and ears had turned red in the cold. "Hand me that plate, would you? Your mom left it on the rail over there. The hot dogs are just about done."

Jeremy grabbed the plate and returned to his father's side. "You know it's pretty cold out here, right?"

"This? It's nothing. Besides, the coals keep me warm."

His father, one of the last of a dying breed, still used charcoal. For Christmas one year, Jeremy had purchased a gas grill, but it ended up gathering dust in the garage until his brother Tom finally asked if he could have it.

His father started piling hot dogs on the plate. "I haven't had the chance to talk to her much, but Lexie seems like a nice young lady."

"She is, Pop."

"Ah, well, you deserve it. I never did like Maria very much," he said. "Right from the get-go, she struck me as wrong somehow."

"You should have told me."

"Nah. You wouldn't have listened. You always knew everything, remember?"

"How did Mom like Lexie? Yesterday at lunch?"

"She liked her. Thought she would be able to keep you in line."

"And that's a good thing?"

"Coming from your mother? That's about the best you're gonna get."

Jeremy smiled. "Do you have any advice?"

His father set aside the plate before finally shaking his head. "Nah. You don't need any advice. You're all grown up. You make your own decisions now. And besides, there's not much I could tell you. I've been married for almost fifty years, and there are times when I still don't have any idea what makes your mother tick."

"That's comforting."

"You get used to it." He cleared his throat. "Hey, maybe there is one thing I could tell you."

"What's that?"

"Two things, actually. Number one, don't take it personally if she gets angry. We all get angry, so don't let it get to you."

"And number two?"

"Call your mother. A lot. She's been crying every day since she found out you were moving. And don't pick up one of those southern accents, either. She wouldn't tell you this, but she had trouble understanding Lexie sometimes."

Jeremy laughed. "I promise."

"It wasn't so bad, was it?" Jeremy asked.

Hours later, they were on the way back to the Plaza. With his apartment in disarray, Jeremy had decided to splurge on a hotel room their last night in town.

"It was wonderful. You've got a special family. I can see why you didn't want to move away."

"I'll still see them quite a bit, whenever I have to check in at the magazine."

She nodded. As they headed into the city, she stared

30

at the skyscrapers and the traffic, marveling at how large and busy everything seemed. Though she'd lived in New York City before, she'd forgotten the crowds, the massive height of the buildings, the noise. So different from where they would live now, another world entirely. The entire population of Boone Creek was probably less than the number of people on a single city block.

"Are you going to miss the city?"

He gazed out the window before answering. "A little," he admitted. "But everything I've ever wanted is down south."

And after one final, wonderful night at the Plaza, they began their new life.

Three

..... ❖ .....

The following morning, as prisms of light began poking through the opening between the drapes, Jeremy's eyes fluttered open. Lexie was asleep on her back with her dark hair splayed over the pillow. Beyond the window, he could hear the faint sounds of the early-morning traffic in New York: the honking of horns and the rise and fall of truck engines as they rolled down Fifth Avenue.

In his opinion, he shouldn't have been able to hear anything. Lord knows it had cost him a small fortune to stay in this particular suite, and he had assumed it would have soundproof windows. Still, he wasn't complaining. Lexie had loved everything about the place: the high ceilings and classic wainscoting, the formality of the server who had brought them chocolate-covered strawberries and the apple cider they'd substituted for champagne, the heavy robe and comfortable slippers, the softness of the bed. All of it.

Touching her hair gently, he thought her beautiful as she lay beside him, and he couldn't help but breathe a sigh of relief when he realized she wasn't wearing the ugly green mask he'd briefly imagined the day before. Even better, she didn't wear curlers or ugly pajamas, either, nor did she dillydally for half an hour in the bathroom as some women were prone to do. Before crawling into bed, she'd only washed her face and run a brush through her hair, and then she was snuggling beside him, just the way he liked it.

See, he did know her, despite what Alvin said. Granted, not everything yet, but there was time for that. He'd learn about her, and she'd learn about him, and little by little they'd settle into their own routine. Oh, he knew there were going to be some surprises—there always were—but it went with the territory of being a couple. In time, she'd get to know the real Jeremy, the Jeremy unburdened by the endless need to impress. Around her, he could be himself, someone who occasionally lounged around in sweats or ate Doritos in front of the television.

He clasped his hands behind his head, feeling suddenly content. She would love the *real* him.

Wouldn't she?

He frowned, wondering suddenly if she knew what she was getting into. Knowing the real him might not be such a good idea, he realized. Not that he viewed himself as bad or unworthy, but like everyone, he had . . . *quirks* that might take her some time to get used to. She was going to learn, for instance, that he always left the seat on the toilet up. He always had and always would, but what if it was a problem for her? It was a big problem for one of his ex-girlfriends, he remembered. And what

33

was she going to think about the fact that, as a general rule, he was far more concerned with how the Knicks were doing than anything having to do with the latest drought in Africa? Or that—as long as it seemed okay—he'd sometimes been known to eat food that had fallen on the floor? That was the *real* him, but what if she wasn't too happy about it? What if she considered them not quirks, but actual flaws in his character? And what about—

"What are you thinking?" Lexie's voice interrupted his thoughts. "You look like you just swallowed a bug."

He noticed that she was staring at him.

"I'm not perfect, you know."

"What are you talking about?"

"I'm just telling you right up front that I've got flaws."

She seemed amused. "Really? And I thought you could walk on water."

"I'm serious. I just think you should know what you're getting into before we get married."

"In case I want to back out?"

"Exactly. I have quirks."

"Like what?"

He thought about it, deciding it might be best if he started small.

"I leave the water faucet running when I brush my teeth. I don't know why, I just do. I don't know if I can change."

Trying to maintain a serious expression, she nodded. "I think I can handle that."

"And sometimes—just so you know—I stand in front of the refrigerator with the door open for a long time while I try to figure out what I want to eat. I know I'm letting the cold air out, but I can't help it. It's who I am."

She nodded again, still amused. "I understand. Anything else?"

He shrugged. "I don't eat broken cookies. If all that's left in the bag are broken cookies, I just throw the bag out. I know it's a waste, but I've always been that way. They taste different."

"Mmm," she said. "It'll be tough, but I suppose I can live with that."

He pursed his lips, wondering whether he should mention the toilet bowl seat. Knowing it was a hot-button issue with some women, he decided to pass for the time being.

"Are you okay with all this?"

"I suppose I have to be."

"Really?"

"Positive."

"What if I told you I cut my toenails in bed?"

"Don't push it, buster."

He grinned, pulling her closer. "You love me even if I'm not perfect?"

"Of course I do."

Amazing, he thought.

As Lexie and Jeremy approached Boone Creek, just as the first stars were appearing in the sky, Jeremy's first thought was that the place hadn't changed a bit. Not that he'd expected it to; as far as he could tell, things around here hadn't changed in the last hundred years. Or maybe three hundred, for that matter. Since they'd left the airport in Raleigh, the view on either side of the highway had been one long version of the movie *Groundhog Day*. Ramshackle farmhouses, barren fields, decaying tobacco barns, stands of trees . . . mile after mile. Sure, they'd passed through the occasional town, but even those had been indistinguishable, unless someone actually knew the difference between Hardee's and Bojangles.

But hey, with Lexie beside him, the drive hadn't been half-bad. She'd been in a good mood all day, and as they neared her home—change that, he thought suddenly: *their* home—she'd become even more cheerful. They'd spent the last couple of hours rehashing their trip to New York, but he couldn't mistake her expression of contentment as they crossed the Pamlico River and reached the final leg of their journey.

The first time he'd been here, Jeremy remembered, he'd barely been able to find the place. The only turn leading toward downtown was located off the highway, so he'd missed the nearest exit and had to pull his car over to check the map. But once he'd turned onto Main Street, he'd been charmed.

In the car, Jeremy shook his head, revising his opinion. He was thinking of Lexie, not the town. The town, while quaint in the way that all small towns were, was anything but charming. At first glance, anyway. He remembered thinking on his first visit here that the town seemed to be slowly rusting away. Downtown occupied only a few short blocks on which too many businesses were boarded up, and decaying storefronts were slowly being stripped of their paint, no doubt helped by the gusts of moving vans headed out of town. Boone Creek, once a thriving town, had been struggling ever since the phosphorus mine and textile mill closed, and there were more than a few times when Jeremy wondered whether the town would survive.

The jury was still out on that one, he concluded. But if this was where Lexie wanted to be, then that was enough. Besides, once you got beyond the "soon to be a ghost town" feel of the place, the town *was* picturesque, in a southern, Spanish-moss-hanging-from-tree-limbs kind of way. At the confluence of Boone Creek and the Pamlico River was a board-walk where one could watch the sailboats cruising along the water, and according to the Chamber of Commerce, in the spring the azaleas and dogwoods planted throughout the downtown "exploded in a cacophony of color that was rivaled only by the ocean sunset of autumn leaves come every October," whatever that meant. Even so, it was the people who made the place special, or so Lexie swore. Like many small-town dwellers, she viewed the people who lived here as her family. What Jeremy kept to himself was the observation that "family" often included a couple of crazy aunts and uncles, and this town was no different. People here gave the term *character* an entirely new meaning.

Jeremy drove past the Lookilu Tavern—the local after-work hangout—the pizza place, and the barbershop; around the corner, he knew, was a massive gothic structure that served as the county library, where Lexie worked. As they edged down the street toward Herbs, the restaurant that Doris, Lexie's grandmother, owned, Lexie sat up straighter. Ironically, Doris had been the reason Jeremy had come to this town in the first place.

As the resident town psychic, she was definitely one of the aforementioned "characters."

Even from a distance, Jeremy could see the lights blazing from inside Herbs. Once a Victorian home, it seemed to dominate the end of the block. Strangely, cars were parked up and down the street.

"I thought Herbs was only open for breakfast and lunch."

"It is."

Remembering the little "get-together" the mayor had thrown in his honor on his previous visit—which had included almost everyone in the county, it seemed—Jeremy stiffened behind the wheel. "Don't tell me they're waiting for us."

She laughed. "No, believe it or not, the world doesn't revolve around us. It's the third Monday of the month."

"And that means?"

"It's the town council meeting. And after that, they play bingo."

Jeremy blinked. "Bingo?"

She nodded. "That's how they get people to come to the meetings."

"Ah," he said, thinking, Don't pass judgment. It's just a different world, that's all. Who cares if no one you know has actually ever played bingo?

Noticing his expression, she smiled. "Don't knock it. Can't you see all the cars? Nobody ever came before they started playing bingo. They offer prizes and everything."

"Let me guess. It was Mayor Gherkin's idea?"

She laughed. "Who else?"

*   *   *

Mayor Gherkin was seated toward the rear of the building, wedged behind two tables that had been pushed together. On either side were two people Jeremy recognized as members of the town council; one was an emaciated lawyer, the other a portly physician. At the corner of the table was Jed, who sat with his arms crossed and a scowl on his face. The largest man Jeremy had ever seen, Jed had a face that was mostly hidden by a beard and a wild mane of hair that made Jeremy think of a woolly mammoth. It was fitting, Jeremy supposed, for not only was Jed the proprietor of Greenleaf Cottages—the only lodging in town—but he also served as the local taxidermist. For a week, Jeremy had slept in a room at Greenleaf surrounded by the stuffed and mounted versions of a variety of creatures known in this part of the world.

It was standing room only; people were crammed around tables with bingo cards spread out before them, frantically stamping the appropriate boxes as Gherkin spoke into the microphone. A cloud of cigarette smoke hung like fog, despite the whirring fans above. Most of the people were clad in overalls, plaid shirts, and NASCAR ball caps, and it seemed to Jeremy that they'd pulled their outfits from the same bin at the local five-and-dime. Dressed head to toe in black—the preferred wardrobe of New Yorkers—Jeremy had the strange sense that he suddenly knew how Johnny Cash must have felt when he stood onstage crooning country-western songs at the county fair.

Above the roar, Jeremy could barely hear the

mayor speaking into the microphone. "B-11 . . . N-26 . . ."

With every number called, the crowd grew louder. Those who weren't lucky enough to have a table were propping the cards against the windowsills and walls; baskets of hush puppies were being mowed through as if the townsfolk needed grease to calm their nerves in their rabid quest for victory. Lexie and Jeremy squeezed their way through the crowd and caught a glimpse of Doris loading more baskets of hush puppies onto a tray. Off to the side, Rachel, the restaurant's rather flirtatious waitress, waved away the cigarette smoke. Unlike New York City, Boone Creek did not frown upon smoking—in fact, it seemed to be almost as popular as the bingo game itself.

"Are those wedding bells I hear?" Jeremy heard the mayor intone. Suddenly, the bingo-number calling stopped, and the only audible sound came from the whirring fans. Every face in the restaurant had turned to stare at Lexie and Jeremy. Jeremy had never seen so many cigarettes dangling from lips in his entire life. Then, remembering what people did around here, he nodded and waved.

People nodded and waved back.

"Out of the way . . . coming through . . . ," Jeremy heard Doris call out. There were rustles of movement as people began pressing into one another, making way, and Doris appeared in front of them. She immediately pulled Lexie into her arms.

When Doris released her, she looked from Lexie to Jeremy and back again. From the corner of his eye, Jeremy noticed the crowd doing the same thing, as if they were part of the reunion as well. Which, considering their proximity, they probably were.

"Well, I'll be," Doris pronounced. Born and bred in the South, she sounded as if she were pronouncing the letters L-I-B. "I didn't expect you home until a little later."

Lexie nodded toward Jeremy. "You can thank lead-foot here. He regards the speed limit as more of a guideline than an actual rule."

"Good for you, Jeremy," Doris said with a wink. "Oh, we've got so much to talk about! I want to hear all about your week in New York. I want to hear all about everything. And where's that ring you've been telling me about?"

Everyone's eyes flashed toward Lexie's ring. Necks were craning as Lexie held up her hand. A couple of oohs and aahs rose from the throng. Folks began closing in to get a better peek, and Jeremy could feel someone breathing on the back of his neck.

"Now, dat dere's a purty ring," Jeremy heard someone say behind him.

"Hold it up a bit, Lex," another added.

"It looks like dem cubic zircomiums from the Home Shopping Network," a woman offered.

For the first time, Lexie and Doris seemed to realize they were the center of attention.

"Okay, okay . . . show's over, folks," Doris said. "Let me talk to my granddaughter alone. We've got some catching up to do. Give us a little room."

Amid murmurs of disappointment, the crowd tried to back away, but there was really nowhere to go. Mainly, people shuffled their feet.

41

"Let's go in the back," Doris finally suggested. "Follow me . . ."

Doris grabbed Lexie's hand and they were off; Jeremy struggled to keep up with them as they headed for Doris's office just beyond the kitchen.

Once there, Doris peppered Lexie with questions in rapid-fire succession. Lexie told her all about their visit to the Statue of Liberty, Times Square, and—of course—the Empire State Building. The faster they talked, the more southern they sounded, and despite Jeremy's attempts to keep up, he was unable to follow everything they were saying. He managed to decipher the fact that Lexie had enjoyed his family but was less than thrilled when she said the evening reminded her of something "you might have seen on *Everybody Loves Raymond*, except six times bigger, with in-laws crazy in a different kind of way."

"Sounds like a hoot," Doris said. "Now, let me get a better look at that ring."

Again Lexie held it out, preening like a schoolgirl. Doris caught Jeremy's eye.

"Did you pick this out yourself?"

Jeremy shrugged. "With a bit of help."

"Well, it's gorgeous."

At that moment, Rachel poked her head in. "Hey, Lex. Hey, Jeremy. Sorry for interrupting, but the hush puppies are running low, Doris. Do you want me to start another batch?"

"Probably. But wait—before you go, come see Lexie's ring."

The ring. Women the world over loved to ogle the ring, even more than they loved saying the word *fiancée*.

Rachel walked over. With her auburn hair and reedlike figure, she was as appealing as ever, although Jeremy thought she seemed more tired than usual. In high school, Rachel and Lexie had been best friends, and although still close—it was impossible not to be close in a town this size—they'd drifted apart when Lexie went off to college. She eyed the ring.

"It's gorgeous," she said. "Congratulations, Lex. And you too, Jeremy. The whole town's been in a tizzy since they found out."

"Thanks, Rach," Lexie said. "How are things going with Rodney?"

Rodney, a local deputy sheriff with a penchant for weightlifting, had pined for Lexie since they were kids and hadn't been all that happy when Lexie and Jeremy became an item. Had it not been for the fact that he started dating Rachel soon afterward, Jeremy was pretty sure Rodney would have preferred that Jeremy stay in New York City.

Rachel's gaze faltered. "They're going."

Lexie watched her, knowing not to push. Rachel brushed a strand of hair from her cheek. "Listen, I'd love to stay and chat, but it's a zoo out there. I have no idea why you let the mayor use this place for these meetings. People get crazy when it comes to hush puppies and bingo. See y'all later. Maybe I'll have some more time to chat."

As soon as she left, Lexie leaned toward Doris. "Is she okay?"

"Oh, it's her and Rodney," Doris said. She waved a hand as if it were old news. "They had some sort of spat a couple days ago."

"Not on account of me, I hope."

"No, no, of course not," Doris assured her, but Jeremy wasn't convinced. Despite the fact that Rodney was dating Rachel, Jeremy had no doubt that he was still sweet on Lexie. Crushes, even in adulthood, were never easily forgotten, and the argument seemed to coincide with the news of their engagement.

"Well, here you are!" said Mayor Gherkin, interrupting Jeremy's thoughts. Gherkin, overweight and balding, was color-blind when it came to clothing. Tonight he wore purple polyester pants, a yellow shirt, and a paisley tie. The consummate politician, he never seemed to draw a breath while speaking. And speak he did—the man was a veritable typhoon of words.

Not surprisingly, Gherkin was still going on.

". . . hiding away in the back . . . why, if I didn't know better, I'd say you were making secret plans to elope and deprive this town of the ceremony it rightly deserves." He lumbered over, grasped Jeremy's hand, and pumped it up and down. "Good to see you. Good to see you," he said almost as an afterthought, before continuing on. "I'm thinking the town square under the lights, or maybe right there on the library steps. With enough hoopla and a little planning, we might be able to get the governor to swing by. He's a friend of mine, and if it coincides with his campaign, well, you never know." He stared at Jeremy with his eyebrows raised.

Jeremy cleared his throat. "We haven't even discussed the wedding yet, but actually, we were thinking about something more low-key."

"Low-key? Nonsense. It's not every day that one of our town's most prominent citizens marries a genuine celebrity, you know."

"I'm a journalist, not a celebrity. I thought we'd been over this—"

"No need to be modest, Jeremy. I can see it now . . ." He squinted as if he actually could. "Today, columns for *Scientific American*; tomorrow, your own talk show, beamed to a worldwide audience from right here in Boone Creek, North Carolina."

"I highly doubt—"

"You've got to think big, my boy. Big. Why, without dreams Columbus would never have sailed to the New World, and Rembrandt would never have picked up a paintbrush."

He slapped Jeremy on the back, then leaned down and kissed Lexie on the cheek. "And you are even lovelier than usual, Miss Lexie. Engagement definitely suits you, my dear."

"Thank you, Tom," Lexie said.

Doris rolled her eyes and was about to shoo him from the room when Gherkin turned his attention back to Jeremy again.

"Do you mind if we talk business for a minute here?" He didn't wait for an answer. "Now, I'd be remiss as a public servant if I neglected to ask if you were planning to write something special about Boone Creek, now that you're living here, I mean. It might be a good idea, you know. And good for the town, too. For instance, did you know that three of the top four catfish ever found in North Carolina have been fished from Boone Creek?

45

Think about that . . . three out of the top four. There just might be some sort of magical quality in the water."

Jeremy didn't know what to say. Oh, his editor would love that one, wouldn't he? Especially the title: "Magic Water Responsible for Giant Catfish." Not a chance. He was already on thin ice for leaving New York; if there were ever any cutbacks at the magazine, he had the sneaking suspicion that he'd be the first to go. Not that he needed the income; most of that had come from the freelance articles he sold to other magazines and newspapers, and he'd invested well over the years. He had more than enough to survive for a while, but the column at *Scientific American* definitely kept his profile higher than it might have been.

"Actually, I have my next six columns done already. And I haven't decided on the next story, but I'll keep the giant catfish in mind."

The mayor nodded, pleased. "You do that, my boy. And listen, I want to officially welcome you both back to town. I can't tell you how thrilled I am that you've chosen our fine community to be your permanent home. But I have to get back to the bingo game. Rhett's been calling the numbers, but with him barely able to read, I'm afraid he's going to make some sort of mistake and a riot'll break out. Lord only knows what the Garrison sisters will do if they feel they've been cheated."

"Folks do take their bingo seriously," Doris agreed.

"Truer words have never been spoken. Now if y'all will excuse me, duty calls."

With a quick turn—remarkable considering the

man's girth—he was out of the room, and all Jeremy could do was shake his head. Doris peeked beyond the door to make sure no one else was coming, then leaned toward Lexie. She motioned toward her granddaughter's belly.

"How are you feeling?"

Listening to Doris and Lexie whisper about Lexie's pregnancy, Jeremy found himself thinking that there was an irony involved in having and raising children.

Most people were aware of the responsibilities of having and raising children, he knew. Having watched his brothers and their wives, he knew how much their lives could change once a child came along; no more sleeping in on the weekends, for instance, or going out to dinner on the spur of the moment. But they claimed they didn't mind, since they viewed parenting as a selfless act, one in which they were willing to make sacrifices for the betterment of their children. Nor were they unique. In Manhattan, Jeremy had come to believe that this view was often taken to extremes. Every parent he knew made sure his or her child attended the best schools, had the finest piano teachers, and participated in the right sports camps, all with the goal of enabling the child to one day attend an Ivy League college.

But didn't this selflessness actually require selfishness?

That's where the irony came in, Jeremy thought. After all, it wasn't as if people needed to have children. No, he knew that having a child was essentially about two things: It was the next logical step in a relationship, but secretly it was also a deep-down desire to create a miniaturized version of "you." As in "you're" so special, it was simply inconceivable that the world should be burdened with the fact that there's only one of "you" to go around. And as for the rest of it? The sacrifices that led to the Ivy League? Jeremy was certain the only reason a five-year-old would even know about the Ivy League was that it was important to the parents. In other words, Jeremy had come to the conclusion that most parents wanted to create not only a "you," but a "better you," because no parent dreams of standing around at a cocktail party thirty years later saying things like "Oh, Jimmie's doing great! He's out on parole and has almost kicked his drug habit." No, they want to say, "Emmett, in addition to becoming a multimillionaire, just finished his PhD in microbiology, and *The New York Times* just ran a feature on how his most recent research is likely to lead to a cure for cancer."

Of course, neither of these issues pertained to Lexie and Jeremy, and Jeremy felt himself puff up just a bit at the realization. They weren't typical parents-to-be for the simple reason that the pregnancy had been unplanned. At the time it happened, they hadn't been thinking of a "little you and me," nor was it the next logical step in their relationship, since technically they hadn't had much of a relationship yet. No, their child had been conceived in beauty and tenderness, without any of the selfishness characteristic of other parents. Which meant that he and Lexie were better and more selfless, and in the long run, Jeremy figured, this selflessness would give their child the ever important leg up when it came to getting accepted to Harvard.

"Are you okay?" Lexie asked. "You've been sort of quiet since we left Herbs."

It was getting close to ten o'clock, and Lexie and Jeremy were at her house, a small, weathered bungalow that backed up to a grove of ancient pines. Beyond the window, Jeremy watched the tips of the trees swaying in the breeze; in the moonlight, the needles appeared almost silver. Lexie was snuggling beneath his arm as they sat on the couch. A small candle flickered on the end table, casting light on a plate of leftovers Doris had prepared for them.

"I was just thinking about the baby," Jeremy said.

"Really?" she said, cocking her head to the side.

"Yeah, really. What? You don't think I think about the baby?"

"No, it's not that. It's just that I got the impression you sort of tuned out when Doris and I were talking about her. So what were you thinking?"

He pulled her closer, figuring it was best not to mention the word *selfish*. "I was thinking how lucky the baby is to have you as a mother."

She smiled before turning to study him. "I hope our daughter has your dimple."

"You like my dimple?"

"I adore your dimple. But I hope she has my eyes."

"What's wrong with my eyes?"

"Nothing's wrong with your eyes."

"But yours are so much better? I'll have you know, my mother loves my eyes."

"I do, too. On you, they're seductive. I just don't

want our daughter to have seductive eyes. She's only a baby."

He laughed. "What else?"

She stared at him, concentrating. "I want her to have my hair, too. And my nose and chin." She tucked a strand of hair behind her ear. "And my forehead, too."

"Your forehead?"

She nodded. "You've got a wrinkle between your eyebrows."

He absently brought his finger to it, as if he'd never noticed it before. "It comes from furrowing my brow." He showed her. "See? It's from deep concentration. Thinking. Don't you want our daughter to think?"

"Are you saying you want our daughter to have wrinkles?"

"Well . . . no, but you're saying that all I get is a dimple?"

"How about if she gets your ears?"

"Ears? No one cares about ears."

"I think your ears are darling."

"Really?"

"Your ears are perfect. Probably the world's most perfect ears. I've heard people talking about how wonderful your ears are."

He laughed. "Okay, my ears and dimple, your eyes, nose, chin, and forehead. Anything else?"

"How about if we stop? I'd hate to think what you'd say if I told you I also want her to have my legs. You seem pretty sensitive right now."

"I'm not sensitive. But I happen to think I've got something more to offer than ears and a dimple.

And my legs . . . well, they've turned heads, if you really must know."

She giggled. "Okay, okay," she said, "you made your point. What are your thoughts on the wedding?"

"Changing the subject?"

"We do have to talk about it. I'm sure you want to have some input."

"I think I'll leave most of that up to you."

"I was thinking about having it take place near the lighthouse. Out by the cottage?"

"I remember," he said, knowing she was referring to the Cape Hatteras Lighthouse, where her parents had been married.

"It's a state park, so we'll need to get a permit. But I was thinking maybe late spring or early summer. I don't want my tummy showing in any pictures."

"Makes sense to me. After all, you don't want anyone to think you're pregnant. What would people say?"

She laughed. "So you don't have any opinions on the wedding? Anything special you've always dreamed about?"

"Not really. Now, opinions on the bachelor party, that's something different . . ."

She punched him playfully in the belly. "Watch it," she teased. Then, settling back, she added, "I'm glad you're here."

"I'm glad I'm here, too."

"When do you want to go house shopping?"

These sudden shifts in conversation served to continually remind Jeremy that his life had suddenly undergone a drastic change. "Excuse me?"

"House shopping. We're going to have to buy a house, you know."

"I thought we were going to live here."

"Here? This place is tiny. Where would you have your office?"

"In the spare bedroom," he said. "There's plenty of room."

"And the baby? Where's she going to sleep?"

Oh yeah, the baby. Amazing that he forgot about that for a second there.

"Do you have anything in mind?"

"I think I'd like something on the water, if that's okay."

"Water sounds nice."

Her face took on an almost dreamy expression as she continued. "And someplace with a big wrap-around porch. Someplace homey, with spacious rooms and windows that let the sun shine in. And a tin roof. You haven't lived until you've heard the rain coming down on a tin roof. It's the most romantic sound in the world."

"I can live with romantic sounds."

She furrowed her brow, considering his responses. "You're being awfully easy about this."

"You're forgetting that I've lived in an apartment for the last fifteen years. We worry about different things, like whether the elevator works."

"As I recall, the one in your building didn't."

"Which should tell you that I'm not picky."

She smiled. "Well, we can't go this week. I'm sure I have a mountain of paperwork at the library, and it'll take a while to catch up. But maybe by the weekend we can go looking."

"Sounds good."

"What are you going to be doing while I'm working?"

"I'll probably pick the petals off flowers while I pine away for you."

"Seriously."

"Oh, you know. I'll try to get settled and get into some sort of schedule. Set up the computer and printer, see if I can get some sort of high-speed access so I can research the Internet. I like to be at least four or five columns ahead so that if a good story comes up, I have the time to work it. It also keeps my editor sleeping easier."

She was quiet as she thought about it. "I don't think you'll be able to get high-speed access out at Greenleaf. They don't even have cable out there."

"Who's talking about Greenleaf? I figure I'll just have it hooked up here."

"Then you might as well use the library. I mean, since you'll be staying at Greenleaf."

"Who says I'm staying at Greenleaf?"

She slid out from beneath his arm and faced him. "Where else would you stay?"

"I thought I'd just stay here."

"With me?" she asked.

"Of course with you," he said, as if the answer were obvious.

"But we're not married yet."

"So?"

"I know it's old-fashioned, but down here couples don't live together before they're married. Folks around town would frown on that. They would assume we're sleeping together."

He stared at her, not bothering to hide his confusion. "But we are sleeping together. You're pregnant, remember?"

She smiled. "I'll be the first to admit that it doesn't make much sense, and if I had my way, you'd stay. And I know that people will eventually find out that I'm pregnant, but the crazy thing is that folks down here understand that people make mistakes. They're perfectly willing to forgive mistakes, but it still doesn't mean we should live together. They'll talk behind our backs, they'll gossip, and it'll take folks a long time to forget that we 'lived in sin.' And for years, that's just how they'll describe us." She shook her head before reaching for his hand. "I know it's a lot to ask, but would you do this for me?"

Leaning back, he remembered what it was like at Greenleaf: a decrepit series of shacks set in the middle of a swamp known for water moccasins; Jed, the scary, nonspeaking proprietor; the mounted animals that decorated every room. Greenleaf. Good God.

"Yeah," he said, "okay. But . . . Greenleaf?"

"Where else is there? I mean, if you want, there's a shed behind Doris's place, and I think it's got a bathroom, but it's not as nice as Greenleaf."

He swallowed, thinking about it. "Jed scares me," he admitted.

"I know he does," she said. "He told me that when I made the reservations, but he promised me that he'll be better now that you're townsfolk. And the good news is that because you'll be staying for a while, he won't charge you the regular rate. You're getting a discount."

"Lucky me," Jeremy forced out.

She traced his forearm with her finger. "I'll make it up to you. For instance, if you're discreet, you can visit me at my place anytime. And I'll even cook you dinner."

"Discreet?"

She nodded. "That means you should probably not leave your car parked out front, or if you do, you should probably leave before the sun's up so no one sees."

"Why does it suddenly feel like I'm sixteen years old and sneaking behind my parents' back?"

"Because that's exactly what we're going to be doing. Except these people are not as understanding as parents. They're much worse."

"Then why are we living here?"

"Because you love me," she said.

Four

·····❖·····

Over the course of the next month, Jeremy began adapting to his life in Boone Creek. In New York City, the first signs of spring began in April, but they started weeks earlier in Boone Creek, right around the beginning of March. Buds began forming on trees, cold mornings gradually gave way to cool ones, and on days when it wasn't raining, the mild afternoon temperatures required nothing more than a long-sleeved shirt. Lawns, brown over the winter as the centipede grass lay dormant, began the slow, almost imperceptible turn toward emerald green, reaching their full color just as the dogwoods and azaleas blossomed. The air was scented with perfume and pine and salted mist, and blue skies broken only by the occasional breath of cloud stretched across the horizon. By the time the ides of March came and went, the town itself seemed brighter and more vivid; it was as if his memory of how the place looked in winter had been nothing but a gloomy dream.

His furnishings, which had finally arrived, were

being stored in the shed behind Doris's, and there were moments while staying at Greenleaf when he wondered whether he would have been better off staying with his furniture. Not that he hadn't adapted to life with Jed as his only neighbor; Jed had yet to say a single word to him, but he was pretty good at taking the occasional message. They were hard to read and sometimes smeared with . . . something—embalming fluid, maybe, or whatever else he used to stuff the critters—but whatever it was helped the notes stick directly to the door, and neither Jed nor Jeremy cared about the syrupy stain left in the aftermath.

He'd also settled into a routine of sorts. Lexie had been right—there wasn't the slightest possibility of high-speed Internet access at Greenleaf, but he'd jerry-rigged a way to dial in to retrieve e-mail and do slow-motion searches, during which time he might wait five minutes for a page to load. On a positive note, the glacial pace of the connection gave him reason to head to the library most days. Sometimes he and Lexie would visit in her office, other times they'd head to lunch, but after an hour or so together, she'd say something like "You know I'd love to visit with you all day, but I do have to get some work done." He'd take the hint and head back to one of the computer terminals, where he'd pretty much taken up residence for his research. His agent, Nate, had been calling him repeatedly, leaving messages and wondering aloud whether Jeremy had any great ideas for a future story, "since the television deal isn't dead yet!" Like most agents, Nate was an optimist above all. Jeremy seldom had an answer other than that Nate would be the first to know. Jeremy hadn't come up with a story, nor had he written even a column, since he'd been down south. With so much going on, it was easy to be distracted.

Or so he tried to convince himself. The fact was he'd had a couple of ideas, but nothing had come of them. Whenever he sat down to write, it was as if his brain turned to mush and his fingers became arthritic. He'd write a sentence or two, spend fifteen to twenty minutes evaluating his work, and then finally delete it. He spent entire days writing and deleting, with nothing to show at the end. Sometimes he wondered why the keyboard suddenly seemed to hate him, but he shrugged it off, knowing he had more important things on his mind.

Like Lexie. And the wedding. And the baby. And, of course, the bachelor party. Alvin had been trying to finalize the date since Jeremy had left, but that depended on the parks department. Despite Lexie's endless reminders on the subject, Jeremy hadn't been able to get through to anyone who might be able to help. In the end, he'd finally told Alvin to schedule the bachelor party for the last weekend in April, figuring the sooner the better, and Alvin hung up with an excited cackle and a promise to make it a night he wouldn't forget.

It wouldn't take much. As much as he was . . . getting used to Boone Creek, it wasn't New York, and he realized he missed the place. Granted, he'd known it would be a major adjustment before he agreed to move down here, but he was still amazed by the utter lack of things to do. In New York, he'd been able to leave his apartment, walk two blocks in either direction, and find a slew of movies to see, everything from the latest action-adventure flick to something arty and French. Boone Creek didn't even have a theater, and the nearest one—in Washington—had only three screens, one of which seemed perennially to show the latest cartoon offering from Disney. In New York, there was always a new restaurant to try and food that suited whatever mood he might be in, from Vietnamese to Italian to Greek to Ethiopian; in Boone Creek, dinner out was either cardboard pizza or home cooking at Ned's Diner, a place where everything was fried and so much oil floated in the air that you had to wipe your forehead with a napkin before leaving. He'd actually overheard folks at the counter talking about the best way to filter bacon grease for maximum flavor and how much fatback—whatever that was— to add to collard greens before topping the whole mess with butter. Leave it to southerners to figure out a way to make eating vegetables unhealthy.

He supposed he was being unkind, but without places to eat or movies to see, what were young couples supposed to do? Even if you wanted to go for a pleasant walk through town, you could walk only a few minutes in any direction before having to turn around. Lexie, of course, found nothing unusual about any of this and seemed perfectly content to sit on the porch after work, sipping sweet tea or lemonade and waving at the occasional neighbor who was strolling around the block. Or, if nature was cooperating and it happened to be storming, another sizzling night of entertainment might entail sitting on the porch and watching for lightning. Lest he be disappointed by the whole idea of porch sitting, Lexie further assured him that "in the summer, you'll see so many fireflies, you'll be reminded of Christmas."

"I can hardly wait," Jeremy replied, sighing.

On the plus side, in the last few weeks Jeremy finally achieved a milestone: the purchase of his very first car. Call it a male thing, but as soon as he realized that he'd be moving to Boone Creek, that was one of the experiences he was most looking forward to. He hadn't saved and invested all these years for nothing. He'd been lucky enough to buy Yahoo! and AOL—after writing an article about the future of the Internet—and had ridden those stocks to the top before cashing out part of his portfolio when he moved to Boone Creek, and he visualized every moment of his purchase—from perusing various automobile magazines and walking the lot to sitting behind the wheel and inhaling the famed "new-car smell." There were countless times that he'd actually regretted living in New York, simply because owning a car in the city was largely superfluous. He couldn't wait to crawl into a sporty two-door coupé or convertible and take it for a test drive along the quiet county roads. On the morning he and Lexie were supposed to head to the lot, he couldn't stop grinning at the fantasy of slipping behind the wheel of his dream car.

What he hadn't quite expected was Lexie's response when he ogled the sporty two-door convertible and ran his finger along its sleek curves. "What do you think?" he asked.

He knew that she, too, couldn't resist.

She stared at the car, confused. "Where would we put the baby seat?"

"We can use your car for that," he said. "This is a car for the two of us. For quick trips to the beach or to the mountains, for weekends in Washington, D.C."

"I don't think my car's going to last that much longer, so don't you think we'd be better off getting something for the whole family?"

"Like what?"

"How about a minivan?"

He blinked. "No way. Not a chance. I didn't wait thirty-seven years for a minivan."

"How about a nice sedan?"

"A sedan? My dad drives a sedan. I'm too young to buy a sedan."

"An SUV? They're sporty and sharp. And you can take them into the mountains."

He tried to imagine how he would look behind the wheel before shaking his head. "Those are the vehicles of choice for suburban mothers. I've seen more SUVs in the Wal-Mart parking lot than I've ever seen in the mountains. And besides, they cause more pollution than regular cars, and I *care* about the environment." He touched his chest for emphasis, doing his best to appear earnest.

Lexie considered his response. "Where does that leave us, then?"

"With my first choice," he said. "Imagine how wonderful life could be . . . zipping along the highway, wind in our hair . . ."

She laughed. "You sound like a commercial. And

believe me, I think it would be great, too. I'd love a flashy little number like this. But you've got to admit it's not very practical."

He watched her, his mouth drying slightly as he felt his dream begin to die. She was right, of course, and he shifted from one foot to the other before finally exhaling.

"Which one do you like?"

"I think this one over here would be good for the family," she said, motioning to a four-door sedan halfway down the lot. "It was rated a 'Best Buy' in *Consumer Reports* for safety, it's reliable, and we can get a warranty up to seventy thousand miles."

Economical. Sensible. Responsible. She covered all the bases, he acknowledged, but his heart nonetheless sank when he saw the car of her choice. In his opinion, it might as well have had wood paneling on the side and whitewall tires for all the sexiness it exuded.

Seeing his expression, she moved toward him and slipped her arms around his neck. "I know it's probably not what you dreamed about, but how about if we order it in fire-engine red?"

He raised an eyebrow. "With flames painted on the hood?"

She laughed again. "If that's what you really want."

"I don't. I was just seeing how far I could go."

She kissed him. "Thank you," she said. "And just so you know, I think you're going to look very sexy whenever you drive it."

"I'm going to look like my father."

"No," she said, "you'll look like the father of

our baby, and no man on earth can touch that."

He smiled, knowing she was trying to make him feel better. Still, his shoulders slumped just a bit with the thought of what might have been when he signed the papers an hour later.

Aside from the tinge of disappointment he felt whenever he slipped behind the wheel, life wasn't all bad. Because he hadn't been writing, he found himself with quite a bit of time on his hands, far more than he was used to. For years he'd chased stories around the world, investigating everything from the Abominable Snowman in the Himalayas to the Shroud of Turin in Italy, exposing frauds, legends, and hoaxes for what they were. In between, he'd hammered out articles exposing con men, psychics, and faith healers, while still finding time to put together his regular twelve columns a year. It was a life of steady pressure, sometimes all consuming, but more often simply unrelenting. In his earlier marriage to Maria, his constant traveling had become a source of tension, and she'd asked him to stop freelancing in exchange for a job that included a regular paycheck from one of the major New York papers. He'd never considered her suggestion seriously, but, reflecting on his life now, he wondered whether he should have. The constant pressure to find and deliver, he realized, had manifested itself in other areas of his life as well. For years he'd needed to do something—anything—every waking moment. He couldn't sit still for more than a few minutes at a time; there was always something to read or study, always something to write. Little by little, he realized, he'd lost the ability to relax, and the result was a long period of his life in which months blurred together, with nothing to differentiate one year from the next.

The last month in Boone Creek, boring as it had been, was actually . . . refreshing. There was simply nothing to do, and considering the hectic pace of his life over the last fifteen years, who could complain about that? It was like a vacation, one he hadn't planned for, but one that left him feeling more rested than he had in years. For the first time in what seemed like forever, he was choosing the pace of his life rather than having his life choose the pace. Being bored, he decided, was an underrated art form.

He especially liked being bored when he was with Lexie. Not so much the porch sitting, but he liked the feel of her beneath his arm while they watched an NBA game. Being with Lexie was comfortable, and he relished their quiet dinner conversations and the warmth of her body as they sat together atop Riker's Hill. He looked forward to those simple moments with an enthusiasm that surprised him, but what he enjoyed most of all were those mornings when they could sleep in, then wake up slowly together. It was a guilty pleasure—she allowed it only when she picked him up at Greenleaf after work, lest his car in the driveway be spotted by nosy neighbors—but whatever the reason, the sneaking around made it that much more exciting. After rising, they would read the newspaper at the small kitchen table while they had breakfast. More often than not, she'd still be wearing her pajamas and fuzzy slippers, her hair would be tousled, and her eyes would carry the slightest puffiness from sleep. But when the morning sun slanted through the windows, he was sure she was the most beautiful woman he had ever seen.

Sometimes she would catch him staring at her and would reach for his hand. Jeremy would begin reading again, and as they sat together holding hands, lost in their own worlds, he would wonder whether there was any greater pleasure in life.

They'd also been shopping for a house, and since Lexie had a pretty good idea of what she had in mind and Boone Creek didn't have that many houses to begin with, Jeremy figured they would find the right one in a couple of days. If he was lucky, maybe even in an afternoon.

He was wrong. For whatever reason, they spent three long weekends walking through every house for sale in town at least twice. Jeremy found the whole situation more disheartening than exciting. There was something about walking through people's homes that left him feeling as if he were passing judgment, and usually not in the kindest of ways. Which, of course, he was. While the town may have been historic and the homes charming from the outside, going inside inevitably led to disappointment. Half the time it was like entering a time warp, one that led back to the 1970s. He hadn't seen so much beige shag carpet, orange wallpaper, and lime green kitchen sinks since *The Brady Bunch* went off the air. Sometimes there were strange odors, a few of which made his nose curl—mothballs and kitty litter, perhaps, or soiled diapers and moldy bread—and more often than not, the furniture was enough to make him shake his head. In his entire thirty-seven years of life, he'd never once considered rocking chairs in his living room and couches on the front porch. But hey, he was learning.

There were countless reasons to say no, but even when they found something that struck their fancy and made them want to say yes, it was often just as ridiculous.

"Look," he exclaimed one day, "this house has a darkroom!"

"But you're not a photographer," Lexie responded. "You don't need a darkroom."

"Yes, but I might become a photographer *one day*."

Or:

"I love the high ceilings," she said in wonder. "I've always dreamed of high ceilings in my bedroom."

"But the bedroom's tiny. We'd barely fit a queen-size bed in here."

"I know. But have you seen how high the ceiling is?"

Eventually they found a place. Or rather, a place that Lexie loved; he, on the other hand, was still unsure. A two-story brick Georgian with an uncovered porch that overlooked Boone Creek, it also had an interior layout that suited her. On the market for nearly two years, the place was a bargain—by New York standards an absolute steal—but it needed quite a bit of renovation. Still, when Lexie insisted that they walk through a third time, even Mrs. Reynolds, the

Realtor, knew the hook was baited and a hungry fish was circling. A thin, gray-haired lady, she wore a selfsatisfied grin on her mousy face as she assured Jeremy the remodeling would cost "no more than the purchase price."

"Great," he said, mentally computing whether his bank account would cover it.

"Don't worry," Mrs. Reynolds added. "It's perfect for a young couple, especially if you're thinking of starting a family. Houses like this don't come along every day."

Actually they do, Jeremy thought. This house could have been purchased by anyone in the past two years.

He was about to make a crack along those lines when he noticed Lexie motioning from the stairs.

"Can I walk through the upstairs one more time?" she asked.

Mrs. Reynolds turned with a smile, no doubt thinking of her commission. "Of course, dear. I'll join you. By the way, are you thinking of starting a family? Because if you are, you've got to see the attic. It would make a fantastic playroom."

As he watched Mrs. Reynolds accompany Lexie upstairs, he wondered if she somehow realized that he and Lexie were already well past the thinking stage.

He doubted it. Lexie was still keeping the pregnancy under wraps, at least until the wedding. Only Doris knew, which he supposed he could live with, except for the fact that lately he'd found himself getting involved in the strangest conversations with Lexie, some of which he would have rather she shared with friends. She might be sitting on the couch, for instance, when she would suddenly turn to him and say, "My uterus will be swollen for weeks after I give birth," or, "Can you believe my cervix is going to dilate ten centimeters?"

Ever since she'd started reading books about pregnancy, he'd been hearing words like *placenta*, *umbilical*, and *hemorrhoids* far too often, and if she mentioned the fact that her nipples would get sore while breast-feeding one more time—"even to the point of bleeding!"—he was sure he'd have to leave the room. Like most men, he had only the vaguest knowledge about how the whole "child growing inside you" thing worked and even less interest; as a general rule, he was far more concerned about the specific act that set the whole thing in motion in the first place. Now *that* he wouldn't mind talking about, especially if she were staring at him over a wineglass in a candlelit room and using her sultry voice.

The point was, she threw out those words as though they were ingredients listed on a cereal box, and instead of getting him more excited about what was happening, more often than not the conversations left him feeling queasy.

Despite those conversations, he was excited. There was something thrilling about the fact that *she* was carrying *his* child. It was a source of pride to know that he had done his part to preserve the species, thereby fulfilling his role as creator of life—so much so, in fact, that half the time he wished Lexie hadn't asked him to keep it secret.

Lost in thought, it took him a second to realize

Lexie and Mrs. Reynolds were making their way back down the stairs.

"This is the one," Lexie said, glowing as she reached for his hand. "Can we buy it?"

He felt his chest puff out a bit, even as he realized he'd have to sell a substantial chunk of his investment portfolio to make this work. "Whatever you want," he said, hoping she could hear the magnanimous tone he used.

That evening, they signed the papers; their offer was accepted the following morning. Ironically, they would close on the house on April 28, the same day he'd be heading to New York for his bachelor party. Only later did it strike him that in the last month he'd become someone else entirely.

Five

..... ❖ .....

"You *still* haven't reserved a date at the light-house?" Lexie asked.

It was the last week of March, and Jeremy was walking with Lexie toward the car after work.

"I've tried," Jeremy explained. "But you can't imagine what it's like trying to get through to these people. Half of them won't talk to me unless I fill out forms, the other half always seem to be on vacation. I haven't even completely figured out what I'm supposed to do."

She shook her head. "It'll be June by the time you make the arrangements."

"I'll figure something out," Jeremy promised.

"I know you will. But I'd really rather not be showing, and it's already almost April. I don't think I can make it until July. My pants are getting tight, and I think my butt is already getting bigger."

Jeremy hesitated, knowing this was a minefield where he had no desire to tread. In the past few days, it had been coming up with more frequency. Speaking the truth—*Well, of course your butt is getting*

70

bigger . . . you're pregnant!—would mean sleeping at Greenleaf every night for a week straight.

"You look exactly the same to me," he ventured instead.

Lexie nodded, still lost in thought. "Talk to Mayor Gherkin," she suggested.

He looked at her, keeping his expression serious. "He thinks your butt is getting bigger?"

"No! About the lighthouse! I'm sure he can help."

"Okay," he said, stifling his laugh. "I'll do that."

They walked a few steps before she nudged him playfully with her shoulder. "And my butt is *not* getting bigger."

"No, of course not."

As usual, their first stop before heading home was to check on how the renovations were proceeding.

Though they wouldn't officially close on the house until late April, the owner—who'd received the place as an inheritance but lived out of state—was willing to let them begin work on it, and Lexie had attacked the situation with gusto. Because she knew pretty much everyone in town—including carpenters, plumbers, tilers, roofers, painters, and electricians— and could see the finished home in her mind's eye, she took control of the project. Jeremy's role was limited to writing the checks, which considering he really hadn't wanted to be in charge of the project seemed to be more than a fair exchange.

Even though he hadn't known quite what to expect, it certainly wasn't this. Entire crews had been working for the past week, and he remembered being amazed at what had been accomplished on the first day. The kitchen had been torn out; shingles were piled on the front lawn, carpeting and a number of windows removed. Huge piles of debris lay scattered from one end of the house to the other, but since then he'd come to believe the only thing the workers did was to shift the debris piles from place to place. Even when he came by during the day to check on the progress, no one ever actually seemed to be working. Standing in circles drinking coffee, maybe, or smoking on the back porch most definitely, but *working*? As far as he could tell, they always seemed to be waiting for a delivery or for the general contractor to return, or they were taking a "short break." Needless to say, the majority of the workers were paid by the hour, and Jeremy always felt a tinge of financial panic whenever he headed back to Greenleaf.

Lexie, however, seemed happy enough with the progress and noticed things that he never did. "Did you see they've started running the new wiring upstairs?" or, "I see they got the new plumbing routed through the walls, so we'll be able to put the sink beneath the window."

Usually, Jeremy would nod in agreement. "Yeah, I noticed that."

Aside from checks to the contractor, he still wasn't writing yet, but on the plus side, he was fairly sure he'd figured out the reason. It wasn't so much a mental block as it was a mental overload. So much was changing, not only the obvious, but little things, too. Like what to wear. For instance, he'd long believed that he had a fairly innate sense of style, albeit one with a distinct New York flair, and his many ex-girlfriends had often complimented him on his appearance. He was a longtime subscriber to *GQ* magazine, favored Bruno Magli shoes and tailored Italian shirts. But Lexie apparently had a different opinion and seemed to want to change him entirely. Two nights ago, she'd surprised him with a gift-wrapped box, and Jeremy had been touched by her thoughtfulness . . . at least until he'd opened it.

Inside was a plaid shirt. *Plaid*. Like the kind lumberjacks wore. And Levi's jeans. "Thanks," he forced out.

She stared at him. "You don't like them."

"No, no . . . I do," he lied, not wanting to hurt her feelings. "It's nice."

"You don't sound like you mean it."

"I really do."

"I just figured you might want to have something in your closet that might help you fit in with the guys."

"What guys?"

"Guys in town. Your friends. In case . . . I don't know, you want to go play poker or go hunting or fishing or something."

"I don't play poker. Or hunt or fish." Or have any friends, either, he suddenly realized. Amazing that he hadn't even noticed.

"I know," she said. "But maybe one day you'll want to. It's what guys do down here with their friends. I know, for instance, that Rodney gets together to play poker once a week, and Jed is probably the most successful hunter in the county."

"Rodney or Jed?" he asked, trying and failing to fathom spending a few hours with either of them.

"What's wrong with Rodney and Jed?"

"Jed doesn't like me. And I don't think Rodney does, either."

"That's ridiculous. How could they not like you? But tell you what, why don't you talk to Doris tomorrow? She might have some better ideas."

"Poker with Rodney? Or hunting with Jed? Oh, I'd pay to see that!" Alvin howled into the receiver. Because Alvin had filmed the mysterious lights in the cemetery, he knew exactly whom Jeremy was talking about, and he still remembered them vividly. Rodney had thrown Alvin in jail on trumped-up charges after Alvin had flirted with Rachel at the Lookilu, and Jed frightened Alvin in the same way he frightened Jeremy. "I can just see it . . . sneaking through the forest in your Gucci shoes and lumberjack shirt . . ."

"Bruno Magli," Jeremy corrected. At Greenleaf for the night, he was still thinking about the fact that he hadn't made any friends.

"Whatever." Alvin laughed again. "Oh, that's just great . . . city mouse goes country, all because the little woman made him do it. You've got to tell me when this happens. I'll make a special trip down there with my camera to record it for posterity."

"That's okay," he said. "I'll pass."

"But she has a point, you know. You do need to make some friends down there. Which reminds me . . . do you remember that girl I met?"

"Rachel?"

"Yeah, that's the one. Do you ever see her?"

"Sometimes. Actually, since she's the maid of honor, you'll see her, too."

"How's she doing?"

"Believe it or not, she's actually dating Rodney."

"The muscle-bound deputy? She could do better. But hey, here's an idea. Maybe you and Lexie could double-date. Lunch at Herbs, maybe a little porch sitting . . ."

Jeremy laughed. "You sound like you'd fit in well here. You know all the exciting things to do."

"That's me. Mr. Adaptable. But if you see Rachel, tell her I said hi and that I'm looking forward to seeing her again."

"Will do."

"How's the writing going? I'll bet you're getting antsy to chase another story, huh?"

Jeremy shifted in his seat. "I wish."

"You're not writing?"

"Not a word since I've been down here," he admitted. "Between the wedding and the house and Lexie, I hardly have a spare minute."

There was a pause. "Let me get this straight. You're not writing at all? Even for your column?"

"No."

"You love writing."

"I know. And I'll get back to it as soon as things settle down."

Jeremy could sense his friend's skepticism at his answer. "Good," Alvin finally said. "Now, about the bachelor party . . . it's going to be awesome. Everyone up here is on board, and as I promised, it's going to be a night you'll never forget."

"Just remember . . . no dancing girls. And I don't want some lady in lingerie jumping out of a cake or anything like that.

"Oh, c'mon. It's a tradition!"

"I'm serious, Alvin. I'm in love, remember?"

"Lexie worries about you," Doris said. "She cares about you."

Doris and Jeremy were having lunch the following afternoon at Herbs. Most of the lunch crowd had finished eating, and the place was clearing out. As usual, Doris had insisted that they eat; whenever they got together, she claimed Jeremy was "skin and bones," and today Jeremy was enjoying a chicken pesto sandwich on pumpernickel bread.

"There's nothing to worry about," he protested. "There's just a lot going on, that's all."

"She knows that. But she also wants you to feel like you belong here. That you're happy here."

"I am happy here."

"You're happy because you're with Lexie, and she knows that. But you have to understand, deep down Lexie wants you to feel the same way about Boone Creek that she does. She doesn't want you here just because of her, she wants you here because this is where your friends are. Because this is where you feel like you belong. She knows it was a sacrifice for you to move from New York, but she doesn't want you to think of it that way."

"I don't. Believe me, I'd be the first to tell her if I felt that way. But . . . c'mon . . . Rodney or Jed?"

"Believe it or not, they're good guys once you get to know them, and Jed tells the funniest jokes I've ever heard. But okay, if you don't relax the way they do, maybe they're not the right ones." She brought a finger to her lips, thinking. "What did you do with friends in New York?"

Went to bars with Alvin, flirted with women, Jeremy thought. "Just . . . guy stuff," he said instead. "Went to ball games, shot pool every now and then. Just hung out, mainly. And I'm sure I'll make friends, but as I said, I'm busy right now."

Doris evaluated his answer. "Lexie says you're not writing."

"I'm not."

"Is it because of . . . ?"

"No, no," he said, shaking his head. "It has nothing to do with feeling out of place or anything like that. Writing isn't like other jobs. It's not just about showing up and going through the motions. It's more about creativity and ideas, and some-times . . . well, you just don't feel creative. I wish I knew how to tap into my creative source whenever I wanted, but I don't. But if I've learned anything about writing in the last fifteen years, it's that I know the inspiration will eventually come."

"You can't come up with an idea?"

"Not an original one. I've printed up hundreds of pages from the library computer, but every time I come up with something, I realize that I've already covered it before. Usually more than once."

Doris thought about it. "Would you like to use my journal?" she asked. "I know you don't believe what's in it, so maybe you could . . . I don't know, write an article about your investigation into it."

She was referring to the journal she'd compiled in which she claimed to be able to predict the sex of babies. Hundreds of names and dates were included in the pages, including the entry that had predicted Lexie's birth and the fact that she was a girl.

To be honest, Jeremy had considered it—Doris had made the offer previously—but although he'd rejected it initially because he knew her abilities couldn't be real, lately he'd rejected it because he didn't want his true feelings to cause a rift with Doris. She was going to be family.

"I don't know . . ."

"I'll tell you what. You can make your decision later, after you've studied it. And don't worry—I promise that I'll be able to handle being famous if you do end up writing about it. You don't have to worry. I'll still be the same charming woman I've always been. It's in the office. Wait here."

Before Jeremy had the chance to object, she was rising from the table and heading for the kitchen. In her absence, the front door opened with a squeak and Jeremy saw Mayor Gherkin enter.

"Jeremy, my boy!" Gherkin exclaimed, approaching the table. He slapped Jeremy on the back. "I didn't expect to find you here. I thought you might be out pulling water samples, searching for clues regarding our latest mystery."

The catfish.

"Sorry to disappoint you, Mr. Mayor. How are you?"

"Good, good. But busy. Town business never stops. There's always so much to do. Barely sleep at all these days, but don't bother worryin' none about my health. Haven't needed more than a few hours of sleep ever since the dehumidifier almost electrocuted me a dozen years back. Water and electricity don't mix."

"I've heard that," Jeremy said. "Hey, listen . . . I'm glad I ran into you. Lexie thought I should talk to you about the wedding."

Gherkin's eyebrows shot up. "You reconsidering my offer to make it an event for the whole town and have the governor come?"

"No, it's not that. Lexie wants to have the ceremony out at Cape Hatteras Lighthouse, and I haven't been able to get through to anyone at the parks department to get the permits. Do you think you could help with that?"

Mayor Gherkin thought for a few moments, then gave a low whistle. "That's a tough one," he said, shaking his head. "Dealing with the state can be mighty tricky business. Mighty tricky. It's like making your way through a minefield. You have to know someone to navigate the territory."

"That's why we need your help."

"I'd love to help, but I've just been so busy trying to straighten things out for the Heron Festival this summer. It's the big event around here—even bigger than the Historic Homes Tour, if you can believe that. We have carnival rides for the kids, concession booths along Main Street, parades, and all sorts of contests. Anyway, the grand marshal of the parade was supposed to be Myrna Jackson from Savannah, but she just called saying she's not going to be able to make it on account of her husband. You know Myrna Jackson?"

Jeremy tried to place the name. "I don't think so."

"The acclaimed photographer?"

"Sorry," Jeremy said.

"Famous woman, Myrna," he said, ignoring Jeremy's comment. "Probably the most famous southern photographer there is. Wonderful work. She actually spent a summer in Boone Creek when she was a girl, and we were lucky to get her. But just like that, her husband comes down with cancer. A terrible, terrible thing, mind you, and we'll all be praying for him—but it also puts us in a bind. We're in quite a spot, and it's going to take some time to find a new grand marshal. I'm going to have to spend hours on the phone trying to line someone up. Someone famous . . . It's just a shame I don't have any connections in the celebrity world. Well, except you, of course."

Jeremy stared at the mayor. "Are you asking me to be the grand marshal?"

"No, no, of course not. You've already got your key to the city. Someone else . . . someone whose name people will recognize." He shook his head. "Despite the breathtaking beauty of our town and the wonder of our fine citizens, it's not easy selling Boone Creek to someone from a major metropolis. Frankly, it's not a duty I look forward to, not with everything else that needs to be arranged for the festival. And then, having to deal with those folks in state government . . ." He trailed off, as if even considering the request were too much to fathom.

Jeremy knew exactly what the mayor was doing. Gherkin had a way of getting people to do just what he wanted and making them think it was their idea. It was obvious he wanted Jeremy to take care of his grand marshal problem in exchange for getting the permit, and the only question was whether Jeremy wanted to play along. Frankly, he didn't, but they did need a date . . .

Jeremy sighed. "Maybe I can help. Who do you want?"

Gherkin brought a hand to his chin, looking as if the fate of the world rested on solving this particular dilemma. "Could be anyone, I suppose. I'm just looking for name recognition, someone who'll make the town ooh and aah and bring in the crowds."

"How about if I find someone? In exchange, of course, for helping us with the permit?"

"Well, now there's an idea. Wonder why I hadn't thought of it. Let me think about that for a bit." Gherkin tapped his finger against his jaw. "Well, I suppose that might work. Assuming you get the right sort of person, I mean. What kind of person are you talking about?"

"I've interviewed a lot of people over the years. Scientists, professors, Nobel Prize winners . . ."

The mayor was already shaking his head as Jeremy continued.

"Physicists, chemists, mathematicians, explorers, astronauts . . ."

Gherkin looked up. "Did you say astronauts?"

Jeremy nodded. "The guys who fly the space shuttle. I did a big story on NASA a couple of years back, and I became friends with a few. I could give them a call . . ."

"You've got yourself a deal." Gherkin snapped his fingers. "I can see the billboards now: 'The Heron Festival: Where Outer Space Is Brought to Your Doorstep.' We can make use of that theme all weekend. Not just a pie-eating contest, but a Moon-Pie-eating contest; we can make floats that look like rockets and satellites—"

"You bothering Jeremy with that ridiculous catfish story again, Tom?" Doris said as she walked back into the room, the journal nestled beneath her arm.

"Nosiree," Gherkin answered. "Jeremy here was kind enough to offer to find a grand marshal for the parade this year, and he's promised us a genuine astronaut. What do you think of outer space, as far as themes go?"

"Inspired," Doris said. "A stroke of genius."

The mayor seemed to puff up just a bit. "Yes, you're absolutely right. I like the way you think. Now, Jeremy, what weekend were you thinking about for the wedding? Summer's mighty tough, what with all the tourists."

"May?"

"Early or late?"

"Doesn't matter," he said. "As long as we get a date, anything will be fine. But if you can, the earlier the better."

"In a rush, huh? Well, consider it done. And I can't wait to hear all about that astronaut as soon as you talk to him."

With a quick turn, Gherkin was gone and Doris was laughing under her breath as she took her seat. "Snookered you again, huh?"

"No, I knew what he was doing, but Lexie's been getting antsy about that permit."

"But other than that, the plans are going well?"

"I suppose. We've had our differences—she wants something small and intimate, I tell her that even if only my side of the family comes, there won't be enough hotels out there to accommodate them all. I want my agent, Nate, to come; she says that if we invite one friend, we have to invite them all. Things like that. But it'll work out. My family will understand no matter what we do, and I've already explained the situation to my brothers. They're not thrilled, but they understand."

Just as Doris was about to say something, Rachel came bursting through the front door, her eyes red and swollen. She sniffled as she saw Doris and Jeremy, froze for a second, and then headed toward the rear of the building. Jeremy could see the concern on Doris's face.

"I think she needs someone to talk to," he observed.

"You don't mind?"

"No, we'll catch up on the wedding plans another time."

"Okay . . . thank you." Doris slid the journal to Jeremy. "And take this. It's a great story, I promise. And you won't find any tricks because there weren't any."

Jeremy accepted the journal with a nod, still undecided as to whether or not he would use it.

Ten minutes later, Jeremy was enjoying the afternoon sunshine and heading for his cottage at Greenleaf when he eyed the office. After hesitating, he turned that way and pushed open the door. There was no sign of Jed, which meant he was probably in the shack set on the far edge of the property, the place where he plied his craft as a taxidermist. Jeremy paused once again before thinking, Why not? He might as well try to break the ice, and Lexie swore the man did talk.

He headed down the rutted path toward the shack. The smell of death and decay hit him long before he pushed his way inside.

Centered in the room was a long wooden workbench covered in stains that Jeremy assumed were blood, and strewn about were dozens of knives and other assorted tools: screws, awls, and a few of the scariest pliers and knives he had ever seen. Along the walls, set atop the shelves, and stuffed into corners were countless examples of Jed's work, everything from bass to opossums to deer, though he had the peculiar habit of making everything he mounted appear as if it were about to attack something. Off to Jeremy's left was what seemed to be a counter where business was transacted. It, too, was stained, and Jeremy found himself growing queasy.

Jed, wearing a butcher's apron while working on a wild boar, looked up as Jeremy entered. He froze.

"Hey, Jed, how are you?"

Jed said nothing.

"I just thought I'd come by to see where you actually do your work. I don't think I've mentioned my interest, but I find your work quite amazing." He waited to see if Jed would speak. Jed merely stared at Jeremy as if he were a bug that had splattered on the windshield.

Jeremy tried again, trying to ignore the fact that Jed was absolutely enormous and furry, was holding a knife, and didn't seem to be in the best of moods. He went on. "You know, how you make them look like they're snarling, claws exposed, ready to pounce. I've never seen that before. At the Museum of Natural History up in New York, most of the animals look friendly. Yours look like they're rabid or something."

Jed scowled. Jeremy had the sense that his conversational gambit wasn't going well.

"Lexie says you're quite a hunter, too," he offered, wondering why it suddenly seemed so hot in there. "I've never been, of course. The only thing we hunted in Queens were rats." He laughed, Jed didn't, and in the ensuing silence, Jeremy found himself growing nervous. "I mean, it's not like we had deer running down the block or anything. But even if we did, I probably wouldn't have shot them. You know, after seeing *Bambi* and all."

Staring at the knife in Jed's hand, Jeremy realized he was beginning to ramble, but he couldn't seem to help it.

"That's just me, though. Not that I think there's anything wrong with hunting, of course . . . NRA, Bill of Rights, Second Amendment. I'm all for that. I mean, hunting is an American tradition, right? Line up the deer in your sights, and bam. Little fella topples over."

Jed moved the knife from one hand to the other, and Jeremy swallowed, wanting nothing more than to get out of there.

"Well, I just dropped by to say hey. And good luck with . . . well, whatever you're doing there. Can't wait to see it. Any messages?" He shifted from one foot to the other. "No? Okay, then. Nice talking to you."

Jeremy took a seat at the desk in his room and stared at a blank screen, trying to forget what had just happened with Jed. He desperately wished he could think of something to write but gradually came to the conclusion that the well had run dry.

It happened to all writers at various times, he knew, and there was no magic cure, simply because all writers approached their craft in slightly different ways. Some wrote in the morning, others in the afternoon, still others late at night. Some wrote to music, others needed complete silence. He knew of one writer who supposedly worked naked, locking himself in his room and giving strict instructions to his assistant that he was not to receive his clothing until he slid five written pages beneath the door. He knew of others who watched the same movie over and over, still others who couldn't write without drinking or smoking excessively. Jeremy wasn't that eccentric; in the past, he'd written whenever and wherever he'd needed to, so it wasn't as if he could make a simple change and all would be right again.

Though he wasn't quite panicked yet, he was getting concerned. More than two months had passed since he'd written anything, but because of the magazine's publishing schedule—it was usually put together six weeks in advance—he'd written enough columns to get him through July. Which meant he still had a bit of breathing room before he'd be in serious trouble with *Scientific American*.

But because freelancing paid most of the bills and he'd practically emptied his brokerage account to buy his car, pay for his living expenses, put the down payment and closing costs in escrow, and continue the ever expanding renovations, he wasn't sure he had even that much time. Money was being sucked from his accounts as if by a vampire on steroids.

And he *was* blocked, he was beginning to think. It wasn't just that he was busy or life had changed, as he'd suggested to Alvin and Doris. After all, he'd been able to write after he'd divorced Maria. In fact, he'd needed to write just to keep from dwelling on it. Writing had been an escape back then, but now? What if he never got over this?

He would lose his job. He would lose his income, and how on earth was he supposed to support Lexie and his daughter? Would he be forced to become "Mr. Mom" while Lexie worked to support the family? The images were disconcerting.

From the corner of his eye, he caught sight of Doris's journal. He could, he supposed, take her up on the offer. It might be just what he needed to get the juices flowing again—supernatural elements, interesting, original. If, of course, it was true. Could she really predict the sex of babies?

No, he decided again. And that was the thing. It couldn't be true. It might be one of the greatest coincidences in history, but it wasn't true. There was simply no way to tell the sex of a baby by placing a hand on a woman's stomach.

Why, then, was he so willing to believe his own baby would be a girl? Why was he as positive about

87

it as Lexie? When he imagined himself holding the baby in the future, she was always wrapped in a pink blanket. He sat back in his chair, wondering, and then decided that in fact he wasn't absolutely positive. Lexie was the one who was sure, not him, and he was merely reflecting her opinion. And the fact that she continually referred to the baby as a little girl only reinforced that.

Instead of dwelling on it further—or trying to write—Jeremy decided to scan his favorite news sites on the Internet, hoping that something might click. Without high-speed access, the progress was slow to the point of making him drowsy, but he pushed on. He visited four sites involving UFOs; the official Web site regarding the latest in haunted houses; and the site put up by James Randi, who like him was devoted to exposing hoaxes and frauds. For years, Randi had a standing offer to pay a million dollars to any psychic who could prove his or her ability under rigorous scientific controls. To date, no one—including those better-known psychics who appeared regularly on television or wrote books—had taken him up on his challenge. Once, in one of his columns, Jeremy had made the same offer (on a much smaller scale, of course) with exactly the same results. People who called themselves psychics were experts in self-promotion, not the paranormal. Jeremy recalled his exposé of Timothy Clausen, a man who claimed to be able to speak to spirits from beyond the grave. It was the last major story he'd worked on before he'd traveled to Boone Creek in search of ghosts and found Lexie instead.

On Randi's site, there was the usual collection of stories, supposedly magical events peppered with the author's disbelief, but after a couple of hours, Jeremy logged off, realizing he was no further along with ideas than when he'd started.

Checking his watch, he saw it was almost five, and he wondered whether he should stop by the house to see how the repairs were going. Maybe they'd moved another pile or something, anything to make it appear as if the project could be completed this year. Despite the endless bills, Jeremy was beginning to doubt whether they would ever move in. What once seemed manageable now seemed daunting, and he decided he'd pass on the visit to the house. No reason to make a dismal day even worse.

Instead, he chose to head to the library to see how Lexie was doing. He threw on a clean shirt, ran a brush through his hair, and slapped on some cologne; a few minutes later, he was passing Herbs on his way to the library. The dogwoods and azaleas were starting to look limp and tired, but along the sides of buildings and at the base of trees, tulips and daffodils were beginning to open, their colors even more vivid. The warm southerly breeze made it seem more like early summer than late March, the kind of day that would bring throngs to Central Park.

He wondered whether he should swing by and pick up a bouquet of flowers for Lexie, finally deciding he should. There was only one florist in town, and the store also sold live bait and fishing tackle; despite a sparse selection, he emerged from the store a few minutes later with a spring bouquet he was sure Lexie would love.

He reached the library within minutes but frowned when he realized that Lexie's car wasn't in its normal spot. Glancing toward the office window, he noticed her light was off. Thinking that she was at Herbs, he headed back that way, looking for but not seeing her car, then swung past her house, figuring she must have made it an early day. She was probably running an errand or shopping.

He turned the car around and retraced his path through town, cruising slowly. When he spotted Lexie's car parked near a Dumpster behind the pizza parlor, he slammed on the brakes and pulled his car in beside hers, figuring she must have wanted to walk the boardwalk on such a beautiful day.

He grabbed the flowers and headed between the buildings, thinking he'd surprise her, but as he rounded the corner, he came to an abrupt halt.

Lexie was there, just as he'd expected her to be. She was sitting on the bench that overlooked the river, but what stopped him from moving forward was the fact that she wasn't alone.

Instead, she was sitting beside Rodney, almost nestled against him. From the back, it was difficult to make out anything more than that. He reminded himself that they were just friends. She'd known him since they'd been kids, and for a moment that was enough.

Until, that is, they shifted on the bench, and he realized they were holding hands.

Six

.... ❖ ....

Jeremy knew that what he saw shouldn't bother him. Deep down, he knew that Lexie wasn't interested in Rodney, but as April rolled in over the next week, he found himself dwelling on the scene he'd witnessed. Even when he'd asked Lexie whether anything unusual had happened that day, she'd said no, telling him that she'd spent the afternoon at the library. While he could have questioned her further about the lie, he hadn't seen the need. She'd been thrilled by the flowers and had kissed him immediately after he'd handed them over. He'd searched for anything different about the kiss—whether it was hesitant or lingered too long, as if over-compensating for guilt—but he'd sensed nothing amiss. Nor was there anything unusual about their conversation over dinner, or their spell on the porch afterward.

Even so, he couldn't forget the image of Lexie holding Rodney's hand. The more he thought about it, the more he realized that they looked like a couple, but he reminded himself that it didn't make sense. Lexie and Rodney couldn't be seeing each other secretly. He spent most days at the library doing research and every evening with Lexie. Jeremy couldn't force himself to believe that Lexie spent a single moment dreaming of what might have been between her and Rodney had Jeremy never come along. She'd told him that Rodney had had a crush on her since they'd been young and that every now and then they'd attended some town function together as a couple, but that was in the past. Lexie had always resisted further development in their relationship, and he couldn't imagine that she would change her mind now. Yes, she'd been holding his hand, but that didn't necessarily mean she was feeling any differently toward him. There had been times when Jeremy held his mother's hand, for goodness' sake. It could have been a sign of affection or support or just a way to show that she was listening to him as he spilled out his troubles. In a relationship like Lexie and Rodney's, it could have been a gesture of comfort, since they'd known each other for years.

It wasn't as if he should expect Lexie to start ignoring people she'd known all her life, right? Or stop caring about other people? Weren't those the reasons he'd fallen in love with her in the first place? Of course they were. Lexie had a way of making everyone she spent time with feel as if they were the center of the world, and though that included Rodney, it didn't mean she was in love with him. Which meant, of course, there was nothing to worry about.

So why on earth was he still thinking about it?

And why, when he saw them, had he felt a stab of jealousy?

Because she'd lied about it. A lie of omission, perhaps, but a lie nonetheless. Finally, unable to stand it a moment longer, he rose from his desk, grabbed his car keys, and drove toward the library.

Slowing as he approached, he saw her car parked exactly where it should be and stared at the light on in her office. He watched for a few minutes, turning away quickly when he caught a glimpse of her. Despite the foolishness he felt at this new obsession, he nonetheless breathed a sigh of relief. He told himself again that he had nothing to worry about, that it was ridiculous to have even considered the possibility that Lexie might be elsewhere, and the foolish feeling lasted until he returned to Greenleaf.

Yes, he thought as he perched himself in front of the screen again, he and Lexie were doing just fine, and he chided himself for his suspicion, promising to make it up to her somehow. He could do that, he thought, he should do that—even if he would never admit the reason. Maybe they'd head out of town tonight for dinner.

Yeah, he decided, aside from porch sitting, there was nothing pressing on the old agenda, and a little change of pace might do them both some good. More than that, she'd be surprised at his thoughtfulness. If there was one thing he'd learned in the dating world, it was that women loved surprises, and if it helped him alleviate the guilt he felt from checking up on her in the first place, all the better.

He nodded to himself. A special night was just

what they needed. He'd even buy her another bouquet of flowers, and he spent the next twenty minutes on the Internet, trying to figure out a good place to go. He found one, called Doris to see if she'd heard of it—she recommended it with gusto—and then made reservations before showering again.

With another couple of hours until she got off work, he sat in front of the computer again, his fingers poised on the keyboard. But even after a day spent mostly at the desk, Jeremy realized that he was no closer to writing than he had been when he'd risen that morning.

"I saw you earlier today," Lexie said, peeking over her menu at him.

"You did?"

She nodded. "I saw you driving past the library. Where were you going?"

"Oh," he said, glad she hadn't caught him staring up at her window. "Nowhere, really. Just driving around to clear my mind before hitting the computer again."

Surprised with a bouquet of daffodils and an out-of-town dinner reservation, she'd been thrilled, just as he'd expected. But of course, being thrilled meant heading back to her house so she could change and get ready, which delayed their departure by nearly forty-five minutes. By the time they arrived at the Carriage House on the outskirts of Greenville, their table had been given away and they'd had to wait at the bar for twenty minutes.

Lexie seemed reluctant to ask the obvious follow-up question, which made sense. Every day she asked how his writing went; every day Jeremy answered there had been no change. It was probably beginning to wear on her the same way it was beginning to wear on him.

"Did you get any ideas?" she ventured.

"A few, actually," Jeremy lied. Technically, it wasn't a lie—he'd had that strange idea about Lexie and Rodney—but he knew it wasn't the sort of idea she was referring to.

"Really?"

"I'm still noodling with it, and we'll see where it leads."

"That's great, honey," she said, her mood brightening even more. "We should celebrate, then." She gazed around the dimly lit room; with the waiters in black and white and candles on every table, the setting was surprisingly elegant. "How on earth did you find out about this place, anyway? I've never been here before, but I've always wanted to go."

"Just a bit of research," he said, "and then I called Doris."

"She loves this place," Lexie said. "If she had her way, I think she'd run a restaurant like this instead of Herbs."

"But you have to pay the bills, right?"

"Exactly," she said. "What are you planning on ordering?"

"I was thinking about the porterhouse," he said, scanning the menu. "I haven't had a good steak since I left New York. And the au gratin potatoes."

"Isn't a porterhouse two steaks? The strip and the filet?"

"That's why it sounds good," he said, closing the menu, his mouth already watering. As he looked across at her, he noticed her nose was wrinkling. "What?" he asked.

"How many calories do you think that has?"

"I have no idea. And I don't care, either."

She forced a smile, returning to the menu again. "You're right," she said. "We don't go out like this all the time, so what's the big deal? Even if it is . . . what? A pound, pound and a half of red meat?"

He felt his brow furrowing. "I didn't say I was going to eat the whole thing."

"It doesn't matter even if you do. It's not my place to say anything. Get what you want."

"I will," he said, feeling defiant. In the silence, he watched her study the menu, thinking about the porterhouse. It *was* a lot of red meat, now that he thought about it, packed with cholesterol and fat. Didn't the experts say you should eat no more than three ounces at a time? And this steak . . . what was that? Sixteen ounces? Twenty-four? It was enough to feed an entire family.

Ah, who cared? He was young, and he'd make it a point to work out tomorrow. Go for a jog, do some extra push-ups. "What are you thinking about getting?"

"I'm still deciding," she said. "I'm not sure which one I'm in the mood for, but it'll either be the broiled tuna or the stuffed chicken breast with the sauce on the side. And steamed vegetables."

Of course that's what you're getting, Jeremy thought. Something light and healthy. She'd stay fit and thin, even though she was pregnant, while he would waddle out of the restaurant.

He reached for the menu again, noticing that she

made a point of ignoring him. Which meant, obviously, that she did notice. Scanning the items, he moved to the seafood and poultry sections. Everything sounded wonderful. Just not as wonderful as the porterhouse. He closed the menu again, thinking this was guilt he could have done without.

Since when had food become such a reflection of character? If he ordered something healthy, he was a good person; if he ordered something unhealthy, he was bad? It wasn't as if he were overweight, right? He would order the porterhouse, he resolved, but reminded himself again to have only half of it, maybe less. It wasn't as if he'd waste it, either. He'd bring the rest home for leftovers. He nodded to himself, pleased with his decision. The porterhouse it was.

When the waiter appeared, Lexie ordered a cranberry juice and the stuffed chicken breast. Jeremy said he'd have the cranberry juice as well.

"And for your dinner?"

He felt Lexie watching him. "The . . . tuna," he said. "Medium rare."

After the waiter left, Lexie smiled. "The tuna?"

"Yeah," he said. "It sounded good when you mentioned it."

She shrugged, unreadable.

"What now?"

"It's just that this place is famous for its steaks. I was kind of hoping to try a bite of yours."

Jeremy felt his shoulders sag. "Next time," he said.

Try as he might, Jeremy wasn't sure he'd ever figure out women. There were times while he'd been dating that he believed he was getting closer, that he would be able to anticipate their subtle expressions and mannerisms and use them to his own advantage. But as his dinner with Lexie demonstrated, he had a long way to go.

The problem wasn't the fact that he'd ordered the tuna instead of the porterhouse. It went deeper than that. The real problem was that most men wanted a woman's admiration; consequently, men were willing to do nearly anything to achieve that. Women, he suspected, had never fully grasped this simple fact. For instance, women might assume that men who spent a great deal of time at the office did so because they viewed their job as the most important thing in their life, when nothing could be further from the truth. It wasn't about power for power's sake—well, okay, for some men it was, but they were in a minority—it was the fact that women were drawn to power for the same reasons men were drawn to attractive young women. These were evolutionary traits, traits passed down since the caveman days, and neither gender had much control over them. Years ago he'd written a column about the evolutionary basis of behavior, pointing out that among other things, men were drawn to young, shapely, attractive women because they tended to be fertile and in good health—in other words, a mate likely to create strong offspring—and that women were likewise drawn to men who were powerful enough to protect and provide for them and their offspring.

He got a lot of mail about that column, he remembered, but what was odd about it were the reactions. While men tended to agree with this representation of evolution, women tended to disagree, sometimes vehemently. A few months later, he wrote another column about the differences, using excerpts from the letters as examples.

But even if he could understand objectively that he'd ordered the tuna because he'd wanted Lexie to admire him—thus making him feel powerful—it still didn't help him decipher what made her tick, and pregnancy only complicated the matter further. He admitted that he didn't know much about pregnancy, but if there was one thing he was sure about, it was the fact that pregnant women often had strange cravings. Lexie might have been an expert on virtually everything else, but he was ready for whatever she might throw at him in that particular department. His brothers had told him to expect anything; one sister-in-law had craved spinach salad, another wanted pastrami and olives, still another would wake up in the middle of the night to eat tomato soup and cheddar cheese. Consequently, when he wasn't trying to write, he found himself heading to the grocery store to fill the car with whatever he could think of, anything that might satisfy Lexie's cravings, no matter how odd they might be.

What he didn't expect, however, were the irrational mood swings. One night, about a week after their dinner at the Carriage House, he woke up to the sound of Lexie sniffling. When he rolled over, he found her sitting up in bed with her back against the headboard. In the dim light, he could barely make out her features, but he noticed a pile of used tissues in her lap. He sat up in bed.

"Lex? Are you okay? What's wrong?"

"I'm sorry," she said, sounding as if she had a bad cold. "I didn't mean to wake you."

"That's okay . . . no problem. What is it?"

"Nothing."

It sounded as though she'd said "nudding." He watched her, still unsure what was going on. The fact that he was staring didn't stop her from crying, and she sniffled again. "I'm just sad," she explained.

"Can I get you anything? Pastrami? Tomato soup?"

She blinked through her tears, as if trying to figure out if she'd heard him right. "Why on earth would you think I want pastrami?"

"No reason," he said. Sliding closer, he slipped his arm around her. "So you're not hungry, though? No strange cravings?"

"No." She shook her head. "I just feel sad."

"And you don't know why?"

All at once she broke down again, big heaving cries that left her shoulders shaking. Jeremy felt his throat constrict. There was nothing worse than the sound of a woman crying, and he found himself wanting to comfort her. "There, there," he murmured. "It'll be okay, whatever it is."

"No, it won't," she blubbered. "It's not going to be okay. It's never going to be okay."

"What is it?"

It took a long time before she was able to regain some semblance of control. Finally, she faced him with red, puffy eyes.

"I killed my cat," she announced.

There were a lot of things he'd expected her to say. Perhaps she was overwhelmed by the changes in her life, for instance. Or maybe, in the surge of hormones, she had found herself missing her parents. He had no doubt her emotional outburst had to do with the pregnancy, but this was not the sort of comment he could ever have anticipated. All he could do was stare.

"Your cat?" he asked at last.

She nodded and reached for another tissue, talking through her sobs. "I . . . killed . . . it."

"Huh," Jeremy said. Frankly, he didn't know what else to say. He'd never seen a cat around her place, never heard her talk about a cat. Didn't even know she liked cats.

Meanwhile, she went on, her voice still raspy. He could tell by her body language that she'd been hurt by his comment. "That's . . . all you can . . . say?"

He was at a loss. Should he agree with her? *You really shouldn't have killed the cat.* Should he empathize? *That's okay. The cat deserved it.* Should he support her? *I still think you're a good person, even if you did kill that cat.* At the same time, he was frantically searching his memory, trying to figure out if there actually had been a cat, and if so, what its name was. Or how on earth he'd gone this long without ever seeing it. But in a burst of inspiration, the perfect response leapt to mind.

"Why don't you tell me what happened," he said, trying his best to sound soothing.

It seemed to be exactly what she'd needed to hear, thank goodness, and her sobs began to subside. Again, she blew her nose.

"I was doing laundry and emptied the dryer to add the next load," she said. "I knew he liked warm places, but I never bothered to check inside before I closed the door. I killed Boots."

Boots, he thought. Got it. The cat was named Boots. Still, it didn't make the rest of the story any clearer.

"When did this happen?" he tried again.

"Over the summer." She sighed. "While I was packing for Chapel Hill."

"Oh, we're talking about when you went to college," he said, feeling triumphant.

She looked over at him, obviously confused and irritated. "Of course I am. What did you think I was talking about?"

Jeremy knew it was probably best not to answer. "I'm sorry for interrupting. Go on," he said, doing his best to sound sympathetic.

"Boots was my baby," she said, her voice soft. "He was abandoned, and I found him when he was just a kitten. All through high school, he slept with me in bed. He was so cute—reddish brown fur and white paws—and I knew that God had given him to me to protect him. And I did . . . until I locked him in the dryer."

She reached for another tissue. "I guess that he crawled into the dryer when I wasn't paying attention. He'd done that before, so I usually checked, but for whatever reason, I didn't do it that day. I just loaded the wet clothes from the washer into the dryer, closed the door, and hit the button." The tears started again as Lexie went on, her words broken. "I was downstairs . . . half an hour later . . . when I heard the . . . the . . . thunking . . . and when I went to check . . . I found him—"

She broke down completely then, leaning against Jeremy. Instinctively, he pulled her closer, murmuring words of support.

"You didn't kill your cat," he reassured her. "It was an accident."

She sobbed even harder. "But . . . don't you . . . see?"

"See what?"

"That . . . I'll be a . . . terrible mother. I . . . I . . . locked my poor cat . . . in the dryer . . ."

"I just held her and she kept on crying," Jeremy said at lunch the next day. "No matter how much I assured her that she'd be a wonderful mother, she wouldn't believe me. She cried for hours. There was nothing I could say or do to console her, but she finally nodded off to sleep. And when she woke up, she seemed fine."

"That's pregnancy," Doris said. "It's like a great big amplifier. Everything gets bigger—your body, your tummy, your arms. Emotions and memories, too. You just go crazy every now and then, and sometimes you do the strangest things. Things you'd never do in other circumstances."

Doris's comment conjured up the image of Lexie and Rodney holding hands, and for an instant he wondered whether to mention it. As quickly as the thought came, he tried to dismiss it.

Doris seemed to read his expression. "Jeremy? Are you okay?"

He shook his head. "Yeah," he said. "Just a lot on my mind these days."

"About the baby?"

"About everything," he said. "The wedding, the house. All of it. There's so much to do. We're closing on the house at the end of the month, and the only permit Gherkin could get was for the first weekend in May. There's just a lot of stress these days." He looked across the table at her. "Thanks for helping Lexie with the wedding plans, by the way."

"No need to thank me. After our last conversation, I thought it was the least I could do. And there's not that much to do, really. I'll be making the cake and bringing some finger food for the outdoor reception, but other than that, there wasn't much left once you got the permit. I'll cover the picnic tables that morning, the florist will put some flowers out, and the photographer is good to go."

"She told me she finally picked a dress."

"She did. For Rachel, too, since she's the maid of honor."

"Does it hide Lexie's tummy?"

Doris laughed. "That was her only stipulation. But don't you worry, she'll look beautiful—you can barely tell she's pregnant. But I think people are beginning to suspect anyway." She nodded toward Rachel, who was clearing another table. "I think she knows."

"How would she know? Did you say anything?"

"No, of course not. But women can tell when other women are pregnant. And I've heard people whispering about it over lunch. Of course, it doesn't help that Lexie's been browsing through baby clothes

104

at Gherkin's store downtown. People notice things like that."

"Lexie's not going to be happy about it."

"She won't mind. Not in the long run, anyway. And besides, she didn't really believe she'd even be able to keep it a secret this long."

"Does that mean I can tell my family now?"

"I think," Doris said slowly, "you'd better ask Lexie about that. She's still worried that they won't like her, especially with the wedding being so small. She feels bad about not being able to invite the whole clan." She smiled. "That was her word, by the way, not mine."

"It works," Jeremy said. "They are a clan. But now it'll be a manageable clan."

When Doris reached for her glass, Rachel returned to their table with a pitcher of sweet tea. "Need a refill?"

"Thanks, Rach," Jeremy said.

She poured. "Are you getting excited about the wedding?"

"Getting there. How'd shopping go with Lexie?"

"It was fun," she said. "It was nice to get out of town for a while. But I'll bet you can understand that."

Sure I can, Jeremy thought. "Oh, by the way, I talked to Alvin and he said to say hello."

"He did?"

"He said he's looking forward to seeing you again."

"Tell him hey from me, too." She fiddled with her apron. "Do you two want some pecan pie? I think there're still a few pieces left."

"No thanks," Jeremy said. "I'm stuffed."

"None for me," Doris said.

As Rachel headed toward the kitchen, Doris put her napkin on the table, returning her attention to Jeremy. "I walked through the house yesterday. It looks like it's coming along."

"Does it? I hadn't noticed."

"It'll be done," she reassured him, hearing his tone. "People may work at a slower pace down here, but it all gets done eventually."

"I just hope it's finished before the baby heads off to college. We just found out that there's some termite damage."

"What did you expect? It's an old house."

"It's like the house in the movie *The Money Pit*. There's always something else that needs to be fixed."

"I could have told you that beforehand. Why do you think it had been on the market so long? And come on, no matter how much it costs, it's still cheaper than anything in Manhattan, isn't it?"

"It's certainly more frustrating."

Doris stared at him. "I take it you're still not writing."

"Excuse me?"

"You heard me," she said, her voice soft. "You aren't writing. That's who you are; it's how you define yourself. And if you can't do it . . . well, it's kind of like Lexie's pregnancy in that it amplifies everything else."

Doris was right, Jeremy decided. It wasn't the cost of the new house, plans for the wedding, the baby, or the fact that he was still adjusting to life as a couple. Any stress he felt was due largely to the fact that he couldn't write.

The day before, he'd sent off his next column, leaving only four prewritten columns left, and his editor at *Scientific American* had begun to leave messages on Jeremy's cell phone, asking why Jeremy wasn't bothering to keep in touch. Even Nate was beginning to get concerned; where he used to leave messages about the possibility of coming up with a story that might appeal to television producers, he now wondered whether Jeremy was working on anything at all.

At first, it had been easy to make excuses; both his editor and Nate understood how much had recently changed in his life. But when he offered the standard litany of excuses, even Jeremy realized they sounded exactly like that: excuses. Even so, he couldn't figure out what was wrong. Why did his thoughts become jumbled every time he turned on the computer? Why did his fingers turn to mud? And why did it happen only when it came to writing something that might pay the bills?

See, that was the thing. Alvin e-mailed regularly; Jeremy could pound out a long response in only a few minutes. The same thing happened if his mother or father or brothers e-mailed, or if he had to write a letter, or if he wanted to take notes about something he found on the Internet. He could write about the shows on television, he could write about business or politics; he knew, because he'd tried. It was easy, in fact, to write just about anything . . . as long as it had nothing to do with topics he had any expertise in. In those instances, he simply went blank. Or worse, he felt as if he would never be able to do it again.

He suspected his problem was a lack of confidence. It was an odd feeling, one he hadn't ever experienced before moving to Boone Creek.

He wondered if that was it. The move itself. That's when the problem started; it wasn't the house or the wedding plans or anything else. He'd been blocked from the time he'd rolled back into town, as if the choice to move here had come with a hidden cost. That suggested that he would be able to write in New York, however . . . but could he? He considered it, then shook his head. It didn't matter, did it? He was here. In less than three weeks, on April 28, he'd close on the house and then head off to his bachelor party; a week later, on May 6, he'd be married. For better or worse, this was home now.

He glanced at Doris's journal. How would he start a story about it? Not that he intended to, but just as an experiment . . .

Pulling up a blank document, he began to think, his fingers poised on the keyboard. But for the next five minutes, his fingers didn't move. There was nothing, nothing at all. He couldn't even think of a way to begin.

He ran his hand through his hair, frustrated, wanting yet another break, wondering what to do. There was no way he was going to the house, he decided, since it would only put him in a worse mood. He decided instead to kill some time on the Internet. He heard the modem dial in, watched the screen load, and scanned the main page. Noting that he had two dozen new messages, he clicked on the mailbox.

Most of it was spam, and he deleted those messages without opening them; Nate had sent a message as well, asking if Jeremy had noticed any of the articles concerning a massive meteor shower in Australia. Jeremy responded that he'd written four columns about meteors in the past, one as recently as last year, but he thanked him for the idea.

He nearly deleted the last message, which lacked a subject heading, but thought better of it and found himself staring at the screen as soon as the message appeared. His mouth went dry, and he couldn't turn away. Nor, suddenly, could he breathe. It was a simple message, and the blinking cursor seemed to taunt him: *HOW DO YOU KNOW THE BABY IS YOURS?*

Seven

·····❖·····

HOW DO YOU KNOW THE BABY IS YOURS?

Jeremy knocked back his chair as he rose from the desk, still focused on the message. *Of course the baby's mine!* he wanted to scream. *I know because I know!*

Yes, the message seemed to ask, you say you know. But *how* do you know?

His mind raced for the answers. Because he and Lexie spent a wonderful night together. Because she told him it was his baby and she had no reason to lie. Because they were getting married. Because it couldn't be anyone else's. Because it was his baby . . .

Wasn't it?

Had he been anyone else, had his history been different, had he known Lexie for years, the answer would have been obvious; but.

That was the thing about life, he knew. There was always a *but*.

He shook the thought away, focusing on the message, trying to get control of his emotions. There was no need to get worked up about this, he told himself, even if the message not only was offensive, but bordered on . . . evil. That's how he viewed it. Evil. What kind of person would write such a thing? And for what reason? Because he thought it was funny? Because he wanted to start an argument between Lexie and Jeremy? Because . . .

He went blank for an instant, fumbling, his mind racing, knowing the answer but not wanting to admit it.

Because . . .

Because, the little voice in his head finally answered, *whoever sent it knew that deep down, there was an instant when you wondered, too?*

No, he suddenly thought, that was a lie. He knew the baby was his.

Except, of course, that you aren't able to get a woman pregnant, the little voice reminded him.

With a flash, it all came rushing back—his first marriage to Maria, the difficulty they'd had getting pregnant, the trips to the fertility clinic, the tests he'd taken, all culminating with the doctor's words: *It's highly unlikely that you'll ever be able to father a child.*

It was a kind choice of words: Jeremy had learned during that visit that for all intents and purposes he was sterile, a reality that eventually led Maria to ask for a divorce.

He remembered the doctor telling him that his sperm count was low—almost negligible, in fact—and those he did produce showed very little motility. Jeremy recalled sitting in the office in shock, grasping at any option. *How about if I wore boxers?*

I've heard that helps, or *How about treatments?* There was nothing they could really do for him, the doctor explained. Nothing likely to be effective.

That day had been one of the most devastating of his life; until that point, he'd always assumed that he'd have children, and after the divorce, he'd reacted by becoming someone else entirely. He had more one-night stands than he could count and assumed he would lead the life of a bachelor forever. Until he met Lexie. And the miracle of her pregnancy, a child created out of passion and love, made him realize how pointless those years had been.

Unless . . .

No, scratch that, Jeremy thought. There was no *unless.* Of course the baby was his. Everything— from the timing, to Lexie's behavior all along, to the way Doris treated him now—assured him that he was the father of the baby. He repeated those thoughts like a mantra, hoping to drown out the reality of the doctor's words so long ago.

The message continued to taunt him. Who sent the e-mail? And, he wondered again, why?

Years of investigative research had taught him quite a bit about the Internet, and though the sender used an address Jeremy didn't recognize, he knew that all e-mails could eventually be traced. With a bit of persistence and the right phone calls to a few contacts he'd made over the years, he could trace the e-mail back to the server and, from there, to the computer from which it had originated. He noticed that the message had arrived less than twenty minutes earlier, right around the time he was getting back to Greenleaf.

But again, the question was *Why?* Why would someone send it?

With the exception of Lexie, Jeremy had never told anyone—not his parents or his friends—about his inability to father children, and though there had been an instant when he'd wondered how the pregnancy had happened despite the odds, he'd shrugged that thought off. But if only Maria and Lexie knew—and neither one, he was sure, had sent it—then again, what was the reason? Was it a prank?

Doris had mentioned that some people had begun to suspect that Lexie was pregnant—Rachel, for instance. But he couldn't picture Rachel being responsible for the e-mail. She and Lexie had been friends for years, and this wasn't the sort of prank friends played on one another.

But if it hadn't been meant as a prank, the only conceivable reason to send the e-mail was to cause trouble between Jeremy and Lexie. But again, who would do that?

The real father? a voice inside whispered, suddenly making him remember Lexie and Rodney holding hands.

Jeremy shook his head. Rodney and Lexie? He'd gone over that a thousand times, and it simply wasn't possible. It was ridiculous even to consider it.

Except that it does explain the e-mail, the voice whispered again.

No, he thought, this time more adamantly. Lexie wasn't like that. Lexie wasn't sleeping with someone else that week; Lexie wasn't even seeing someone else. And Rodney wasn't the kind of man who would write an e-mail; he would have confronted Jeremy in person.

Jeremy pressed the button to delete the e-mail. When the screen flashed the confirmation, however, his finger seemed to freeze. Did he really want to delete it now, without finding out who had sent it?

No, he decided, he wanted to know. It would take some time, but he'd find out and speak to whoever sent it, make him see how tasteless it was. And if it was Rodney . . . well, not only would Jeremy confront him, but there was no doubt that Lexie would give him a piece of her mind as well.

He nodded. Oh, he'd find out who did it all right. He saved the message, with the intent to begin the search immediately. And once he learned anything, Lexie would be the first to know.

Spending the evening with Lexie assuaged any doubts he had that he was indeed the father. At dinner, Lexie chatted away as usual; in fact, over the next week, Lexie acted as if nothing was bothering her at all. Which, in all honesty, Jeremy considered somewhat strange, considering that the wedding was now only a little more than two weeks away, they would close on the house a week from Friday—though it was still a long way from being habitable—and Jeremy had begun to wonder aloud where he was going to work in Boone Creek, since he'd obviously forgotten how to write an article. He'd sent another prewritten column, leaving only three left to submit. He hadn't been able to trace the e-mail yet; whoever had done it had covered his tracks well. The address was not only anonymous, it had been routed through a series of different servers—one offshore and another that was unwilling to divulge information without a court order. Luckily he knew someone in New York who thought he could hack in, but it was going to take a little time. The guy freelanced for the FBI and they kept him busy.

On the plus side, aside from another teary episode in the middle of the night, Lexie seemed far less stressed than he was. Of course, that didn't mean she was exactly the woman he'd imagined her to be. She was, he'd come to realize, completely in charge of the pregnancy. Granted, she was the one carrying the baby, she was the one with the crazy mood swings, and she was the one who read all the books, but it wasn't as if Jeremy were clueless. Or that he was bored with the details she seemed to find so intriguing. On the following Saturday morning, with the bright April sun coming down hard, Lexie jingled her keys as they were about to leave to go shopping, as if giving him one last chance to back out of his fatherly duties.

"Are you sure about coming with me today?" Lexie asked.

"Positive."

"Wasn't there a basketball game on television that you want to watch? You're going to miss it."

He smiled. "I'll be fine. There are more games tomorrow."

"You do know this is going to take some time."

"So?"

"I just don't want you to get bored."

"I won't get bored. I love shopping," Jeremy promised.

"Since when? And besides, it's just baby stuff."

"I live to buy baby stuff."

She shook her head. "Suit yourself."

An hour later, after arriving in Greenville, Jeremy entered one of those warehouse baby stores and suddenly wondered whether Lexie might have been right. The place was unlike anything he'd ever seen in New York. Not only was it cavernous, with wide aisles and towering ceilings, but the choice of items on sale was dizzying. If buying things proved how much you loved your children, this was obviously the place to go. Jeremy spent the first few minutes wandering around in disbelief, and wondering who had come up with all this stuff.

Who knew, for instance, that there were literally thousands of different mobiles a parent could attach to the crib? Some with animals, others with colors, some with black-and-white geometric shapes, some that played music, others that spun in slow circles. It went without saying that each mobile had been scientifically shown to stimulate the intellectual development of the baby, and he and Lexie must have stood in the aisle examining the choices for nearly twenty minutes, during which time Jeremy learned that his opinion was usually no help whatsoever.

"I've read that babies respond mostly to black and white," Lexie said.

"Then let's go with this one," Jeremy said, pointing to one with black-and-white designs.

"But I was going to go with an animal theme, and I don't think it'll match."

"It's just a mobile. No one's going to notice."

"I'll notice."

"Then let's go with this one. With the hippos and giraffes."

"But it's not black and white."

"Do you really think it matters? That if our baby doesn't have a black-and-white mobile as an infant, she's going to flunk out of kindergarten?"

"No, of course not," Lexie said. Still, she stood in the aisle, her arms crossed, seemingly no closer to a decision.

"What about this one?" Jeremy finally offered. "It's got panels that you can switch from black and white to animals, and it spins and plays music to boot."

Her expression was almost sad as she peered at him. "Don't you think she might get overstimulated by something like that?"

Somehow, they were able to select the mobile (black-and-white animals, able to spin, but no music), and for some reason, Jeremy made the assumption that everything would go more smoothly from that point on. And over the next few hours, some choices *were* easy—blankets, pacifiers, and, surprisingly, the crib itself—but when they hit the aisle offering car seats, they were flummoxed again. Jeremy had never imagined that it wasn't possible to make do with only one car seat; instead, there were the "less than six months old facing backward" car seat, the "easy to remove and lightweight" car seat, the "can be attached to a stroller" car seat, the "toddler forward facing" car seat, and the "heavy duty if there's an accident" car seat. Add in the endless patterns and colors, the ease or difficulty with which it could be removed from the car, and the buckling mechanisms, and by the end, Jeremy felt lucky that they ended up with only two, both rated as a "Best Buy" for safety in *Consumer Reports*. This Best Buy status seemed ironic in light of the exorbitant price and the fact that the infant car seat would more than likely end up in the attic only a few months after the baby was born.

But safety was paramount. As Lexie reminded him, "You want our baby to be safe, don't you?"

It wasn't as if he could disagree, was it?

"You're right," he answered, loading the two boxes atop the mountain of items they'd accumulated. Two carts were already filled, and they were working on the third. "By the way, what time is it?"

"It's ten after three. About ten minutes later than the last time you asked."

"Really? It seems later."

"That's what you said ten minutes ago."

"Sorry about that."

"I tried to warn you that you'd be bored."

"I'm not bored," he lied. "Unlike some fathers, I care about my baby."

She seemed amused. "Good. But we're almost done here anyway."

"Really?"

"I just want to look at some clothes real quick."

"Great," Jeremy forced out, thinking that was an unlikely scenario if ever there was one.

"It'll only be a minute."

"Take your time," he said, as if proving his gallantry.

She did. All in all, he figured they spent nearly six years looking at clothing that afternoon. With aching legs and feeling something like a pack mule, Jeremy found a ledge to sit on while Lexie seemed intent on examining each and every baby outfit the store had to offer. One by one, she'd select an item, hold it up, and either frown or smile in delight, as she imagined their little girl wearing it. Which, of course, made no sense at all to Jeremy, since they had no idea what their baby was going to look like.

"How about Savannah?" Lexie said while holding up yet another outfit. This one, Jeremy noticed, was pink with purple bunnies.

"I've only been there once," he said.

She lowered the outfit. "I'm talking about a name for the baby. How about Savannah?"

Jeremy thought about it. "Nah," he said, "it sounds too southern."

"What's wrong with that? She is southern."

"But her daddy's a Yankee, remember?"

"Fine. What names do you like?"

"How about Anna?"

"Aren't half the women in your family named Anna?"

This was true, Jeremy thought. "Yes, but think how flattered every one of them will be."

Lexie shook her head. "We can't go with Anna. I want her to have her own name."

"How about Olivia?"

119

Lexie shook her head again. "No. We can't do that to her."

"What's wrong with Olivia?"

"There was a girl I went to school with who was named Olivia. She had a terrible case of acne."

"So?"

"Brings back bad memories."

Jeremy nodded, thinking it made sense. He wouldn't name his daughter Maria, for instance. "What are some of your other ideas?"

"I was thinking about Bonnie, too. What do you think of that?"

"No, I dated a woman named Bonnie. She had nasty breath."

"Sharon?"

He shrugged. "Same thing, except the Sharon I dated was a kleptomaniac."

"Linda?"

He shook his head. "Sorry. That one threw a shoe at me."

Lexie studied him carefully. "How many women have you dated in the last ten years?"

"I have no idea. Why?"

"Because I'm getting the sense that you've dated just about every name out there."

"No, that's not true."

"Name one, then."

Jeremy thought about it. "Gertrude. I can honestly say I've never dated a woman named Gertrude."

After rolling her eyes, Lexie held up the outfit again, examined it once more, then set it aside before reaching for another. Only ten zillion more outfits to go, Jeremy thought. At this rate, we should be leaving the store right about the same time the baby is born.

She held up a new outfit before glancing at him. "Hmm . . ."

"Hmm what?"

"Gertrude, huh? I had an aunt named Gertrude, and she was just about the sweetest lady you've ever met." She seemed to be conjuring up the memory. "Now that I think about it, there might be something there. I'll have to consider that."

"Wait," Jeremy said, trying and failing to imagine calling any infant Gertrude, "you're not serious."

"We could call her Gertie for short. Or Trudy."

Jeremy stood up. "No," he said. "I can put up with a lot of things, but we are not going to name our baby Gertrude. I'm putting my foot down here. As the father, I think I have some say in this, and we're not naming our daughter Gertrude. You asked for a name that I hadn't dated."

"Fine," she said, putting down the outfit, "I was just teasing, anyway. I never liked that name." She walked toward him and slipped her arms around his neck. "Tell you what—why don't you let me make it up to you for dragging you around today. Maybe a nice romantic dinner at my place? With candles and wine . . . well, for you, anyway. And maybe after dinner, we'll figure out something else to do."

Only Lexie could make a day like today suddenly seem worth it, he realized. "I think I can come up with something."

"I can't wait to hear all about it."

"I may have to show you."

"Even better," she teased, but when she leaned in to kiss him, her cell phone suddenly chimed to life. The mood broken, she pulled back and fumbled through her purse for the phone and answered on the third ring.

"Hello?" she said, and though she didn't say anything else right away, Jeremy suddenly knew that something was wrong.

An hour later, after checking out and quickly loading the car, they were sitting at a table at Herbs across from Doris. Though they'd already gone over it, Doris had been talking so fast that Jeremy had trouble keeping up.

"Let's start from the beginning," he said, raising his hands.

Doris took a long breath. "I just can't explain it," she said. "I mean, I know Rachel can be flighty, but never like this. She was supposed to work today. And no one knows where she's gone."

"What about Rodney?" Jeremy asked.

"He's as upset as I am. He's been looking for her all day. So have her parents. It just isn't like her to vanish without telling anyone where she's going. What if something happened to her?"

Doris looked as if she were about to cry. Rachel had worked at the restaurant for a dozen years and had been friends with Lexie before that; Jeremy knew that Doris regarded her as family.

"I'm sure there's nothing to worry about. Maybe she just needed a break and headed out of town."

"Without telling anyone? Without bothering to

call and tell me that she wasn't going to show up? Without talking to Rodney?"

"What did Rodney say, exactly? Did they have an argument, or . . . ?" Jeremy finally asked.

Doris shook her head. "He didn't say anything. He came in this morning and asked if Rachel was around, and when I told him she hadn't come in yet, he took a seat to wait for her. When she didn't show, he decided to swing by her house. The next thing I knew, he was back here, asking if she was in yet since she wasn't at home."

"Was he angry?" Lexie asked, finally joining the conversation.

"No," Doris said, reaching for a napkin. "He was upset, but he didn't seem angry."

Lexie nodded but said nothing else. In the silence, Jeremy shifted in his seat. "And she hadn't stopped anywhere else? Like at her parents'?"

Doris worked the napkin in her hand, wringing it like a washrag. "Rodney didn't say, but you know how he is. I know he didn't stop after swinging by her house. He probably looked everywhere for her."

"And her car was gone, too?" Jeremy pressed.

Doris nodded. "That's why I'm so worried. What if something happened to her? What if someone took her?"

"You mean abducted her?"

"What else could I mean? Even if she wanted to leave, where would she go? She grew up here, her family's here, her friends are here. I've never even heard her talk about someone from Raleigh or Norfolk, or anywhere else, for that matter. She's not the type to just up and leave without telling anyone where she's going."

Jeremy said nothing. He glanced at Lexie, and though it appeared that she was listening, her gaze was unfocused, as if she were occupied by other thoughts.

"How have Rachel and Rodney been getting along?" Jeremy asked. "You mentioned that they were having some trouble before."

"What does that have to do with anything?" Doris asked. "Rodney's more worried than I am. He didn't have anything to do with this."

"I'm not saying he did. I was just trying to figure out why she might have left."

Doris eyed him, her expression unwavering. "I know what you're thinking, Jeremy. It's easy to blame Rodney, to think that he did something or said something that drove Rachel away. But that's not it. Rodney had nothing to do with this. Whatever happened has to do with Rachel. Or someone else. Leave Rodney out of it. Something happened to Rachel. Or Rachel took off. It's that simple."

Her voice brooked no argument about the matter. "I'm just trying to figure out what's going on," he reasoned.

At his words, Doris's tone softened. "I know you are," she said, "and I know there's probably nothing to worry about, but . . . but this is wrong somehow. Unless there's something I don't know about, Rachel just wouldn't do this."

"Has Rodney put out an APB?" Jeremy asked.

"I don't know," Doris said. "All I know is he's

out looking for her now. He promised to keep me informed, but I've got a bad feeling about this. I just know that something terrible is going to happen, if it hasn't already." She paused. "And I think it has something to do with you two."

When she finished, Jeremy knew she was talking less about her feelings than her instincts. Though she readily claimed to be a diviner and someone who could predict the sex of babies before birth, she'd been less willing to claim clairvoyance regarding other matters. Nonetheless, her words left Jeremy with no doubt that she believed she was right. Rachel's disappearance was somehow going to affect them all.

"I don't understand what you're trying to tell us," he said.

Doris sighed and stood up, tossing the crumpled napkin on the table. "I don't know, either," she said, turning toward the windows. "I can't make sense of it. Rachel's gone and I know I should be worried about that, and I am . . . but there's something else about this . . . something I can't make sense of. All I know is that none of this should have happened, and that—"

"Something bad is going to happen," Lexie finished.

Both Doris and Jeremy turned toward her. Lexie sounded as convinced as Doris, but more than that, a note of understanding underscored her pronouncement, as if she knew exactly what it was that Doris had trouble formulating. Jeremy felt again like an outsider.

Doris said nothing; she didn't have to. Whatever

wavelength the two of them were sharing, whatever information passed between them, was incomprehensible to him. All at once, Jeremy was sure that each of them could be more specific if she wanted to be, but for some reason both had decided to keep him in the dark. Just as Lexie had kept him in the dark about that afternoon on the bench with Rodney.

As if on cue, Lexie reached across the table and rested her hand on Jeremy's. "Maybe I should stay with Doris for a while."

Jeremy pulled his hand back. Doris remained silent.

He nodded and rose from the table, again feeling like a stranger. He tried to convince himself that Lexie simply wanted to stay and comfort Doris, and he forced a smile. "Yeah, I think that's a good idea."

"I'm sure that Rachel's fine," Alvin's voice boomed out of the cell phone. "She's a big girl, and I'm sure she knows what she's doing."

After leaving Herbs, Jeremy had swung by Lexie's and dropped off the baby items. He debated whether or not to wait for her there, then decided to head off to Greenleaf. Not to write, but to talk to Alvin. Despite himself, he was beginning to wonder how well he really knew Lexie. To his mind, she'd seemed more concerned about Rodney than she had about Rachel, and he wondered again what Rachel's sudden departure meant.

"I know, but it is strange, don't you think? I mean, you met her. Did she strike you as the type who would just up and leave without telling anyone?"

"Who knows," Alvin said. "But it probably has something to do with Rodney."

"What makes you say that?"

"She's dating him, isn't she? I don't know, maybe they had a fight. Maybe she thinks he's still hung up on Lexie or something like that and just wanted to get away to clear her mind for a few days. The same way Lexie did when she bolted off to the coast."

Jeremy took that in, remembering his experience with Lexie, wondering if it was some sort of southern woman thing.

"Could be," he said. "But Rodney didn't say anything to Doris."

"So Doris says. You don't know that for sure. Maybe that's what Lexie and Doris are talking about now, and it's the reason they wanted to be alone. Maybe Doris is as worried about Rodney as she is about Rachel."

Jeremy said nothing, wondering whether his friend was right. When Jeremy remained quiet, Alvin added, "Then again, it probably doesn't mean anything. It'll all work out, I'm sure."

"Yeah," Jeremy said. "You're probably right."

Jeremy could hear Alvin breathing into the line.

"What's really going on?" Alvin asked.

"What do you mean?"

"You . . . all this. Every time I talk to you, you seem more depressed."

"Just busy," Jeremy said, falling back on his standard answer. "There's a lot going on."

"Yeah, so you've told me. The repairs are bleeding you dry, you're getting married, you're going to have a baby. But you've been under pressure before, and you've got to admit your life isn't as stressful as when you and Maria were getting divorced. But unlike now, then you still had a sense of humor."

"I still have a sense of humor. If I wasn't able to laugh at this stuff, I'd probably curl up in a little ball and mumble nonsense all day long."

"Are you writing yet?"

"Nope."

"Any ideas?"

"Nope."

"Maybe you should work naked and have Jed hold your clothes for you while you work."

For the first time, Jeremy laughed. "Oh, that would work well. I'm sure Jed would just love that."

"And the upside is, you know he wouldn't tell anyone. Since he doesn't talk, I mean."

"No, he talks."

"He does?"

"According to Lexie, he does. He just doesn't talk to me or you."

Alvin laughed. "You getting used to all the crazy animals in your room yet?"

Jeremy realized he barely noticed them anymore. "Believe it or not, I am."

"I don't know whether that's a good thing or a bad thing."

"To be honest, neither do I."

"Well, listen, I've got someone here, and I'm not being a good host, so I should let you go. Give me a call later this weekend. Or I'll call you."

"Sounds good," Jeremy said, and a moment later

he hung up the phone. Staring at the computer, he shook his head. Maybe tomorrow, he thought. Just as he was rising from his desk, the phone rang again. Expecting Alvin had forgotten to tell him something, he answered, "Yeah?"

"Hey, Jeremy," Lexie said. "That's a funny way to answer the phone."

"Sorry. I just hung up with Alvin and thought he was calling back. What's up?"

"I hate to do this to you, but I'm going to have to cancel our dinner tonight. Let's do it tomorrow, okay?"

"Why?"

"Oh, it's Doris. We're heading to her place, but she's still upset and I should probably stay for a while."

"Do you want me to come by? I can bring some dinner with me."

"No, that's okay. Doris has plenty of food, and to be honest, I don't know if she's in the mood to eat. But with her heart troubles, I'd just feel better if I made sure she was okay."

"All right," Jeremy said, "I understand."

"Are you sure? I feel bad about this."

"Really, it's okay."

"I promise to make it up to you, though. Tomorrow. Maybe I'll even wear something skimpy while I cook dinner for you."

Despite his disappointment, Jeremy kept his voice steady. "Sounds good."

"I'll give you a call later, okay?"

"Sure."

"I love you. You know that, right?"

"Yeah," Jeremy said, "I know."

Lexie was quiet on the other end, and it was only after hanging up that Jeremy realized he hadn't said the words in return.

Does trust have to be earned? Or is it simply a matter of faith?

Hours later, Jeremy still wasn't sure. No matter how many times he went over the questions, he wasn't sure what to do. Should he stay at Greenleaf? Head to Lexie's to wait for her? Or check to see if she was really at Doris's?

That's what it came down to, he thought. Was she really there? He supposed he could come up with some sort of plausible excuse and call Doris to find out, but wouldn't that mean he didn't trust her? And if so, why on earth were they getting married?

Because you love her, an inner voice answered.

And he did, he admitted, but alone in his quiet room at Greenleaf, he couldn't help but wonder whether or not it was blind love. In the years he'd been married to Maria, he'd never once been suspicious of her whereabouts, even toward the end of their relationship. He'd never called over to her parents to check to see if she was really there, seldom called her at work, and only rarely popped in unexpectedly. She'd never given him a reason to question her about anything, and for the life of him, he couldn't remember even considering it. But what did that mean when it came to him and Lexie?

It seemed as if he had two views of her—one in

which they spent time together and he chided himself for his paranoia; the other when they were apart and he allowed his imagination to run wild.

But it wasn't completely wild now, was it? He had seen Lexie and Rodney holding hands. When asked directly what she'd done that day, she hadn't mentioned even seeing him. He had received a strange e-mail, one from someone who'd taken great pains to hide who he or she was. And when Doris was talking about Rachel, Lexie's only question had been whether or not Rodney seemed angry.

On the other hand, if she did have feelings for Rodney, why not just admit them? Why agree to marry Jeremy? Why buy a house and go shopping for the baby and spend almost every evening with Jeremy? Because of the baby? Lexie was traditional, Jeremy knew, but she didn't have a 1950s mind-set. She'd lived with a boyfriend in New York, had a passionate fling with Mr. Renaissance . . . she wasn't the type to throw away a life with the man she truly loved—assuming it was Rodney—for the sake of a baby. Which meant, of course, that she loved Jeremy, just as she'd told him on the phone. Just as she told him every time they were together. Just as she whispered when they were entwined in each other's arms.

There was no reason not to believe her, he decided. None at all. She was his fiancée, and if she said she was at Doris's, then that's where she was. End of story, except for one thing: He somehow doubted she was there.

Outside, the sky had turned to black, and from his seat he could see the limbs of trees swaying gently in the breeze. New spring leaves covered the once barren branches, and they glowed silver in the light of the crescent moon.

He should stay here and wait for her call, he thought. They were getting married, and he trusted her. How many times since seeing Lexie and Rodney together had he checked on her, only to feel foolish when he spotted her car at the library? Half a dozen? A dozen? Why would tonight be any different?

It wouldn't be, he told himself, even as he reached for his keys. Like a moth drawn to light, he seemed to have no other choice, and he continued to chide himself as he slipped out the door and crawled behind the wheel of his car.

The night was quiet and dark; downtown was deserted, and in the shadows, Herbs seemed oddly forbidding. He passed by without slowing and headed toward Doris's, knowing that he'd find her there. When he saw Doris's car parked in the driveway, he sighed, feeling a strange mixture of relief and regret. Until that instant, he'd forgotten that he'd simply left Lexie at Herbs without a car in which to get around, and he nearly laughed aloud.

Okay, he thought, that was settled, and he began making his way to Lexie's, thinking he would wait for her there. When she got home, he'd be supportive and quiet, listen to her worries, and make her a cup of hot chocolate if she wanted one. He'd made way too much out of nothing.

Yet when he turned onto Lexie's street and saw her house up the block, he found himself feeling instinctively for the brake pedal. Slowing the car and leaning nearer to the windshield, he blinked to make sure he was seeing things right, then suddenly squeezed the steering wheel hard.

Her car wasn't in the drive, nor were the lights on. He slammed on the brakes and turned his car around, not caring about the screech that sounded from his tires. After gunning the engine and careening around the corner, he sped through town, knowing exactly where she was. If she was not at the library or Greenleaf, not at Doris's or Herbs, there was only one place she could be.

And he was right, for when he pulled onto the street where Rodney Harper lived, he saw her car parked in the drive.

Eight

·····❖·····

Jeremy waited on the porch at Lexie's house.

He had the key, he could have gone inside, but he didn't want to. He wanted to sit on the step outside. Or, rather, seethe on the step outside. It was one thing to talk to Rodney, it was completely another to lie about it. And she had lied. She'd broken their dinner date, she'd called him on the phone and lied about her whereabouts. Lied to him directly.

He watched for her car, his jaw tight.

He really didn't care what her excuse was. There was no excuse for something like this. All she'd had to do was tell him that she wanted to talk to Rodney, that she was worried about him, and he would have been okay with that. Not thrilled, mind you, but okay. So why all the secrecy?

This wasn't the way things should be. This wasn't the way she was supposed to treat him . . . or anyone she cared about, for that matter. And what if actions like these continued after they were married? Did he really want to spend his days wondering if she was really where she said she'd be?

No, no way. Not a chance. That wasn't what marriage was supposed to be, and he hadn't moved down here, hadn't given up *everything*, to be deceived. She either loved him or she didn't; it was as simple as that. And blowing off dinner with him so she could spend time with Rodney made it seem pretty obvious how she felt.

He didn't care if they were friends, and he honestly didn't care whether she thought she was just being supportive, either. All she'd had to do was tell the truth. That's what this was about.

As angry as he was, he had to admit he was hurt as well. He'd come down here to share a life with Lexie, he'd moved here because of her. Not because of the baby, not because he had dreams of settling into a life with white picket fences, not because he'd harbored a secret belief in the romanticism of the South. He'd come here because he wanted her to be his wife.

And now she was lying to him. Not once, but twice, and as he felt his stomach tighten, he was uncertain whether to punch the wall in anger or simply cry into his hands.

He was still sitting on her steps when she arrived an hour later. As she got out of the car, she seemed surprised to see him but then walked toward him as if nothing were amiss.

"Hey," she said, flipping her purse over her shoulder. "What are you doing here?"

Jeremy rose from his seat on the steps. "Just waiting," he said. Glancing at his watch, he noted

135

it was a few minutes before nine. Late, but not too late . . .

Though he made no move toward her—and she seemed to notice this—she leaned in to kiss him anyway. If she noticed his relative nonresponse, she gave no sign.

"It's good to see you," she said.

He looked at her; despite his anger (or his fear, if he was still being honest), she looked beautiful. The idea of someone else taking her in his arms was devastating.

Sensing his roiling emotions, she tugged at his sleeve. "Are you okay?"

"Fine," he answered.

"You seem upset."

It was the perfect opportunity to say what was on his mind, but he found himself hedging. "Just tired," he said. "How was Doris?"

Lexie tucked a strand of hair behind her ear. "Worried. Rachel still hasn't called or checked in."

"And she still thinks something might have happened to her?"

"I'm not sure. You know how Doris is. Once she gets something in her head, it tends to stick, and there's never a logical explanation for it. I get the feeling that she thinks Rachel is . . . okay, for lack of a better word, but that the reason she left . . ." She shook her head again. "Actually, I don't know what Doris is thinking. She just has the feeling that Rachel shouldn't have left, and she's really upset."

Jeremy nodded, even if he didn't quite understand. "If she's okay, then it'll all work out, right?"

Lexie shrugged. "I don't know. I've given up trying to figure out the way Doris's mind works. All I know is that she's usually right. I've learned it time and time again."

Jeremy watched her, sensing she was telling the truth . . . about her time with Doris. She'd volunteered nothing about where she'd been afterward.

He stood straighter. "I take it that you spent the whole evening with Doris, huh?"

"Pretty much," she answered.

"Pretty much?"

Jeremy sensed that she was trying to gauge how much he knew.

"Yeah," she finally said.

"What does that mean?" he asked.

Lexie didn't answer.

"I swung by Doris's this evening," he challenged, "but you weren't there."

"You went to Doris's?"

"Here too," he added.

Taking a small step backward, she crossed her arms. "Were you checking up on me?"

"Call it what you want," Jeremy said, trying to stay calm. "But either way, you haven't told me the truth."

"What are you talking about?"

"Where were you tonight? After you left Doris's?"

"I came here," she said.

"And before that?" Jeremy asked, hoping she would volunteer the information, praying she would be honest, feeling the pit in his stomach grow.

"You *were* checking on me, weren't you?"

Perhaps it was the righteousness in her tone that caused his temper to flare. "This isn't about me!" Jeremy snapped. "Just answer the question!"

"Why are you yelling?" she asked. "I told you where I was."

"No, you didn't!" Jeremy shouted. "You told me where you were before you went somewhere else. You went someplace else after you left Doris's, didn't you?"

"Why are you yelling at me?" Lexie demanded, her own voice rising. "What's gotten into you?"

"You went to Rodney's!" Jeremy shouted.

"What?"

"You heard me!" he said. "You went to Rodney's! I saw you there!"

Lexie took another step backward. "You followed me?"

"No," he snapped, "I didn't follow you. I went to Doris's, then here, and then went looking for you. And guess what I found?"

She paused, as if trying to decide how best to respond. "It's not what you think," she protested, her voice softer than he'd expected.

"And what do I think?" Jeremy demanded. "That my fiancée shouldn't be at another man's house? That maybe she should have told me where she was going? That if she trusted me, she would have said something? That if she cared about me, she wouldn't have broken our dinner date to spend time with another man?"

"This isn't about you!" she said. "And I didn't break our date. I asked if we could do it tomorrow and you said it would be fine!"

Jeremy inched closer. "This isn't just about the dinner, Lexie. This is about the fact that you went to another man's house tonight."

Lexie stood her ground. "And what? Do you think I slept with Rodney? Do you think we spent the last hour making out on the couch? We talked, Jeremy! That's all we did. Just talked! Doris was getting tired, and before I went home, I wanted to know if Rodney could tell me what was going on. So I stopped by, and all we did was talk about Rachel."

"You should have told me."

"I would have! And you wouldn't have even had to ask. I would have told you where I went. I don't keep secrets from you."

His eyebrows lifted. "Oh no? What about that day at the boardwalk?"

"What day at the boardwalk?"

"Last month when I saw you holding Rodney's hand."

She stared at him as if she had never seen him before. "How long have you been spying on me?"

"I haven't been spying! But I did see you holding his hand."

She continued to stare at him. "Who are you?" she finally asked.

"Your fiancé," Jeremy said, his voice continuing to rise, "and I think I deserve an explanation. First, I find you two holding hands, then I find out that you're breaking our dates to spend time with him—"

"Shut up!" she shouted. "Just be quiet and listen."

"I'm trying to listen!" he shouted back. "But

you're not telling me the truth! You've been lying to me!"

"No, I haven't!"

"No? Then why not tell me about your little hand-holding adventure!"

"I'm trying to tell you that you're making this into something it isn't—"

"Oh, really?" he snarled, cutting her off. "And what if you had caught me holding hands with an ex-girlfriend and found out that I was sneaking away to spend time with her?"

"I wasn't sneaking away!" Lexie said, throwing up her hands. "I told you . . . I stayed with Doris almost all night, but I still wasn't sure what was going on. I was worried about Rachel, so I stopped by Rodney's to find out if he knew anything."

"After holding his hand, of course."

Lexie's eyes flashed, but as she spoke he could hear her voice beginning to break. "No," she said, "I didn't. We sat on the porch out back and talked. How many times do I have to tell you this?"

"Maybe enough to admit that you were lying!"

"I wasn't lying!"

He stared at her, his voice taking on a hard edge. "You lied, and you know it." He pointed an accusing finger at her. "That's bad enough, but that isn't the only thing that hurts. What hurts worse is that you keep trying to deny it."

With that, he stepped off the porch and strode to his car, not bothering to look behind him.

Jeremy sped blindly through town, not knowing what to do. He knew he didn't want to go back to

Greenleaf, nor could he imagine heading to the Lookilu Tavern, the only bar still open in town. Though he'd stopped in once or twice, he had no desire to spend the rest of the evening seated at the bar, simply because he knew the ruckus it would cause. If he'd learned one thing about small towns, it was that news traveled fast, especially bad news, and he had no desire to have anyone else in town start speculating about him and Lexie. Instead, he simply drove through town, making a big circuit, without any destination in mind. Boone Creek was not New York City—there was no place to go if one wanted to vanish into a crowd. There were no crowds.

Sometimes he hated this town.

Lexie could talk all she wanted about the beautiful scenery and townsfolk she viewed almost as family, but he supposed he should have expected that. As an only child and an orphan to boot, she'd never been part of a large family as Jeremy had been, and he sometimes felt like telling her that she had no idea what she was talking about. Granted, most of the people he'd met in town were gracious and friendly, but he was beginning to wonder whether that wasn't just an attempt to keep up appearances. Behind the facade, there were secrets and machinations, just like everywhere else, but folks here tried to hide it. Like Doris, for instance. While he was asking questions, Doris and Lexie were passing hidden signals, all with the intention of keeping him in the dark. Or Mayor Gherkin. Instead of simply helping Jeremy get the permits, he'd had his own agenda. There was, Jeremy thought, something to be said about New Yorkers.

When they were angry, they let you know, and they didn't try to sugarcoat it, especially when it concerned family. People just said what was on their minds.

He wished Lexie had behaved more like that. Driving around, he couldn't decide whether his anger was growing or dissipating; he didn't know whether to head back to her house and try to get things sorted out or try to figure it out on his own. He suspected she was hiding something, but for the life of him, he couldn't figure out what it was. Despite his anger and the evidence, he couldn't bring himself to believe that she had a secret affair going on with Rodney. Unless he'd been completely hoodwinked by Lexie, which he doubted, the idea was ridiculous. But something was going on between them, something that Lexie felt uncomfortable talking about. And then, of course, there was the e-mail . . .

He shook his head, trying to clear his mind. After circuiting the town for the third time, he headed into the country. He drove in silence for a few minutes, then turned again, and a few minutes later pulled to a stop in front of Cedar Creek Cemetery— home to the mysterious lights and the place that had brought him to Boone Creek.

This was where he'd first seen Lexie. After arriving in town, he'd come here to take a few photographs before beginning to research the article he'd intended to write, and he could still recall how she'd appeared suddenly, catching him off guard. He could still visualize the way she'd moved and how the breeze rippled through her hair.

It was also in this cemetery that she'd told him about the nightmares she'd had as a child.

Getting out of the car, Jeremy was struck by how different the place was without fog. On the night he'd first seen the mysterious lights, the mist-shrouded cemetery had seemed unearthly, as if lost in time. Tonight, under a clear April sky and a glowing moon, he could make out the shapes of individual headstones and was even able to retrace the route he'd once taken while trying to capture the lights on film.

He moved past the wrought-iron gates and heard the soft crunch of gravel underfoot. He hadn't been here since returning to Boone Creek, and as he made his way past the broken tombstones, his thoughts turned again to Lexie.

Had she told him the truth? Partially. Would she really have told him where she'd gone? Maybe. And did he have a right to be angry? Yes, he thought again, he did.

He didn't like arguing with her, though. And he hadn't liked the way she'd looked at him when she realized that he'd been following her. Nor, he admitted, did he like that aspect of himself, either. Truth be told, he wished he had never seen Lexie and Rodney together in the first place. All it had done was make him suspicious, and he reminded himself again that there was no reason to be suspicious. Yes, she'd gone to see Rodney, but Rachel was missing, and Rodney was without doubt the one she should have talked to.

But the e-mail . . .

He didn't want to think about that, either.

In the silence, it seemed that the cemetery was beginning to grow brighter. It wasn't possible, of course—the ghostly lights appeared only on foggy nights—but when he blinked, he realized he wasn't seeing things. The cemetery was growing brighter. As he frowned in confusion, he heard the unmistakable sound of a car engine. Glancing over his shoulder, he saw the headlights of a car rounding a curve. He wondered who would be driving out this way and was surprised when he noticed the car slowing, then pulling to a stop right behind his car.

Despite the darkness, he recognized the car as Mayor Gherkin's, and a moment later he watched the shadowy figure emerge.

"Jeremy Marsh?" the mayor called out. "You out there?"

Jeremy cleared his throat, surprised for the second time. He debated whether or not to answer before realizing that his car gave him away. "Yeah, Mr. Mayor, I'm over here."

"Where? I can't see you."

"Over here," Jeremy called. "Near the big tree."

The mayor started toward him. As he approached, Jeremy could hear him going on.

"I'll say, you do come to the strangest places, Jeremy. It was all I could do to find you. I suppose I shouldn't be surprised, though, knowing your history with this place and all. But still, I can think of a dozen better places to go if a man wants to be alone. I guess a man feels the urge to go back to the scene of the crime, don't he?"

By the time he finished, he was standing before Jeremy. Even in the dark Jeremy could make out what he was wearing: red polyester pants, a purple Izod shirt, and a yellow sport jacket. He looked something like an Easter egg.

"What are you doing here, Mr. Mayor?"

"Well, I came to talk to you, of course."

"Is this about the astronaut? I left a message at your office—"

"No, no, of course not. I got your message, so don't you worry about that none. I had no doubt you'd come through, being that you're a celebrity and all. What happened was that I was working in my office, just finishing up some paperwork at my store downtown, and I happened to see your car passing by. I waved, but I suppose you didn't see me, and I said to myself, I wonder where Jeremy Marsh could be going in such a hurry."

Jeremy held up his hands to stop him. "Mr. Mayor, I'm really not in the mood—"

The mayor went on as if he hadn't heard him. "But I didn't think anything of it, of course. Not at first, anyway. But wouldn't you know it, you drove by a second time and then a third, and I started wondering if maybe you needed someone to talk to. So I asked myself, Where would Jeremy Marsh go, and . . ." The mayor paused for dramatic effect, then slapped his leg for emphasis as he went on. "Like a *bolt of lightning*, it hit me. Why, he'd go to the cemetery!"

Jeremy simply stared at him. "Why did you think I would go to the cemetery?"

The mayor smiled in satisfaction, but instead of answering directly, he pointed to the magnificent magnolia tree in the center of the cemetery.

"You see that tree, Jeremy?"

Jeremy followed his gaze. With gnarled roots and sprawling limbs, the tree had to be well over a hundred years old.

"Did I ever tell you the story about that tree?"

"No, but—"

"That tree was planted by Coleman Tolles, one of the town's most prominent citizens, back before the War of Northern Aggression. He operated the feed store and the general grocers, and he had himself the prettiest wife for miles around. Her name was Patricia, and though the only painting of her was destroyed in the library fire, my daddy used to swear that he'd sometimes go to the library just to take a gander at her."

Jeremy shook his head impatiently. "Mr. Mayor—"

"Let me finish now. I think this might just shed some light on your little problem."

"What problem?"

"Why, the problem you're having with Miss Lexie. If I were you, I don't suppose I'd be too thrilled to find out she's been spending time with another man."

Jeremy blinked in shock, speechless.

"But as I was telling you, this Patricia was one beautiful lady, and before she married Coleman, he had courted her for years. Pretty much everyone in the county was courting her—and she loved the attention—but old Coleman won her heart in the end, and their wedding was the biggest the county had ever seen. They could have lived happily ever after, I suppose, but it was not to be.

Coleman was the jealous type, you see, and Patricia wasn't the type to be rude to those other young men who'd been courting her. Coleman just couldn't take it."

The mayor shook his head. "They ended up having a terrible argument, and the stress was just too much for Patricia to bear. She took ill and spent two weeks in bed before the good Lord called her home. Coleman was brokenhearted, and after she was buried in the cemetery, he planted this tree in her honor. And here it grows, this living version of our very own Taj Mahal."

Jeremy stared at the mayor. "Is that a true story?" he asked at last.

The mayor raised his right hand as if taking an oath. "May I be struck down if it isn't."

Jeremy wasn't sure how to respond; nor did he have any idea how the mayor knew the source of his troubles.

The mayor shoved his hands in his pockets. "But as you can see, it's quite appropriate considering your own circumstances. Like a flame draws a moth, this here tree must have drawn you to the cemetery."

"Mr. Mayor—"

"I know what you're thinking, Jeremy. You're wondering why I didn't mention the story when you were planning to write about the cemetery before."

"No, not exactly."

"Then you were wondering how on earth there could be so many fascinating stories concerning elements of our fine town. All I can say is that we're a bastion of history here. Why, I could tell you stories about half the buildings downtown that would have you simply enthralled."

"That's not it, either," Jeremy said, still trying to grasp what was happening.

"Then, I suppose you're wondering how I knew about Miss Lexie and Rodney."

Jeremy met Gherkin's eyes. Gherkin simply shrugged. "In small towns, word gets around."

"You mean everyone knows?"

"No, of course not. Not about this, anyway. I suppose there are only a few of us who know, but we know better than to go spreading gossip that might be hurtful to someone. The fact is, I'm as concerned as anyone about Rachel's mysterious absence. Before you talked to Doris tonight, I spent some time with her, and she was a wreck. She loves that girl, you know. I was there, in fact, when Rodney came by, and I stopped in again after you'd gone back to Greenleaf."

"But the rest of it?"

"Oh, that was simple deduction," Gherkin said with a shrug. "Rodney and Rachel are seeing each other but having problems, Rodney and Lexie are friends, and I see you circling town and driving too fast, almost like a blind man was behind the wheel. It didn't take much to realize that Lexie had gone to Rodney's to talk to him and you were upset about it, what with all the other stress you're under."

"Stress?"

"Sure. What with the wedding and the house and Lexie being pregnant."

"You know about that, too?"

"Jeremy, my boy, since you're now a resident

of our fine town, you've got to understand that folks are mighty perceptive around these parts. There's not much to do other than try to figure out what's going on in other folks' lives. But don't you worry; my lips will remain sealed until the official announcement. As an elected official, I try to stay above all the gossip that goes on in town."

Jeremy made a mental note to hide out at Greenleaf as much as possible.

"But the main reason I came to find you was to tell you a story about women."

"Another story?"

Gherkin raised his hands. "Well, less of a story than a lesson. It's about my wife, Gladys. Now, she's as fine a woman as you'll ever come across, but there have been times when she's been less than truthful during the course of our marriage. For a long time it bothered me, and there were times when we actually raised our voices at each other, but what I eventually came to understand was that if a woman truly loves you, you can't always expect her to tell the truth. You see, women are more attuned to feelings than men are, and if they're not being truthful, more often than not it's because they think the truth might hurt your feelings. But it doesn't mean they don't love you."

"You're saying that it's okay for them to lie?"

"No, I'm saying that if they do lie, it's often because they care."

"What if I want her to tell me the truth?"

"Well, then, my boy, you better be prepared to accept the truth in the spirit with which it was offered."

Jeremy thought about that but said nothing. In the silence, Mayor Gherkin shivered. "It's getting a bit chilly out here, ain't it? So before I go, I just want to leave you with this. You know in your heart that Lexie loves you. Doris knows it, I know it, the whole town knows it. Why, when folks see you two together, it's almost as if we expect you to break out in song, so there's no reason to be concerned about the fact she went to see Rodney in his time of need."

Jeremy glanced away. Even though the mayor was still standing beside him, he suddenly felt very much alone.

Back at Greenleaf, Jeremy debated whether or not to call Alvin again. He knew that if he talked to Alvin, he'd end up rehashing the entire evening, and he didn't want that. Nor was he ready to accept Gherkin's advice. Occasional lies might work in the mayor's marriage, but that wasn't what he wanted with Lexie.

He shook his head, tired of his troubles with Lexie, tired of wedding plans and house renovations, tired of not being able to write. Ever since he'd come down here, his life had become one misery after another, and for what? Because he loved Lexie? Then how come he was bearing all the stresses and she seemed just fine? Why did he have to be the fall guy?

No, he admitted, that wasn't completely fair. She was under stress, too. Not only with the wedding plans and the house, but she was the one who was pregnant, she was the one who woke up crying in the middle of the night, and she was the one who had to watch everything she ate or drank. She just seemed better able to handle it than he did.

At loose ends, Jeremy gravitated toward his computer, knowing he couldn't write but figuring he could at least check his e-mails. When he came to the first message, however, all he could do was stare.

HAS SHE TOLD YOU THE TRUTH? READ DORIS'S JOURNAL. YOU'LL FIND THE ANSWER THERE.

Nine

..... ❖ .....

"I don't know what to tell you," Alvin offered, sounding at a loss. "What do you think it means?" After reading the message a dozen times, Jeremy had finally reached for the phone.

"I don't know," he said.

"Have you checked Doris's journal?"

"No," Jeremy answered, "I just got the e-mail. I haven't had time to do anything. I'm just trying to make some sense of it."

"Maybe you should do what the message says," Alvin suggested. "Look through Doris's journal."

"For what?" Jeremy asked. "I don't even know what I'm supposed to be looking for. And I can guarantee that Doris's journal has nothing to do with what's been going on lately."

"What are you talking about?"

Jeremy leaned back in his seat, then got up to pace, then collapsed into his seat again as he related the events of the last few hours. When he finished, Alvin was quiet.

"I just want to make sure I heard you right," Alvin finally said. "She was at Rodney's?"

"Yeah," Jeremy said.

"And she didn't tell you?"

Jeremy leaned forward in his seat, trying to figure out the best way to answer. "No, but she said that she was going to."

"And you believe her?"

That was the crux of the matter, wasn't it? Would she really have told him?

"I don't know," Jeremy confessed.

After a brief pause, Alvin said, "Again, I don't know what to tell you."

"What do you think it means? Why is someone sending me e-mails like this?"

"Maybe they know something you don't," Alvin pointed out.

"Or maybe they just want to have us break up," Jeremy said.

Alvin didn't respond directly. Instead he asked, "Do you love her?"

Jeremy ran a hand through his hair. "More than life."

As if trying to make his friend feel better, Alvin spoke cheerfully. "Well, at least you'll head into the next phase of life with one heck of a party next weekend. Six days and counting."

For the first time in what seemed like hours, Jeremy smiled. "It'll be fun."

"Without a doubt. It's not every day that my best friend gets married. I'm looking forward to seeing you, too. And besides, a little trip to the city will do you good. I've been down there, remember? I know for a fact there's nothing to do other than watch your toenails grow."

And study people, Jeremy thought. He said nothing, however.

"But listen, you call me if you learn something from Doris's journal. As much as I hate to admit it, I'm beginning to live vicariously through your adventures."

"I wouldn't consider these e-mails adventures."

"Call them what you will. But you've got to admit they've been making you think, right?"

"Oh yeah," Jeremy admitted. "They've been making me think."

"In the end, if you're going to marry her, you've got to trust her, you know."

"I know," Jeremy said. "Believe me, I know."

For the second time that evening, Jeremy found himself wondering what it meant to trust someone. That's what it came down to. Most of the time, yes, but lately it hadn't been easy.

But the e-mails. Not one, but two. And the second one . . .

If he picked up the journal, suppose he learned something about Lexie, something he didn't know or might not want to know? Would that affect the way he felt about her? Would it make him throw in the towel and storm away without ever looking back?

He tried to fit the pieces together. Whoever sent the e-mails not only knew that Lexie was pregnant and that Jeremy had Doris's journal, but was also bold enough to suggest he would learn something Lexie had been hiding. The implication, again, was that someone wanted to break them up.

But who? Granted, anyone in town might know Lexie was pregnant; few, however, knew he had the journal, and aside from Lexie, he could think of only one person who knew the contents of the journal.

Doris.

But it made no sense. She was the one who'd pushed Lexie toward Jeremy in the first place; she was the one who explained Lexie's behavior so Jeremy could understand Lexie better. Doris was also the one Jeremy talked to about his writer's block.

He was so lost in thought, it took a moment for him to realize that someone was knocking at the door. He crossed the room and opened it.

Lexie forced a smile. Despite her brave expression, her eyes were red and swollen, and he knew she'd been crying. At first, neither of them said anything. Then:

"Hey," she offered.

"Hi, Lex," he said. When he made no move toward her, she stared down at the floor.

"I guess you're wondering why I'm here, huh? I was sort of hoping that you would come back, but you didn't."

When Jeremy didn't respond, she tucked a strand of hair behind her ear. "I just wanted to tell you I'm sorry. You were right about everything. I should have told you, and I was wrong to have done what I did."

Jeremy studied her before taking a step back from the door. With that tacit permission, Lexie entered his room and took a seat on the bed. Jeremy reached for the chair in front of the desk.

"Why didn't you tell me?" he asked.

"I didn't plan on going," she said. "I know you might not believe it, but when I left Doris's, I was intending to go home and . . . I don't know . . . it just hit me that I should probably talk to Rodney. I figured he'd be able to tell me where Rachel might have gone."

"What about before?" Jeremy said. "At the boardwalk. Why didn't you tell me about that?"

"Rodney's just a friend, and he's going through a rough time. I know how it might have looked to you, but we go back a long way, and I was just trying to be supportive."

Jeremy noticed the careful way she'd avoided answering the question. He leaned forward in the chair. "No more games, Lexie, okay?" he said, his voice steady and serious. "I'm not in the mood. I just want to know why you didn't tell me."

Lexie turned toward the window, but he could see the reflection of the lamplight in her eyes. "It was . . . hard. I didn't want to be involved in the first place. And I didn't want to involve you, either." She laughed, sounding shaken. "But I guess I did, huh?" She shook her head and drew a long breath before going on. "The thing is, Rodney and Rachel have been arguing a lot lately because of me."

Her voice grew softer. "Rachel has been having a hard time with the fact that Rodney and I dated. But more than that, she knows how Rodney felt about me. And that's the thing. Rachel still thinks Rodney has feelings for me, and—according to Rachel, anyway—Rodney still brings my name up now and then, usually at exactly the wrong times. But if you talk to Rodney, he claims she's exaggerating. That's what we were talking about at the boardwalk."

Jeremy brought his hands together. "Does he have feelings for you?"

"I don't know," she said.

When she saw Jeremy's expression of disbelief, she went on quickly. "I know that's a cop-out, but I'm not sure what else to say. Does Rodney still care about me? Yeah, I think he does, but we've known each other ever since we were little. The question you want me to answer is whether he would be seeing Rachel if we weren't engaged, and all I can say is that I think he would. I've told you before that I always thought those two belonged together. But . . ."

She trailed off, her brow knit with concern.

"You don't know for sure," Jeremy finished for her. If he were Lexie, he wasn't sure he would have been able to come up with an answer either.

"No," she said. "But he does understand that I'm engaged to someone else. He accepts that it's not going to work between us, and I know he does care for Rachel. But Rachel is sensitive about me, and I think that Rodney inadvertently makes things worse. He told me that Rachel got mad at him one afternoon when they were driving because he glanced up at the library. She accused him of looking for me, and they ended up arguing for hours. He was telling her that it was just a habit, that he didn't mean anything, and Rachel kept saying that he was never going to get over me and that he was making excuses. The next day, he was still upset and dropped by the library to get my advice, so we went to the boardwalk to talk."

She straightened up with a sigh. "And tonight, like I said, it just happened. Since I know both of them, since I care about both of them and want it to work out between them, I feel like I should try to fix it. Or at least listen when one of them wants to talk to me. I feel like I'm stuck in the middle of something, and I don't know how to get out or what I'm supposed to do."

"Maybe you were right not to tell me. These southern soap operas aren't my thing."

For the first time since she'd arrived, she seemed to relax.

"Mine either. There are times when I wish I were back in New York where everyone was a stranger. Things like this get old, and it's even worse because I made you angry. I made you suspicious, and then I made it worse by trying to cover it up. You have no idea how sorry I am about that. It's never going to happen again."

Her voice had grown even softer and began to break; when she swiped at the corner of her eye, Jeremy rose from his chair and took a seat beside her on the bed. When he reached for her hand, her shoulders began to tremble and she drew a ragged breath.

"Hey," Jeremy whispered, "it's okay. Don't cry."

His words seemed to release her emotions, and she lowered her face into her hands. Her sobs were deep and heavy, as if she'd been holding them in for hours, and when he slipped his arm around her, her crying only intensified.

"It's all right," he whispered.

"No . . . it's . . . not," she choked out between sobs, her face still buried in her hands.

"I mean it," he said, "I forgive you."

"No . . . you . . . don't. I saw . . . the way you were . . . looking at me . . . at the door . . . when I got here."

"I was still mad then. But not now."

She shuddered, her face still hidden. "Yes, you are. You . . . hate me . . . We're having a baby, and all we ever do . . . is fight . . ."

This wasn't going well. Feeling lost, Jeremy reminded himself again about her surging hormones. Like most men, he assumed that hormones were the explanation for every emotional outburst, but in this instance it really seemed to be true.

"I don't hate you. I was mad at you, but that's over now."

"I don't love . . . Rodney. I love you . . ."

"I know."

"I won't ever talk to Rodney ever again . . ."

"You can talk to him. Just not at his house, okay? And don't hold his hand, either."

If possible, his comment made her cry even harder.

"I knew you were . . . still mad at me . . ."

It took almost half an hour for Lexie to stop crying; by the end, Jeremy had decided it was best if he didn't say anything, other than to deny that he was still mad. Anything else seemed only to make it worse. Like a small child after a severe meltdown, every thirty seconds or so she would draw a series of jagged breaths, and her face would screw up as if she were about to start crying once more. Unwilling to risk provoking another crying fit, Jeremy sat in silence as Lexie tried to recover.

"Wow," she said, her voice raspy.

"Yeah," Jeremy agreed. "Wow."

"I'm sorry," she said, seemingly as dazed as he felt. "I don't know what happened there."

"You cried," Jeremy said.

She shot him a look; with puffy eyes, it didn't have quite the same effect as it usually did, though.

"Did you find out anything about Rachel?" he asked.

"Not too much. Except for the fact that Rodney's pretty sure she didn't leave today. He thinks she left after work yesterday. They'd had an argument on Thursday night, and according to Rodney, she told him it was over and that she never wanted to see him again. Later, when he passed by her house, her car wasn't in the driveway."

"He was spying on her?" Jeremy prompted, glad he wasn't the only one.

"No, he wanted to smooth things out. But anyway, if she left on Friday after work . . . I don't know, maybe she's planning to be gone the whole weekend. Still, it doesn't explain why she didn't call Doris to tell her she wouldn't be in this morning, and it still doesn't tell us where she's gone."

Jeremy thought about it, remembering that both Doris and Lexie said she'd never mentioned friends from out of town. "And she wouldn't have just headed to the beach or something? Maybe she wanted to be alone. Or at least away from Rodney for a while."

"Who knows." Lexie shrugged. "But even before this . . . I don't know." She seemed to be trying to choose her words carefully. "She's been acting strange lately, even with me. Almost like she's going through a midlife crisis."

"She's too young for that," Jeremy pointed out. "Like you said, it probably has something to do with her relationship with Rodney."

"I know . . . but it's more than that. Like she's being secretive. Normally, she talks all the time, but when we went out shopping for her bridesmaid's dress, she didn't say much at all. Like she was hiding something."

"Maybe she's been planning this weekend for a while."

"Maybe," Lexie said. "I just don't know."

For a long moment, neither of them said anything. In the silence, Lexie tried to stifle a yawn, looking sheepish when she finished. "Sorry," she said. "I'm getting tired."

"Crying for an hour will do that to a person."

"So will pregnancy," she said. "I've been tired a lot lately. At work, I've even been closing my door so I can rest my head on the desk."

"Well, take it easy. You're carrying my baby, you know. And you should probably head home so you can get some sleep."

She arched an eyebrow at him. "Do you want to come over?"

He thought about it. "I'd better not," he said. "You know what happens when I sleep over."

"You mean we don't actually sleep for a while?"

"I can't help it."

161

She nodded, suddenly serious. "You sure you're not staying here because of—"

"No," he said, cutting her off with a smile. "I'm not mad. Now that I understand what's been going on, I'm all better."

She kissed him, then rose from the bed. "Okay," she said, stretching. He noticed her belly didn't flatten as much as it once did, and his gaze settled there for an instant too long.

"Don't stare at my fat," she chided, sounding self-conscious.

"You're not fat," he said automatically, feeling pleased. "You're pregnant, and you look beautiful."

She watched him as he answered, as if wondering again whether he'd been telling the truth about the reason he wasn't coming over, then seemingly thought better of rehashing the conversation. Jeremy rose and walked her to the door. After kissing her good-bye, he watched as she made her way to the car, replaying the entire evening in his mind.

"Hey, Lexie?"

She turned. "Yes?"

"I forgot to ask you. Do you know if Doris has a computer?"

"Doris? No."

"Not even at work?"

"No," Lexie answered. "She's as old-fashioned as they come. I doubt if she even knows how to turn one on. Why?"

"No reason," he said.

He saw the confusion in her face but didn't want to get into it. "Sleep well," he said. "I love you."

"Love you, too," she said, her voice subdued. She opened the car door and slid behind the wheel.

Jeremy watched as she started the car, backed up, and headed down the gravel drive, the rear lights fading as she rolled out of sight. A few minutes later, he was at his desk, leaning back in his chair with his feet propped up.

A lot had been explained tonight, and it all made perfect sense. His suspicions about Rodney had been put to rest—assuming he'd ever really believed them in the first place—but there was still the matter of the e-mails.

If Lexie was telling the truth, Doris hadn't sent them. But if she hadn't, who had?

On his desk was Doris's journal, and he found himself staring at it once more. How many times had he debated whether or not to read it in the hopes of finding an article to write? For whatever reason, he'd avoided it, but he thought again about the latest e-mail.

HAS SHE TOLD YOU THE TRUTH? READ DORIS'S JOURNAL. YOU'LL FIND THE ANSWER THERE.

What truth? And what would he find in Doris's journal? What answer was he supposed to find?

He didn't know. Nor was he even sure he wanted to find out. But with the message still playing in his mind, he found himself reaching for the journal.

Ten

····❖····

Jeremy studied the journal for much of the next week.

For the most part, Doris had been meticulous with her notations. In all, there were 232 names in the book, all written in pen; another 28 women were listed by initials, though no reason was offered as to why they weren't further identified. Fathers were usually, but not always, identified. For the most part, Doris had included the date of the visit, an estimate of how far along the mother was, and the predicted sex of the baby. The mothers signed their names after her prediction. In three instances, the women she'd written about hadn't even known they were pregnant.

Beneath each prediction, Doris had left a space where she'd later written in the name and sex of the baby once it had been born, sometimes with a different-color pen. Occasionally she included the birth notice from the newspaper, and as Lexie had told him, Doris had been correct with every prediction. At least with those she'd actually made. There were thirteen instances where Doris hadn't predicted the sex of the baby—a fact that neither Lexie nor Doris had mentioned. In those cases, Jeremy assumed by further notes that Doris made, the mother would eventually miscarry.

The entries, one after the next, seemed to blend together.

February 19, 1995, Ashley Bennett, 23,
twelve weeks along.
Tom Harker the father. BOY *Ashley Bennett*
Toby Roy Bennett, born August 31, 1995.
July 12, 1995, Terry Miller, 27, nine weeks
along. Lots of morning sickness. Second baby.
GIRL *Terry Miller*
Sophie May Miller, born February 11,
1996.

He continued reading, searching for patterns, trying to spot anything unusual. He read through the journal, entry by entry, half a dozen times. By midweek, he began to feel something gnaw at him, as if he were missing something, and he read through the journal again, this time starting from the back. Then he read through it again.

It was Friday morning when he finally found it. In half an hour, he was supposed to pick up Lexie so they could close on the house. He still hadn't packed for his trip to New York, but all he could do was stare at the entry that Doris had scrawled in shaky penmanship.

Sept. 28, 1996: L.M.D. Age 28, seven weeks along. Trevor Newland, likely father. Found out accidentally.

Nothing else was listed beneath, which meant the mother had miscarried.

Jeremy gripped the journal, suddenly finding it difficult to breathe. Only one name, one he didn't recognize, but initials that he did.

L-M-D. *Lexie Marin Darnell.*

Pregnant with someone else's baby. Another lie of omission.

Another lie . . .

His thoughts started racing with the realization. Lexie had lied about this, just as she'd lied to him about spending time with Rodney. Just as she'd once lied about where she went after seeing Doris . . . and before that, lied about knowing the truth about the mysterious lights in the cemetery.

Lies and hidden truths . . .

A pattern?

His lips tightened into a grim line. Who was she? Why was she doing this? And why on earth wouldn't she have told him? This he would have understood.

He didn't know whether to be angry or hurt. Or both. He needed time to think things through, but that was the thing: There was no time. Soon he and Lexie would own a house; in a week they'd be married. But Alvin had been right all along. He didn't know her, had never known her. Nor, he suddenly realized, did he completely trust her. Yes, she'd explained her deceptions, and taken in isolation, each had been explained. But was this going to be a regular occurrence? Would he have to live with twisting of the truth? *Could* he live that way?

And who had sent the e-mail? Again, it came back to that, didn't it? The acquaintance he had looking into the routing information for the mysterious e-mails had called earlier in the week to let Jeremy know that the e-mail most likely came from out of town and that soon he hoped to have an answer. Which meant . . . *what*?

He didn't know, and he didn't have time to figure it out. The meeting with the lawyer to close on the house was scheduled in twenty minutes. Should he postpone the closing? Could he, even if he wanted?

Too much to think about; too much to do.

Moving on autopilot, he left his room at Greenleaf; ten minutes later, with his thoughts in disarray, he pulled to a stop in front of Lexie's house. Through the window, he saw movement, and she stepped onto the porch.

Idly, he noticed she'd dressed for the occasion. Wearing tan pants and a matching jacket over a light blue blouse, she smiled and waved as she skipped down the porch steps. For an instant, it was easy to forget she was pregnant.

Pregnant . . .

Just like before. The realization brought his feelings of anger to the surface once more, but she didn't seem to notice as she slid into the car.

"Hey, hon, how are you? For a minute there, I wasn't sure we would make it on time."

He couldn't bring himself to respond. Couldn't bring himself to look at her. He wasn't sure whether

167

he wanted to confront her now or wait until he had more time to process what all this meant.

She put a hand on his shoulder. "You okay?" she ventured. "You seem distracted."

He squeezed the steering wheel, trying to keep control. "Just thinking."

She watched him. "Do you want to talk about it?"

"No," he said.

She continued to stare, unsure whether to be concerned. After a moment, she settled back and buckled her seat belt.

"Isn't this exciting?" she said, trying simultaneously to change the subject and lighten the mood. "Our first house. We should celebrate after this. Maybe have lunch before you head off to the airport. Besides, I'm not going to see you for a couple of days."

He slipped the car into drive, and it lurched forward. "Whatever."

"Don't sound so enthusiastic about it."

He pretended to be absorbed in the road as he pulled away, his hands tight on the wheel. "I said I'd go."

She shook her head and turned toward the window. "Thanks a lot," she muttered.

"What? Now *you're* mad?"

"I just don't understand why you're in such a bad mood. This is supposed to be exciting. We're buying a house; you're heading off to the bachelor party. You're supposed to be happy. Meanwhile, you're acting like we're heading to a funeral."

Jeremy opened his mouth to say something but thought better of it. If they had an argument now, there was no way it would end before they got to the attorney's office. He knew that. He didn't want to make this public, nor was he even sure how to begin. But they would talk about this later. No doubt about it.

Instead, they drove the rest of the way in silence, the mood inside the car growing heavier with every passing minute. By the time they reached the office and saw Mrs. Reynolds waiting out front for them, Lexie was unwilling to look his way. As soon as the car stopped, Lexie opened the door and got out; she headed toward Mrs. Reynolds without waiting.

Fine, he thought. She was angry? Welcome to the club, my dear. He shut the door and trailed slowly behind her, showing no desire to catch up.

"Today's the big day," Mrs. Reynolds said, smiling as Lexie approached. "You two ready?"

Lexie nodded; Jeremy said nothing. Mrs. Reynolds looked from Lexie to Jeremy and back again. Her smile faded. She'd been around long enough to recognize a spat when she saw one. Buying a house was stressful, and people reacted in different ways. But it wasn't her business. What *was* her business was getting them both inside to sign the papers before the spat evolved into something that might cancel the deal.

"I know they're already waiting for us," she prompted, pretending not to notice their sullen expressions. "We'll be in the conference room." She took a step toward the door. "It's this way. You two are getting one heck of a deal. Once the house is finished, you're going to own a real showplace."

She held the door open, waiting for a response.

"Down the corridor," she urged again. "The second door on your left."

Once inside, she hurried past them, almost forcing them to follow. They did, but as fate would have it, the lawyer wasn't in the room.

"Take a seat. I'm sure he just stepped out for a minute. Let me check on him, okay?"

Lexie and Jeremy sat kitty-corner to each other as Mrs. Reynolds disappeared from view. Jeremy reached for a pencil and began tapping it absently on the table.

"What's wrong with you today?" Lexie finally asked.

Jeremy could hear the challenge in her tone but said nothing.

"You're not going to speak to me?"

Slowly he lifted his gaze to meet hers. "Tell me what happened with Trevor Newland," he said, his voice quiet. "Or should I call him Mr. Renaissance?"

Lexie's eyes widened only slightly, and she seemed on the verge of answering when Mrs. Reynolds reappeared in the doorway with the lawyer in tow. They took a seat at the table, and the lawyer spread the file in front of them.

The lawyer began to explain the proceedings, but Jeremy barely heard him. Instead, his mind flashed back to the past. The last time he'd been in a room like this, he'd been finalizing his divorce with Maria. Everything seemed the same, from the large cherry table surrounded by padded chairs, to the shelves filled with legal books and the large windows that let in the sunlight.

For the next few minutes, the lawyer explained the

contract page by page. He walked them through the numbers, showed them the totals of the bank loan and the home inspection, the appraisal, and the prorated taxes. The total suddenly seemed overwhelming, as did the fact that he'd spend the next thirty years paying for the house. With a sinking feeling in his stomach, Jeremy signed where needed and then slid the pages to Lexie. Neither of them asked questions, neither one held up the process. At one point, Jeremy saw the lawyer exchange glances with Mrs. Reynolds, who simply shrugged in response.

In time, the lawyer reassembled the three files: one for the seller, one for his own records, and another for Jeremy and Lexie. He offered the file, and Jeremy reached for it as he rose from the table.

"Congratulations," the lawyer said.

"Thank you," Jeremy answered.

There was no small talk as Mrs. Reynolds led Jeremy and Lexie from the room; once they got outside, Mrs. Reynolds congratulated them as well before heading quickly for her car.

Outside, in the sunlight, neither Jeremy nor Lexie seemed to know what to say until Lexie finally broke the silence.

"Can we go to the house?" she asked.

Jeremy studied her before responding. "Don't you think we should talk first?"

"Let's talk when we get there."

The first thing Jeremy noticed when they pulled up to the house was the balloons tied on the post near the front door; he saw the WELCOME HOME banner beneath them. He glanced over at Lexie.

"I put the balloons and banner up this morning," she explained. "I thought it would be a nice surprise."

"It is," he said. He knew he should say more but didn't.

Lexie shook her head, a tiny, almost imperceptible movement that spoke volumes. Without speaking, she opened the car door and stepped out. Jeremy watched her walk toward the house, noting that she neither waited for him nor glanced back.

Jeremy sensed she was as disappointed in him as he was with her; that his anger mirrored her own. He knew what had happened with Trevor Newland; she knew that he knew as well.

Still, she seemed to want to avoid talking about it.

Jeremy got out of the car. By that point, Lexie was standing on the front porch with her arms crossed, facing away from him, toward an ancient grove of cypress trees. Jeremy walked toward her, aware of the sound of his steps as he moved onto the porch. He stopped when he was close.

Her voice was almost a whisper.

"I had it all planned, you know? About today? I was so excited when I got the balloons and the banner from the store, and I had it all planned out in my mind. I figured that after we closed, I'd suggest a picnic and we'd grab some sandwiches and sodas at Herbs and I'd surprise you by bringing you here. To our house, on the first day we owned it. I thought we'd sit on the back porch and . . . I don't know, just be excited because we both knew that a day like this would never come again." She paused. "It's not going to be like that, is it?"

Her words made him regret his actions, if only for an instant. But none of this was his fault; all he'd done was learn something about Lexie that she hadn't trusted him enough to tell him. And he'd called her on it.

He heard her draw a long breath before she faced him. "Why do you want to know about Trevor Newland? I already told you about him. He showed up in town one summer a few years ago, we had a fling, and he left. That's all."

"That wasn't what I asked. I asked what happened."

"I don't see why that matters," she said. "I cared for him and he left and I never saw him again. I never heard from him again."

"But something happened," he pressed.

"Why are you doing this?" she demanded. "I was thirty-one before we ever met, Jeremy. I didn't come out from under some rock, and I didn't spend my life hiding in an attic. Yes, I dated people before you were around, okay? And yeah, I even cared for some people, too. But so did you, and you don't see me asking about Maria or your old girlfriends. I don't know what's gotten into you lately. It's like I have to tiptoe around every subject so I don't offend you. Yeah, maybe I should have told you about Trevor, but with the way you're acting lately, we still would have ended up fighting."

"The way I'm acting?"

"Yeah," she said, her voice rising. "A little jealousy is normal, but this is ridiculous. First Rodney, now Trevor? Where's it going to stop? Are you going to ask me the names of every guy I dated in college? Do you want to know who I went to the prom with? Or how about the first boy I ever kissed? You want all the details? Like I said, when's it going to stop?"

"This isn't about jealousy!" he snapped.

"No? Then what's it about?"

"It's about trust."

"Trust?" Her expression was incredulous. "How am I supposed to trust you if you don't trust me? This whole week I've been afraid to even say hello to Rodney, especially since Rachel got back, for fear of what you might think. I still don't know where she went or what's going on with her, but I've been on pins and needles trying to keep you happy, so I haven't even had time to ask. But just when I think things are getting back to normal between us, you start asking about Trevor. It's like you're looking for excuses to pick a fight, and I'm tired of it."

"Don't blame me for this," Jeremy answered. "I'm not the one who keeps hiding things."

"I'm not hiding anything."

"I read Doris's journal!" Jeremy retorted. "I saw your initials in there!"

"What are you talking about?"

"Her journal!" he said again. "It's right there in her notes—that LMD was pregnant, but that Doris couldn't tell the sex of the baby. That to Doris, it meant that the woman would miscarry. L-M-D. Lexie Marin Darnell! It was you, wasn't it?"

She swallowed, not hiding her confusion. "It was in the journal?"

"Yeah, and so was the name Trevor Newland."

"Wait . . . ," she said, her confusion growing more evident.

"Just tell me," he demanded. "I saw your initials, I saw his name, and I put two and two together. You were pregnant, weren't you?"

"So what?" she cried. "Why does it even matter?"

"It just hurts to think that you didn't believe in me enough to tell me. I'm tired of these secrets between us—"

She cut him off before he had a chance to finish. "It hurts? Did you ever stop to think about my feelings when you saw the journal? That I might have been hurt? That maybe I didn't tell you because I don't like to remember what happened? That it was a horrible period of my life, and I never wanted to relive it again? It has nothing to do with trusting you. It has nothing to do with you at all. I got pregnant. I had a miscarriage. So what? People make mistakes, Jeremy."

"You're missing my point."

"What point? That you wanted to pick another fight this morning and were looking for any excuse to start one? Well, you did find one, so congratulations. But I'm getting tired of this. I know you're under stress, but you don't have to keep taking it out on me."

"What's that supposed to mean?"

"With your writing!" she said, throwing up her hands. "That's what this is all about, and you know it! You can't write, and you're taking it out on me, like it's somehow my fault. You've been blowing everything out of proportion, and I'm on the receiving end. A friend is in trouble, so I talk to him, and all of a sudden, I don't trust you. I don't tell you that I had a miscarriage four years ago, and it's because I don't trust you. I'm sick of being made to feel like I'm the bad guy because you can't come up with an article."

"Don't blame all this on me. I'm the one who made the sacrifice to come down here—"

"See!" she said. "That's exactly what I mean! You made the *sacrifice*." She practically spat out the word. "That's exactly how you've been acting! Like you ruined your whole life by moving down here!"

"I didn't say that."

"No, but that's what you meant! You're stressed about writing, and you take it out on me! It's not my fault! And did you ever stop to think that I'm stressed, too? I'm the one who made all the wedding plans! I'm the one who's been in charge of renovating the house! I'm the one who's doing all this while carrying a baby! And what do I get? '*You didn't tell me the truth.*' Even if I did, even if I'd told you everything, you still would have found another reason to be mad at me! Nothing I do is right anymore. It's like you've changed into a person I don't even know."

Jeremy felt his own anger flare again. "That's because you don't think I do anything right, either! I don't dress right, I don't order the right foods, I want the wrong kind of car, I didn't even get to pick the house I'm going to live in. You've been making all the decisions, and my ideas count for nothing!"

Her eyes flashed. "That's because I'm thinking about our family. All you think about is yourself!"

"And what about you?" he shouted. "I'm the one who had to give up my family because you wouldn't. I had to risk my career because you wouldn't. I live in a piece-of-crap motel surrounded by dead animals because you didn't want people in town to get the wrong impression! And I've been the one paying for things you want—not the other way around!"

"Money? You're mad about the money, too?"

"I'm going broke down here, and you don't even notice! We could have waited on some of these renovations! We didn't need a five-hundred-dollar crib! We didn't need an entire dresser full of clothes! The baby's not even here yet!" He threw his hands in the air. "So you can see why I'm stressed about writing. It's how I pay for all this stuff you want, and I can't do it here. There's no news to draw on, there's no energy, there's nothing here!"

When he finished, they both stared at each other for a long time without speaking.

"Is that what you really think? That there's *nothing here*? What about the baby and me? Doesn't that mean anything?"

"You know what I mean."

Lexie crossed her arms. "No, I don't. Why don't you tell me?"

Jeremy shook his head, suddenly exhausted. All he'd wanted her to do was listen. Without a word, he started off the porch.

177

He walked toward the car, then decided to leave it. Lexie would need it; he'd figure something out later. He fished the keys from his pocket and threw them near the tire. Heading up the drive, he didn't bother to look back.

Eleven

..... ❖ .....

Hours later, Jeremy sat in the easy chair at his parents' brownstone in Queens, staring out the window. He'd ended up borrowing Doris's car earlier that afternoon to change clothes and grab his things from Greenleaf, then rushing to the airport. Noting his expression, Doris hadn't questioned his request, and during the drive he'd replayed the argument a hundred times.

At first, it had been easy to stay angry at the way Lexie had twisted the facts to her own advantage, but as the miles rolled past and his emotions settled, he began to wonder whether she might have been right. Not about all of it—she had some responsibility for the way the argument had escalated—but certainly on some counts. Had he really been angry about her lack of trust, or was he reacting to the stress he was under and taking it out on her? If he was completely honest, he might admit his stress was part of the equation, but it wasn't only work-related stress. There was still the matter of the e-mails.

E-mails meant to make him question whether the baby was his. E-mails intended to make him suspicious of Lexie. E-mails that seemed to have served their purpose. But who had sent them? And why?

Who knew that Lexie was pregnant? Doris, of course, which again made her the obvious choice. But he just couldn't see her doing that, and according to Lexie, she didn't even know how to use a computer. Whoever had sent the e-mails was an expert.

Then there was Lexie. He remembered her expression when he'd told her that he'd seen her name. Unless her confusion had been faked, she hadn't known her name was in the journal. Had Doris ever told her that she knew? Had Lexie ever told Doris? Depending on when the miscarriage had happened, neither one might have said anything at all to the other.

So who knew?

He placed a call to his hacker friend again and left a message, telling him it was urgent and that he really needed the information. Before hanging up, he asked him to call his cell phone as soon as he came up with anything.

In an hour, he'd be heading out to the bachelor party, but he wasn't in the mood. As good as it would be to spend some time with Alvin, he didn't want to get into all of this with him. Tonight was supposed to be fun, but right now having fun didn't seem possible.

"Shouldn't you be getting ready?"

Jeremy saw his father coming in from the kitchen. "I am ready," he said.

"What's with the shirt? You look like a lumberjack."

In his haste to pack and get out of town—and realizing he'd sweat through the clothes he'd worn earlier at the closing—Jeremy had pulled the flannel shirt off its hanger. Glancing down, he wondered whether it was a subconscious effort to admit that Lexie had been right. "You don't like it?"

"It's different, that's for sure," his father remarked. "You buy that down there?"

"Lexie got it for me."

"You might want to talk to her about style. Now, I might look good in something like that, but it just doesn't seem right on you. Especially if you're going out tonight."

"We'll see," Jeremy said.

"Suit yourself," his father said, taking a seat on the couch. "So what's going on? You have a fight with Lexie before you left?"

Jeremy raised his eyebrows. First the mayor, now his father. Was he that easy to read?

"What makes you say that?" he asked instead.

"The way you've been acting. She mad about you having a bachelor party?"

"No, not at all."

"'Cause some women get mad about that. Oh sure, they all say it's okay, that it's tradition, but deep down they don't like the thought of their fiancés gawking at beautiful women."

"It's not going to be that kind of party. I told Alvin I didn't want that."

His father made himself comfortable. "Then what was the fight about? You want to talk about it?"

Jeremy debated whether or not to tell him, then decided not to. "Not really. It's private."

His father nodded. "Always a good idea, by the way. Take it from me. What a couple fights about should always remain private. If it doesn't, there's hell to pay. But that doesn't mean I can't give you some advice anyway, does it?"

"It's never stopped you before."

"All couples argue. That's what you've got to remember."

"I know that."

"Yeah, but what you're thinking is that you and Lexie argue more than you should. Now, I can't tell you whether you do or you don't, but I met that young lady when she came up here and I'll tell you straight up that she's good for you and you'd be dumb if you didn't try to resolve whatever problems there are. She's one of a kind, and your mother thinks you got mighty lucky. So does everyone up here, by the way."

"You don't even know her. You only met her once."

"Did you know she's been writing to your mother every week since you've been down there? And your sisters-in-law?"

Jeremy's face registered his surprise.

"That's what I thought," his father said. "Been calling, too. And sending pictures. Your mom has seen what she looks like in her wedding dress, what the cake looks like, how the house is coming. She even sent some postcards with a picture of the lighthouse on them, so your mom knows what that looks like, too. All that so your mom and the rest of us feel like we're part of what's going on. Your mom can't wait to go down there so they can spend some more time together."

Jeremy was silent. "Why didn't I know about this?" he asked at last.

"I don't know. Maybe she wanted you to be surprised at the wedding, and I'm sorry if I blew it. But my point is that most people wouldn't do all that. She knew your mom wasn't happy about you leaving, but she didn't take it personally. Instead, she just went about trying to make things better. It takes a special person to care like that."

"I can't believe it," Jeremy mumbled, thinking that Lexie was full of surprises. But this time it was okay.

"Now, I know you've been married before, but you're starting all over again. The one thing you've got to remember is to see the big picture. When things get tough, remind yourself why you fell in love with her in the first place. She's a special woman, and you were lucky to find her, just as she was lucky to find you. She's got a heart of gold, and you can't fake something like that."

"Why do I get the sense that you're on her side and you think the argument was my fault?"

"Because I've known you all my life," his father said with a wink. "You've always been good at picking fights. What do you think you've been doing when you write those articles?"

Despite everything, Jeremy laughed. "What if you're wrong about me? What if it was her fault?"

His father shrugged. "Well, then I'd say it takes two to tango. My guess is that both of you are right and both of you are wrong. That's the way most arguments go, anyway. People are who they are and no one is perfect, but marriage is about becoming a team. You're going to spend the rest of your life learning about each other, and every now and then, things blow up. But the beauty of marriage is that if you picked the right person and you both love each other, you'll always figure out a way to get through it."

Later that night, Jeremy was leaning against the wall of Alvin's apartment with a beer in his hand, surveying the crowd, many of whom were watching the TV. Mostly because of the tattoo connection, Alvin was a big Allen Iverson fan, and as fate would have it, the 76ers were facing the Hornets in the play-offs. Though most of those in attendance would probably have preferred to watch the Knicks, they'd played on Wednesday. Nonetheless, people were around the television, using the bachelor party as an excuse to watch the game with a rowdiness not normally permitted by the wives they'd left at home. If they had wives, that is. Jeremy wasn't so sure about some of them, who were as heavily tattooed and pierced as Alvin. But they seemed to be having a good time; a few had been drinking since they'd arrived and were already slurring their words. Every now and then, someone would suddenly seem to remember why he was at Alvin's apartment in the first place and wander toward Jeremy.

"You having fun?" he might say, or, "How about I get you another beer?"

"I'm doing fine, thanks," Jeremy would answer.

Though he hadn't seen these people in a couple of months, few seemed to feel the need to catch up, which made sense considering that most of them were more Alvin's friends than his. In fact, as he scanned the room, he realized that he didn't recognize half the people here, which struck him as somewhat amusing since it was supposed to be his party. He would have been just as happy spending the evening with only Alvin, Nate, and his brothers, but Alvin was notorious for seizing any excuse to have a good time. And Alvin seemed to be having a great time, especially considering the 76ers were leading by two halfway through the third period. He was among those whooping and hollering every time the 76ers scored. As were Jeremy's brothers. Only Nate, who'd never been much of a sports fan, seemed uninterested in the game; he was busy loading his plate with another slice of pizza.

The party had started out on a good note; he'd stepped into the room and had been greeted as if he'd recently returned from war. His brothers had crowded around and bombarded him with questions about Lexie and Boone Creek and the house; Nate had been kind enough to bring a list of possible story ideas, one of which concerned the increasingly popular use of astrology as a way to invest. Jeremy listened, making mental notes, and admitted to himself that it was original enough for a column, if not an article; he thanked Nate, with the promise to keep it in mind. Not that it would do any good.

Nonetheless, it had been easy to forget his problems for the time being. Distance had a strange way of making the aggravations of Boone Creek life seem humorous; while telling his brothers about the renovations, they couldn't stop laughing at his description of the workers, and Jeremy found himself laughing as well. They roared at the fact that Lexie made him stay at Greenleaf and pleaded with Jeremy to take pictures of his room so they could see the stuffed critters themselves. They wanted a photo of Jed, too, who in the course of the conversation had grown to almost mythic proportions in their minds. And they begged, just as Alvin had, to let them know as soon as he went hunting so they could hear all about it.

In time, they drifted toward the television along with everyone else, getting in the spirit of the evening. Jeremy felt content to watch from a distance.

"Nice shirt," Alvin commented, coming up.

"I know," Jeremy said. "You've already told me twice."

"And I'm going to keep telling you. I don't care whether Lexie bought it or not. You look like a tourist."

"So?"

"So? We're going out tonight. We're going to storm this city, party it up in honor of your last few nights as a single man, and you're dressed like you just spent the afternoon milking cows. It's not you."

"It's the new me."

Alvin laughed. "Weren't you the one who was complaining about the shirt in the first place?"

"I think it grew on me."

"It certainly grew somewhere. But I'll tell you, my friends are getting a kick out of it."

Jeremy lifted his beer and took another sip. He'd

been nursing it for an hour, and it was getting warm. "I can't say that bothers me. Half of them are wearing T-shirts they bought at rock concerts, and the other half are covered in leather. I'd look out of place no matter what I wore."

"That may be true," Alvin said with a grin, "but notice the energy they're bringing to your party. I couldn't imagine having to spend the whole night with just Nate along for the ride."

Jeremy spotted his agent across the room. Nate was wearing a tight three-piece suit, the top of his head was shiny with perspiration, and there was a spot of pizza sauce on his chin. He seemed more out of place than Jeremy. Noticing Jeremy's stare, he waved a slice of pizza.

"Yeah, that reminds me . . . thanks for inviting your friends to my bachelor party."

"Who was I supposed to invite? I tried the guys at *Scientific American*, but they didn't seem all that interested. Other than them, the only names I could come up with, besides your brothers and Nate, were females. I didn't realize that you were such a hermit while you lived here. And besides, this is just the pre-party to get us in the proper mood for the evening."

"I hesitate to ask what's on the agenda later."

"Don't bother. It's a surprise."

A roar from the crowd erupted as people high-fived. Beer sloshed here and there as the replay showed Iverson sinking a long three-pointer.

"Hey, did Nate talk to you yet?"

"Yeah. Why?"

"Because I don't want him ruining the evening

by talking about writing all night. I know that's a sore subject with you right now, but you're going to have to leave it behind when we hit the limo."

"Not a problem," Jeremy lied.

"Yeah, sure. That's why you're over here leaning against the wall instead of watching the game, right?"

"I'm preparing myself for the evening."

"Looks more like you're pacing yourself so you don't get in trouble. If I didn't know better, I'd say you're still on your first beer."

"So?"

"So? It's your bachelor party. You're allowed to cut loose. In fact, you're supposed to cut loose. So how about I get you another beer and we'll get this party started."

"I'm fine," Jeremy insisted. "I'm having a good time."

Alvin studied him. "You've changed," he said.

Yeah, Jeremy thought, I have. But he said nothing.

Alvin shook his head. "I know you're getting married, but . . ."

When he trailed off, Jeremy stared at him. "But what?"

"This," Alvin answered. "All of it. The way you're dressed, the way you're acting. It's like I don't know who you are anymore."

Jeremy shrugged. "Maybe I'm growing up."

Alvin began peeling the label off his beer bottle as he answered. "Yeah," he said. "Maybe."

Once the game ended, most of Alvin's friends lingered near the food, doing their best to finish off the last of the pizza until Alvin finally shooed them from the apartment. When they were gone, Jeremy followed Alvin, Nate, and his brothers down the stairs, where they piled into the waiting limousine. Another case of beer was on ice inside, and even Nate was getting into the spirit of things. A lightweight when it came to alcohol, he was swaying after only three beers, and his eyelids were already at half-mast.

"Clausen," he was saying. "You need to do another story like the one you did with Clausen. That's what you need to find. You need to bag another elephant. Are you hearing me here?"

"Bag an elephant," Jeremy said, trying to ignore the boozy breath. "Got it."

"That's it. That's exactly what you need to do."

"I know."

"But it's got to be an elephant."

"Of course."

"An elephant. Do you hear me?"

"Giant ears, long trunk, eats peanuts. Elephant. Got it."

Nate nodded. "Now you're thinking."

Across the car, Alvin moved toward the front to give directions to the driver. A few minutes later, the car rolled to a stop; Jeremy's brothers finished the rest of their beers before crawling out.

Jeremy was the last to get out, and he realized they were at the same trendy bar where he'd gone to celebrate his appearance on *Primetime Live* in January. With a long granite bar and dramatic lighting, the place was as sleek and crowded as it was back then. Beyond the glass windows, it seemed to be standing room only.

"I thought you might like to start here," Alvin said.

"Why not?" Jeremy said.

"Hey!" Nate called out. "I recognize this place." He turned around. "I've been here before."

"C'mon, big boy," Jeremy heard one of his brothers say. "Let's go on in."

"But where are the dancing girls?"

"Later," he heard another brother add. "The night's still young. We're just getting started."

When Jeremy turned to Alvin, he simply shrugged. "I didn't plan anything, but you know how some guys get when it comes to bachelor parties. You can't hold me accountable for everything that happens tonight."

"Sure I can."

"Gee, you're just a big bundle of fun tonight, aren't you?"

Jeremy followed Alvin toward the front door; Nate and his brothers had already made their way inside, wedging their way around groups. Once inside, Jeremy found himself breathing in the atmosphere that had once felt like home. Most of the people here were stylishly dressed; a few others in suits looked as if they'd come straight from the office. He soon zeroed in on a gorgeous brunette at the far end of the bar who seemed to be drinking something tropical; in his earlier life, he would have offered to buy her a drink as an opener. Tonight, seeing her made him think of Lexie, and he fingered his cell phone, wondering if he should call just to let her know that he'd arrived okay. Maybe even apologize.

"What do you want to drink?" Alvin called out. He'd already elbowed his way to the bar and was leaning in, trying to get the attention of the bartender.

"I'm okay right now," Jeremy shouted over the noise. Through the waves of people, he could see his brothers congregating at the other end of the bar. Nate seemed to be wobbling as he made way for another group to pass.

Alvin shook his head and ordered two gin and tonics; after paying, he handed one to Jeremy.

"No can do," he said, handing over the drink. "It's your bachelor party. As the best man, I'm putting my foot down here and insisting you lighten up."

"I'm having fun," Jeremy insisted again.

"No, you're not. What? Did you and Lexie have another fight?"

Jeremy surveyed the bar; in the corner, he thought he saw someone he'd once dated. Jane something. Or was it Jean?

It didn't matter, but he supposed that it was simply a way of avoiding Alvin's question. He straightened up. "Sort of," he admitted.

"You two fight all the time," Alvin said. "Did you ever think that might be telling you something?"

"We don't fight all the time."

"What's this latest one about?" Alvin asked, ignoring Jeremy's comment. "Did you forget to kiss her the right way before you left for the airport?"

Jeremy frowned. "She's not like that."

"Well, something's going on," Alvin persisted. "You want to talk about it?"

"No," Jeremy said. "Not now."

Alvin arched an eyebrow. "Must be big, huh?"

Jeremy took a drink, feeling the burn at the back of his throat. "No," he said.

"Whatever," Alvin said, shaking his head. "Fine, you don't want to talk to me, maybe you should talk to your brothers. All I'm saying is that ever since you've been down there, you haven't been happy." He paused to let that sink in. "Maybe that's the reason you haven't been able to write."

"I don't know why I'm not writing, but I can say that it has nothing to do with Lexie. And I'm not unhappy."

"You can't see the forest for the trees."

"What's gotten into you?" Jeremy said.

"I'm just trying to get you to think clearly about all this."

"All what?" Jeremy demanded. "You sound like you don't want me to marry her."

"I don't think you should marry her," Alvin snapped. "That's what I tried to tell you before you moved down there. You don't even know her, and I think part of your problem is that you're finally realizing it. It's not too late—"

"I love her!" Jeremy said, his voice rising in exasperation. "Why are you saying this?"

"Because I don't want you to make a mistake!" Alvin shot back. "I'm worried about you, okay? You can't write, you're practically broke, you don't seem to trust Lexie, and she doesn't trust you enough to tell you she's been pregnant before. And now you two are fighting again for the umpteenth time . . ."

Jeremy blinked. "What did you say?"

"I said I don't want you to make a mistake."

"After that!" Jeremy shouted.

"What?"

"You said that Lexie has been pregnant before."

Alvin shook his head. "My point is—"

"How did you know about that?" Jeremy demanded.

"I don't know . . . I guess you must have mentioned it earlier."

"No," Jeremy said, "I didn't. I didn't learn about it until this morning. And I didn't tell you. So again, how did you know?"

It was in that instant, while staring at his friend, that he felt the pieces suddenly fall into place: the untraceable e-mails . . . Alvin's brief infatuation with Rachel and his offer to let her visit . . . the fact that Alvin had made a point of bringing her up in conversation, which meant he was still thinking about her . . . Rachel's recent unexplained absence coupled with Alvin's need to hang up the phone because he had company.

Jeremy found himself holding his breath as the rest of it came together like the neatest of puzzles, too far-fetched to believe, too obvious to ignore . . .

Rachel, who had been Lexie's best friend for years . . . who had access to Doris's journal and knew what was in it . . . who would have known that Doris had given it to Jeremy . . . who was having trouble with Rodney because of Lexie . . .

And Alvin, his friend, who still talked to Jeremy's ex, old friends who shared everything . . .

"Rachel was here, wasn't she?" Jeremy finally said, his voice cracking with anger. "Rachel came to visit you in New York, didn't she?"

"No."

"You sent those e-mails," he went on, the depth

of Alvin's betrayal finally penetrating. He stared at Alvin as if he were a stranger. "You lied to me."

People around them turned to watch; Jeremy barely noticed. Alvin took an involuntary step backward.

"I can explain—"

"Why would you do that? I thought you were my friend."

"I am your friend," Alvin said.

Jeremy didn't seem to hear him. "You knew how stressed I've been . . ."

He shook his head, trying to grasp the full reality of the situation. Alvin reached for his arm. "Okay, yeah—Rachel did come up, and I was the one who sent the e-mails," he admitted. "I didn't even know she was coming until the day before when she called, and I was as surprised as you were. You've got to believe me on that. And as for the e-mails, I only sent them because I care about you. You haven't been yourself since you went down there, and I didn't want you to make a mistake."

Jeremy said nothing. In the silence, Alvin squeezed his arm and went on. "I'm not saying that you shouldn't marry her. She seems nice, she really does. But you rushed into this thing, and you weren't listening to reason. She might be the best lady ever, and I hope she is, but you should know what you're getting into."

Jeremy exhaled, still unable to face Alvin. "Maria told you, didn't she?" he said. "About the real reason we divorced."

"Yeah," Alvin said, seemingly relieved that Jeremy seemed to be getting it. "She did. She said there was no way it could happen. She was even more suspicious than I was, if you want to know the truth, and it just got me thinking, so I sent the e-mail." He sighed. "Maybe I was wrong to do that, and I honestly figured you'd blow it off, but then you called me and you were upset, and I suddenly realized that you were having the same doubts about how she got pregnant that I was."

He stopped, letting that sink in before going on. "And then Rachel shows up, we have a few drinks, and she starts telling me about how much Rodney still cares about Lexie, and I'm remembering the fact that Lexie copped to the fact she'd spent the evening with Rodney. Meanwhile, the more Rachel talked, the more I found out about Lexie's past— about this guy she'd dated and how she'd gotten pregnant before—and it just confirmed how little you knew about her."

"What are you trying to say?"

Alvin drew a long breath, choosing his words carefully. "I'm just saying that this is a big decision, and you should know what you're getting into."

"Are you saying that you think the baby is Rodney's?" Jeremy asked.

"I don't know what to think about it," Alvin answered, "but that's not the point—"

"No?" Jeremy said, his voice rising. "Then what is the point? You want me to dump my fiancée while she's pregnant so I can move back to New York and party with you?"

Alvin held up his hands. "I'm not saying that."

"It sure as hell sounds like that's what you're

saying!" Jeremy shouted, not wanting to hear any more. Again the people around him turned to stare; again he ignored them. "And I'll tell you what!" he went on. "I don't care what you think I should do. It's my baby! I'm going to marry Lexie! And I'm going to live in Boone Creek because that's where I belong!"

"You don't have to yell—"

"You lied to me!"

"I was trying to help—"

"You betrayed me—"

"No!" Alvin said, his voice rising to meet Jeremy's. "All I did was ask questions you should have been asking yourself all along."

"It wasn't any of your damn business!"

"I didn't do this to hurt you!" Alvin shouted back. "I'm not the only one who thought you were moving too fast with all this! Your brothers think the same thing!"

The comment made Jeremy freeze for a second; Alvin took the opportunity to press his case.

"Getting married is a big deal, Jeremy! We're not talking about going out to dinner with her; we're talking about you waking up for the rest of your life with her by your side. People don't fall in love in just a couple of days. And no matter what you think, you didn't, either. You thought she was great, you thought she was intelligent or beautiful or whatever . . . but to suddenly decide to spend the rest of your life with her? To give up your home and your career on a whim?"

His voice had a pleading note, one that reminded Jeremy of a teacher trying to get through to a gifted, though obstinate, student. He could conjure up any number of responses. He could have told Alvin that he had no doubt the baby was his; he could have told Alvin that sending the e-mails was not only wrong, but sinister; he could have told Alvin that he loved Lexie and had loved her all along, and he always would. But they'd gone over all that, and even if Alvin was wrong, he wouldn't want to admit it.

And Alvin was wrong. About every bit of it.

Instead, Jeremy stared into his drink and swirled it before meeting Alvin's eyes. With a quick jerk of his arm, he threw the rest of his drink in Alvin's face and then grabbed him by the collar. Hurtling forward, he shoved an off-balance Alvin back a few steps, pinning him against a column.

He almost hit him. Instead, he brought his face close to Alvin's, near enough to smell his breath.

"I never want to see or talk to you again."

With that, he turned and strode out the door.

Twelve

···· ❖ ····

"I haven't heard from him," Lexie admitted the following afternoon, eyeing Doris across the table at Herbs.

"I'm sure it's going to be all right," Doris said.

Lexie hesitated, trying to figure out whether Doris was telling the truth or simply saying what she wanted to hear. "You didn't see his expression at the house yesterday. The way he stared at me . . . like he hated me."

"Can you blame him?"

Lexie looked up. "What's that supposed to mean?"

"Just what I said," Doris replied. "How would you like it if you discovered something about Jeremy that made you feel you couldn't trust him?"

Lexie stiffened in protest. "I didn't come here to listen to this."

"Well, you're here, and you're going to listen. You came here hoping for sympathy, but when you told your story, I kept thinking about how Jeremy might have seen all this. He sees you holding hands with Rodney, you break your date to spend the evening with Rodney, and then he finds out that you've been pregnant before. It's no wonder he was angry."

Lexie opened her mouth to say something, but Doris raised her hands to cut her off.

"I know it's not what you want to hear, but he's not the only one at fault here."

"I apologized. I explained everything."

"I know you did, but sometimes that's not enough. You hid things from him, not once or twice, but three times. You can't do that, not if you want his confidence. You should have told him what happened with Trevor. I thought you already had, or I never would have given him the journal."

"Why did I have to tell him? I hadn't thought about it in years. It happened a long time ago."

"Not to him. To him, it happened on Friday. I'd probably be angry, too."

"You sound like you're on his side."

"On this, I am."

"Doris!"

"You're engaged, Lexie. I know Rodney's been your friend for years, but you're engaged to Jeremy, and the rules change. It would have been fine if you had told him up front what you were doing, but you were sneaking behind his back."

"That's because I knew how he'd react."

"Oh really? How did you know?" Doris fixed her with an unwavering gaze. "All you would have had to do was call and tell him that you wanted to talk to Rodney, that you were trying to find out where Rachel went, that you wanted to find out whether you were somehow responsible. I'm sure he would

199

have understood that. But you didn't tell the full story, and not for the first time. And then he finds out that you were pregnant before?"

"You mean I'm supposed to tell him everything?"

"That's not what I'm saying. But this? Yeah, you probably should have told him. It wasn't like it was a big secret in town, and even if it was something you wanted to forget, you had to figure that he was going to find out anyway. It would have been better for you to tell him than for him to have found out the way he did. Or worse, what if he'd heard it from someone else?"

Lexie turned toward the window, her mouth a stubborn line, and Doris thought she might leave. But she stayed seated, and Doris reached across the table to take her hand.

"I know you, Lexie. You can be headstrong, but you're not a victim. And neither is Jeremy. What's going on with you two, all this stress you're both under . . . that's called life. And life has a tendency to throw curveballs when you least expect them. Every couple has ups and downs, every couple argues, and that's the thing—you're a couple, and couples can't function without trust. You have to trust him, and he's got to trust you."

In the silence, Lexie thought about Doris's comment while continuing to stare through the window. A cardinal landed on the window ledge, hopped from spot to spot as if the ledge were on fire, then flew off. She'd seen the bird land here a hundred times before, maybe a thousand times, but as she watched she was struck by the absurd conviction that somehow this bird was trying to tell her something.

She waited, watching for the cardinal to reappear, hoping it would come back. But it didn't, and she realized how foolish the thought had been. Above her, the ceiling fans whirred, moving the air in empty circles.

"You think he'll come back?" Lexie finally asked, her voice betraying her fear.

"He's coming back," Doris said, squeezing her hand with conviction.

Lexie wanted to believe it, even if she wasn't so sure herself. "I haven't heard from him since he left," she whispered. "He hasn't called once."

"He will," Doris said. "Give him time. He's trying to sort through everything, and he's with his friends this weekend. It's his bachelor party, don't forget."

"I know . . ."

"Don't read anything extra into this. When's he coming back?"

"Supposedly Sunday night. But—"

"Then that's when he'll be here," Doris said. "And when he does show up, just be happy to see him. Ask about his weekend, and listen with interest when he tells you all about it. And afterwards, make sure he knows how special you think he is. Believe me, I was married for a long time."

Despite the turmoil she was feeling inside, Lexie grinned. "You sound like a marriage counselor."

Doris shrugged. "I know men. Let me tell you, they can be rip-roaring mad or frustrated or worried about work or life, but in the end, they're pretty simple to figure out if you know what makes them tick. And one of the things that make them tick is an almost desperate need to feel appreciated and admired. You make them feel that way, and you'll be amazed at what they'll do for you."

Lexie simply stared at her grandmother. Doris had a mischievous grin as she went on. "Of course, they want great sex and want you to keep the house clean and neat and organized while looking beautiful and still having the energy to do fun things together, but admiration and appreciation are right up there."

Lexie's jaw dropped. "Gee, really?" she asked. "Maybe I should go barefoot and stay pregnant, except when I'm wearing lingerie."

"Don't act so indignant." Doris had turned serious again. "You're not the only one who has to make a sacrifice when it comes to being a couple. You think you're getting the short end of the stick? Men have to make sacrifices, too. Correct me if I'm wrong, but you want Jeremy to hold your hand and snuggle as you watch a movie, you want him to share his feelings and listen, you want him to spend time with your daughter and earn enough not only to buy but renovate the house. Well, I'll tell you straight up that no man says to himself as he's walking down the aisle, Gee, I'm going to work hard and sacrifice so I can provide a good living for my family, and I'm going to spend hours with my kids even when I'm tired, all the while hugging and kissing and listening to my wife and telling her all my troubles, and meanwhile, *I'm not going to expect a single thing*." Doris didn't wait for a response. "A man promises to do the things to keep you happy in the hopes that you, too, will do the things that keep him happy."

She reached for Lexie's hand. "Like I said, you're in this together. Men have certain needs, women have different needs; that's the way it was hundreds of years ago, and that's the way it's going to be hundreds of years from now. If you both realize that, and you both work on meeting each other's needs, you'll have a good marriage. And part of that, for both of you, is trust. In the end, it's that simple."

"I don't know why you're telling me this."

Doris gave a knowing smile. "Yes, you do. But my hope is that you remember this when you're married. If you think it's tough now, wait until then. Just when you think it can't get any worse, it can. And just when you think it can't get any better, it will. But as long as you remember that he loves you and you love him—and both of you remember to act that way—you'll be just fine."

Lexie mulled over Doris's words. "I suppose this is the premarriage talk, huh? The one you've been saving up for all these years?"

Doris let go of Lexie's hand. "Oh, I don't know. I suppose it might have come out eventually, but I didn't plan on saying all this beforehand. It just came up."

Lexie was silent as she considered it. "So, you're sure he's going to come back?"

"Yeah, I'm sure. I've seen the way he looks at you and I know what it means. Believe it or not, I've been around the block more than once."

"What if you're wrong?"

"I'm not. Don't you remember? I'm psychic."

"You're a diviner, you're not psychic."

Doris shrugged. "Sometimes the feeling comes across exactly the same way."

Lexie stopped outside of Herbs, squinting in the bright afternoon sunlight. Searching for her keys, she found herself contemplating the wisdom of Doris's words. It hadn't been easy hearing her grandmother's assessment of her situation, but was it ever easy hearing that you might be wrong? Since Jeremy had left her standing on the porch, she'd fumed with self-justification, as if anger might keep her worries in check, but now she couldn't escape how petty the memory made her feel. She didn't want to fight with Jeremy; she was as tired of the arguments as he was. This was no way to start their marriage, and she decided it would end here and now. Unlocking her car and sliding behind the wheel, she nodded with determination. She would change if she had to—and also because it was the right thing to do.

Pulling out of the parking lot, she wasn't sure where to go. Drawn by instinct, however, she soon found herself at the cemetery, standing before the headstones of her parents. Seeing their names carved in granite, she thought of the couple she didn't remember and tried to imagine what they had been like. Did her mother laugh a lot, or was she quiet? Was her father a fan of football or baseball? Pointless thoughts, but she nonetheless found herself wondering how much like Doris her mother had been, and whether her mother would have given her the same lecture Doris had. More than likely, she guessed. They were mother and daughter, after all. For a reason she couldn't explain, the thought made her smile. She would call Jeremy as soon as she got home, she decided. She'd tell him again that she was sorry and that she missed him.

And, as if her mother were listening, a light breeze stirred the air, making the leaves of the magnolia sway, almost in hushed agreement.

Lexie spent nearly an hour in the cemetery, conjuring up images of Jeremy and what he might be doing. She pictured him sitting in the worn easy chair in his parents' living room, talking to his father, and it seemed as if she were in the adjoining room, listening in. She caught herself remembering how she felt when she first entered his childhood home, surrounded by those who knew him far longer than she had. She recalled the flirtatious way he'd watched her that evening and the tender way he'd traced her belly with his finger later that night at the Plaza.

Sighing as she glanced at her watch, she realized that there was a lot she should be doing: grocery shopping, paperwork at the library, gift buying for some employees' upcoming birthdays . . . But as she jingled her keys, she suddenly felt an undeniable urge to go home, one so powerful that she felt little choice in the matter. She turned from her parents' headstones and walked back to her car, puzzled by the urgency.

She drove slowly, careful to avoid the rabbits and raccoons that typically scampered across this stretch of road, but as she drew nearer to her home, an inexplicable sense of anticipation made her press down more firmly on the accelerator. She turned onto the road that fronted her property, blinking in confusion at the sight of Doris's car parked along the street—until she caught sight of the figure perched on her front steps, elbows on his knees.

Fighting the urge to jump from the car, she stepped out slowly and began to walk up the driveway as if nothing about the scene struck her as unusual.

Jeremy had risen even before she'd slung her purse over her shoulder. "Hi," he said.

She forced herself to steady her voice and smile as she approached. "Down here, people say, 'hey,' not 'hi.'"

Jeremy studied his feet, seemingly oblivious to the playfulness in her tone.

"I'm glad to see you, stranger," she added, her voice gentle. "It's not often that I come home to see such a handsome man waiting on my porch."

When Jeremy looked up, she could see the exhaustion in his face.

"I was just beginning to wonder where you were."

She stood before him, recalling her earlier memory of his touch against her skin. For an instant, she thought about throwing herself into his arms, but there was something so fragile and tentative about his demeanor that she held back.

"I'm glad to see you," she said again.

Jeremy responded with the ghost of a smile but said nothing.

"Are you still mad at me?" she asked.

Instead of answering, he simply stared at her. When she realized he was debating how to answer, weighing what he wanted to say against what he thought she wanted to hear, she reached for his arm. "Because if you are, you have every right to be." She spoke in a breathless rush, anxious not to leave out anything she needed to say. "You were right. I should have told you about everything, and I won't keep things like that from you again. I'm sorry."

He seemed amused. "Just like that?"

"I've had some time to think about it."

"I'm sorry, too," he conceded. "I shouldn't have overreacted the way I did."

In the silence that followed, Lexie took in the fatigue and sorrow that seemed to hang from his figure. Instinctively, she moved toward him. He hesitated only briefly before opening his arms. She moved into them, kissed him gently on the lips, and then put her head on his chest. With his arms wrapped around her, they held each other for a long time, but she was conscious of the lack of passion in his embrace.

"Are you okay?" she whispered.

"No, not really," he answered.

She took his hand and led him inside, pausing in the living room, unsure whether to sit beside him on the couch or in the chair beside it. Jeremy moved around her and collapsed onto the couch. Then, leaning forward, he ran a hand through his hair.

"Sit by me," he said. "I have something to tell you."

At his words, her heart skipped a beat. She moved next to him, feeling the warmth of his leg against her own. When he exhaled sharply, she felt herself stiffen.

"Is it about us?" she asked.

He stared in the direction of the kitchen, his eyes unfocused. "You could say that."

"And the wedding?"

When he nodded, Lexie steeled herself for the worst. "Are you moving back to New York?" she whispered.

It took a moment for him to grasp what she was asking, but when he faced her, she saw his confusion.

"Why would you think something like that? Do you want me to move back?"

"Of course not. But the way you're acting, I don't know what to think."

Jeremy shook his head. "I'm sorry. I didn't mean to be so evasive. I guess I'm still trying to make sense of everything myself. But I'm not mad at you or thinking of calling off the wedding. I probably should have explained that right away."

She felt herself relax. "What's going on? Did something happen at the bachelor party?"

"Yeah," Jeremy said. "But there's more to it than just that."

He started at the beginning, finally telling her about the depths of his struggles with writing, his worries about the cost of the house, the sense of frustration he sometimes felt in the limited confines of Boone Creek. She'd heard bits and pieces of it all before, though she admitted to herself that she hadn't sensed how difficult it had really been for him. He spoke in a voice that omitted blame, as if talking to himself as much as to her.

She wasn't sure where he was going but knew enough to stay silent until he'd finished. He sat straighter.

"And then," he added, "I saw you and Rodney holding hands. Even when I saw it, I knew it shouldn't bother me. I told myself that over and over, but I guess that the other stresses I was under made me think it was something more. I knew how ridiculous the belief was, but I guess I was looking for a reason to take it out on you." He gave a half-hearted smile. "Which was exactly what you told me the other day. Then you went over to Rodney's again, and I just snapped. But there was something else I haven't told you. Something that happened after each of those events."

She reached for his hand, feeling relief when he accepted it.

He told her about the e-mails he'd received, describing the anger and anxiety they'd caused. At first, she had trouble understanding what had happened, and she tried to keep her voice steady in an attempt to stifle her growing sense of shock.

"That's how you knew what was in the journal?" she asked.

"Yeah," he said. "I don't know whether I would have noticed it otherwise."

"But . . . who would have done something like that?"

Jeremy sighed as he answered. "Alvin."

"Alvin? Alvin sent them? But . . . that doesn't make sense. There was no way he could know—"

"Rachel told him," he said. "When she left? She went to see Alvin in New York."

Lexie shook her head. "No. I've known her forever. She wouldn't do that."

He told her the rest of the story as best he could

piece it together. "And after I stormed out of the bar, I didn't know what to do. I just walked for a while until I heard people running up behind me. My brothers . . ." He shrugged. "They could see how angry I was, and that got them going. Put a couple of drinks in them, and they're more than happy to start a brawl. They kept asking what Alvin did and whether they should have a 'talk' with him. I told them to let it go."

In a role reversal, Jeremy seemed to find it easy to keep talking; Lexie was still trying to digest what he'd told her.

"They ended up bringing me back to my parents, but I couldn't sleep. I couldn't talk to anyone up there about everything that had gone on, so I changed my flight to the first one out this morning."

When he finished, Lexie felt as if she couldn't breathe.

"I thought he was your friend."

"So did I."

"Why would he do something like that?"

"I don't know," Jeremy said.

"Because of me? What did I ever do to him? He doesn't even know me. He doesn't know us. This was . . ."

"Evil," Jeremy said, finishing for her. "I know it was."

"But . . ." She dabbed at an unexpected tear. "He . . . I just don't . . ."

"I don't know what to say, either," Jeremy said. "I've been trying to make sense of it since it happened, but the only thing I've figured out is that in his own twisted way, he thought he was helping me avoid a potential disaster. It's sick, I know. In any case, I'm through with him."

She met his gaze with sudden fierceness. "Why didn't you tell me about the e-mails earlier?"

"Like I said, I wouldn't have known what to say. I didn't know who sent them, I didn't know why. And then, with everything else . . ."

"Does your family know?"

"About the e-mails? No, I didn't say anything—"

"No," Lexie interrupted, trembling. "That you were worried about whether it was your baby."

"I know it's my baby."

"It is your baby," she said. "I've never slept with Rodney. You're the only one I've slept with in years."

"I know . . ."

"But I want you to hear me say it. It's our baby, yours and mine. I swear."

"I know."

"But you wondered, didn't you?" Her voice was beginning to crack. "Even if it was only for an instant, you wondered about it. First you find me over at Rodney's, and then you discover that I hadn't told you about being pregnant before, and with all your other stress . . ."

"It's okay."

"No, it's not. You should have told me. If I'd known any of this . . . we could have gone through all this together." She struggled for self-control.

"It's over, okay? There's nothing we can do about it, and we'll get through this and move on."

"You must have hated me."

"I never hated you," he said, pulling her close. "I love you. We're getting married next week, remember?"

She turned her face into his chest, finding comfort in the circle of his arms. In time, she sighed. "I don't want to see Alvin at the wedding."

"I don't, either. But there's something else I have to tell you."

"No, I don't want to hear it. Not just yet. I've had enough shock for one day."

"This is good," he promised. "You'll want to hear this."

She looked up at him, as if hoping he wasn't lying.

"Thank you," he said.

"For what?"

With a gentle smile, he kissed her on the lips. "For the letters you sent to my family. Especially my mother. It's those things that remind me that marrying you is the best thing I'll ever do."

Thirteen

···· ❖ ····

A cold, slashing rain, unseasonable in its fury, crashed water against the windows in waves. The gray clouds, which had drifted in uneventfully the night before, brought with them morning mist and a wind that shook the last of the blossoms from the dogwood trees. It was early May, and there were only three days until the wedding. Jeremy had made arrangements to meet his parents at the Norfolk airport, where they'd follow him in a rented car to Cape Hatteras Lighthouse in Buxton. Until they arrived, he busied himself with helping Lexie make final calls to verify that everything was ready.

The gloomy weather did nothing to dampen the renewed passion Lexie and Jeremy felt for each other. On the night he'd returned, they made love with an intensity that surprised them both, and he could vividly recall the electric feel of her skin against his own. It was as if, in their lovemaking, they were trying to erase all of the pain and betrayals, the secrets and anger, of the past few months.

Once the burden of their respective secrets had

been removed, Jeremy felt lighter than he had in months. With his impending marriage, he had a valid excuse to avoid thinking about work and had little trouble doing so. He went jogging twice and made the decision to take it up regularly again as soon as the wedding was behind him. Although the renovations on the house weren't complete, the contractor promised that they would be able to move in well before the baby was born. It would probably be the end of August, but Lexie felt confident enough to go ahead and put her bungalow up for sale, promising to bank the entire proceeds to shore up their dwindling savings.

The one place they didn't go was Herbs. After learning what Rachel had told Alvin, Lexie couldn't fathom the idea of seeing her—not yet, anyway. The night before, Doris had called, asking why neither Jeremy nor Lexie had even dropped in to say hello. On the phone, Lexie assured Doris that she wasn't angry with her and admitted that Doris had been right to take her to task when they last spoke. When Lexie didn't follow up with a visit, Doris called again.

"I'm beginning to think there's something that you're not telling me," Doris said, "and if you don't tell me what's going on, I'm going to march over to your house and perch myself on your porch until you fill me in."

"We're just busy and making sure everything is ready for the weekend," Lexie said, trying to appease her.

"I didn't just fall off the turnip truck," Doris said, "and I know avoidance when I see it, and the fact is, you're avoiding me."

"I'm not avoiding you."

"Then why not swing by the restaurant a little later?" When Lexie hesitated, Doris made an intuitive leap. "Does this have something to do with Rachel, by any chance?"

When Lexie didn't answer, Doris sighed. "That's it, isn't it? I should have known. On Monday, she seemed to be avoiding me, too. Same thing today. What did she do now?"

Lexie was wondering how much to say when she heard Jeremy enter the kitchen behind her. Thinking he was coming in for a glass of water or a snack, she gave him a distracted smile before she noticed his expression.

"Rachel's here," Jeremy said. "She wants to talk to you."

Rachel flashed a nervous smile when Lexie entered the living room, then quickly looked away. Lexie stared at her without speaking. In the doorway, Jeremy shifted his weight from one foot to the other, then decided to slip out the back door so the two could be alone.

Lexie heard the back door close before she took a seat across from Rachel. Devoid of makeup, Rachel looked anxious and exhausted. In her hands, she twisted a tissue compulsively.

"I'm sorry," she said without preamble. "I never meant for any of this to happen, and I can only guess how angry you are. I just want you to know I didn't want to hurt you. I had no idea that Alvin had done what he did."

When Lexie didn't respond, Rachel brought her

hands to her head, massaging her temples. "He called me at home this past weekend and tried to explain, but I was just so horrified. If I'd known, if I'd even had an inkling of what he was doing, I would never have talked to him. But he fooled me . . ."

She trailed off, still unable to meet Lexie's eyes.

"You're not the only one. He fooled Jeremy, too," Lexie said.

"But it was still my fault."

"Yeah," Lexie agreed, "it was."

Lexie's comment seemed to stop Rachel's train of thought. In the silence that followed, Lexie watched her, trying to assess whether she was feeling contrite because of what she'd done or because she'd been caught. She was a friend, someone Lexie had trusted, but then again, Jeremy would have said the same thing about Alvin.

"Tell me how it happened," Lexie finally said.

Rachel sat up straighter; when she spoke, it sounded as if she'd been rehearsing her words for days.

"You know that Rodney and I have been having problems, right?"

Lexie nodded.

"That's where it started," Rachel said. "I know that you and Rodney always saw your relationship differently. To you, he was just a friend, but to Rodney . . . well, you were like some kind of fantasy, and even now, I'm not sure whether he's ever going to get over you. When he looks at me sometimes, it's like he really wants to be seeing you instead. I know that sounds crazy, but I felt it every time he showed

216

up at my door. It's like I was never quite good enough, no matter what I was wearing or what we planned to do. And then, one day when I was running something into Doris's office, I found Alvin's phone number, and . . . I don't know . . . I was feeling depressed and lonesome, and I just decided to give him a call. I didn't know what to expect—I really didn't expect anything—but we just got to talking, and I started telling him about the troubles that Rodney and I have been having in our relationship and how he can't seem to get over you. Well, Alvin got real quiet and then told me you were pregnant. The way he said it let me know that he wasn't sure Jeremy was the father. And that maybe Rodney was."

Lexie felt her stomach sink.

"I want you to know that I never thought it was Rodney's baby. Never, not once. I knew that you and Rodney had never slept together, and I said something to that effect. I didn't think twice about it. Honestly, once I hung up, I didn't even think we'd talk again, but then Alvin called me sometime later, and all I could think was that it was nice to hear from him. And after Rodney and I got into another fight, I just wanted a break from it all . . . so on a whim I decided to head to New York for a few days. I can't explain it other than to say I had to get out of town and it was a place I'd always wanted to go. So I called Alvin when I got there, and we ended up spending most of the night talking. I was upset and maybe I drank too much, but somehow you came up again and I let it slip that you'd been pregnant before and that it was even noted in Doris's journal."

When Lexie raised her eyebrows, Rachel hesitated before going on.

"Doris kept the journal in her office and I was looking through it when I saw your initials and Trevor's name in there. I know it wasn't any of my business and I know I shouldn't have said anything, but I was just talking. I didn't have any idea that he was sending Jeremy e-mails and trying to break you two up. I didn't find out about that until this past weekend, after Jeremy was already back here. Alvin called me in this panic on Saturday and blurted out everything, and I got this sick feeling. Not only because of what I'd helped to set in motion, but because he'd been using me all along." Her voice wavered as she stared at her shredded tissue. "I swear, I didn't mean to hurt you, Lex. I thought we were just talking."

Rachel's eyes filled with tears. "You have every right to be angry with me, and I wouldn't be surprised if you never wanted to see me again. If I were you I don't know that I would want to see me. It's taken me this long to even work up the courage to come here. I haven't been able to eat for the last couple of days. I know that probably doesn't matter, but I wanted you to know the truth. You've been like a sister to me over the years, and I'm closer to Doris than I am to my own mother . . . It breaks my heart to think that I hurt you or even to think that I might have played a part in what Alvin was doing. I am so sorry. You'll never know how sorry I am for what happened."

When she finished, silence settled between them. Rachel had spoken without pause, and the effort seemed to have drained her. The tissue was in tatters, small pieces raining onto the floor, and Rachel bent over to pick them up. As she did, Lexie tried to figure out whether Rachel's story diminished her responsibility, and how she wanted to respond. She was ambivalent. She felt justified in telling Rachel that she never wanted to see her again, but overpowering her anger was a growing sense of sympathy. She knew that Rachel was flighty and jealous, insecure and occasionally irresponsible, but she also knew that betrayal wasn't in her nature. Lexie sensed that she'd been telling the truth when she said she had no idea what Alvin had been up to.

"Hey," she said.

Rachel looked up.

"I'm still angry," Lexie said. "But I know you didn't mean it."

Rachel swallowed. "I'm so sorry," she repeated.

"I know you are."

Rachel nodded. "What will you tell Jeremy?"

"The truth. That you didn't know."

"And Doris?"

"That I'll have to think about. I haven't told Doris anything yet. To be honest, I don't know that I will, either."

Rachel exhaled, her relief evident.

"That goes for Rodney, too," Lexie added.

"What about us? Will we be able to stay friends?"

Lexie shrugged. "I suppose we have to, being that you're my maid of honor."

Rachel's eyes brimmed over. "Really?"

Lexie smiled. "Really."

Fourteen

···· ❖ ····

On their wedding day, the sun rose over a calm
Atlantic Ocean, casting prisms of light across the
water. A light mist lingered on the beach as Doris
and Lexie cooked breakfast for the guests at the
cottage. Doris met Jeremy's parents for the first
time and hit it off particularly well with Jeremy's
father; Jeremy's brothers and their wives were their
normal, boisterous selves and spent most of the
morning leaning over the railing of the porch, marveling at the brown pelicans that seemed to ride the
backs of porpoises just beyond the break line.

Because Lexie had been so insistent about limiting
the number of guests, his brothers' presence was a
surprise. When he saw them getting off the plane in
Norfolk the day before, he wondered whether they'd
been hastily invited in the last couple of days because
of the situation with Alvin. But he knew better when
his sisters-in-law rushed into his arms, chattering
about how Lexie had invited each of them personally and how much they were looking forward to
getting to know her.

In all, there were sixteen guests: Jeremy's family, along with Doris, Rachel, and Rodney; the final guest was a last-minute fill-in for Alvin. Hours later, as Jeremy was standing on the beach waiting for Lexie to appear, he felt Mayor Gherkin pat him on the back.

"I know I've told you before," Gherkin said, "but I am truly honored to have been chosen as your best man for this wondrous occasion."

Clad in blue polyester pants, a yellow shirt, and a plaid sport jacket, the mayor was a sight to behold, as always, and Jeremy knew that the ceremony wouldn't have been the same without him. Or Jed, for that matter.

Jed, it turned out, in addition to being the local taxidermist, was an ordained minister. His hair was combed, he was dressed in what was probably his best suit, and it was the first time he'd ever been close to Jeremy without wearing a scowl.

Just as Lexie had wanted, the ceremony was both extremely intimate and romantic. Jeremy's mother and father stood closest; his brothers and sisters-in-law formed a small semicircle around them. A local guitarist sat off to the side, playing quiet music, and a narrow path had been lined with seashells—something his brothers had done right after lunch. With the sun descending in the sky, the flames from a dozen tiki torches amplified the golden colors of the sky. Rachel was already tearing up, clutching the flowers in her hand as if she would never let them go.

Lexie was barefoot, as was Jeremy; on her head was a small crown of flowers. Doris beamed as she walked beside her; Lexie wouldn't consider letting anyone but Doris give her away. When Lexie finally came to a halt, Doris kissed her on the cheek and made her way to the front. From the corner of his eye, Jeremy saw his mother loop an arm through Doris's and pull her closer.

Lexie seemed almost to glide as she moved slowly toward him. In her hand was a bouquet of wildflowers. When she reached Jeremy, he could smell the slightest trace of perfume lingering in her hair.

They turned to face Jed as he opened the Bible and began to speak.

Jeremy was startled by the soft, melodic timbre of his voice, entranced as he listened to Jed welcome the guests and read a few passages from the Bible. Fixing them with a serious expression from beneath his heavy brow, he spoke of love and commitment, of patience and honesty, and of the importance of keeping God in their lives. He told them that life wouldn't always be easy, but that if they kept their faith in God and each other, they would always find a way to overcome anything. He spoke with surprising eloquence, and like a teacher who had long ago earned the respect of his students, he led them deftly through their vows.

Mayor Gherkin handed Jeremy the ring, and Lexie gave him one as well. As they slipped them on each other's fingers, Jeremy could feel his hands shaking. At that moment, Jed pronounced them man and wife. Jeremy kissed Lexie softly, taking her hand in his. In front of God and his family, he'd promised his love and devotion for all eternity, and he'd never believed it could feel so natural and right.

After the ceremony, the guests lingered on the beach. Doris had prepared a small buffet, and the food was spread out on a nearby picnic table. One by one, Jeremy's family congratulated them with hugs and kisses, as did Mayor Gherkin. Jed vanished after the ceremony before Jeremy could thank him but reappeared a few minutes later, carrying a plain cardboard box the size of a small refrigerator. In the interim, he'd changed back into his overalls and his hair had reverted to its wild state.

Lexie and Jeremy walked up to him just as he was placing his gift on the ground.

"What's this?" Lexie asked. "You weren't supposed to bring any gifts."

Jed said nothing. He just shrugged, somehow implying that he'd be hurt if she didn't accept. She leaned in and hugged him, then asked if she should open it. When Jed shrugged again, Lexie took that as a yes.

Inside was the stuffed boar Jeremy had seen him working on; in his signature style, he'd made the boar look as if it were about to maul anyone who got close.

"Thank you," Lexie said, her voice soft, and though Jeremy believed it was the first time it ever happened, he swore he saw Jed blush.

Later, after most of the food had been eaten and the event was winding down, Jeremy wandered away from the guests toward the water. Lexie joined him.

"You okay?"

Jeremy kissed her. "I'm fine. Wonderful, actually. But I'm thinking of going for a little walk."

"Alone?"

"I want to let this—all of it—sink in."

"Okay," Lexie said with a quick kiss. "But don't be long. We're going back to the cottage in a few minutes."

He waited until Lexie had gone off to talk to his parents, then turned and walked slowly through the sand, listening to the sound of the waves as they rolled onto shore. As he walked, he replayed the wedding in his mind: how Lexie had looked walking toward him; the quiet power of Jed's oratory; the dizzying sensation he'd experienced only hours before when pledging his eternal love. With every step, he was struck by a growing sense that anything was possible and that even the sky, with its exquisite colors, seemed to be flying a banner of celebration. When he reached the lengthening shadow of Cape Hatteras Lighthouse, he noticed a group of wild horses congregating on the grassy dune before him. While most of the mustangs were grazing, there was one that stared back at him. Jeremy moved forward, noting the sturdiness of the horse's muscled haunches and the soft, rhythmic flicking of his tail, believing for an instant that he would be able to get close enough to the horse to actually touch him. It was an absurd notion, one he would never test, but when he suddenly slowed to a stop, he found himself raising his hand in a gesture of friendship. The horse's ears rose in curiosity, as if trying to understand, then just as suddenly he bobbed his head up and down in a seemingly friendly gesture of his own. Jeremy watched in silence, marveling at the idea that they were somehow communicating. And when he turned around and saw Lexie and his mother entwined in a tender embrace, all he could think was that he was experiencing the most wonderful day of his life.

Fifteen

···· ❖ ····

The weeks that followed passed in a dreamlike state. An early summer heat wave blanketed Boone Creek, and the town settled into a slow, gentle rhythm. By mid-June, Lexie and Jeremy had also fallen into a comfortable routine, the traumas of the past weeks now behind them. Even the renovations seemed to be proceeding more smoothly, albeit slowly and expensively. The ease with which they'd adapted to their new life didn't particularly surprise them; what they hadn't expected were the many ways in which married life was so unlike being engaged.

After a brief honeymoon at the cottage, with lazy mornings spent lounging in bed and long afternoon walks along the sandy beach, they returned to Boone Creek, cleaned out Jeremy's cabin at Greenleaf, and moved into Lexie's bungalow. For the time being, Jeremy set up his office in the guest room, but instead of attempting to write, he spent most of his afternoons getting the house ready to show prospective buyers. He mowed and edged the yard, planted dianthus around the trees, trimmed the hedges, and painted the porch outside; inside, he also painted and moved a bit of the clutter into the storage shed behind Doris's. With only one or two people walking through the bungalow every couple of weeks and a sale necessary to help with the financing—and renovations—of the new house, both he and Lexie wanted the place looking its best. Other than that, life in Boone Creek went on as usual. Mayor Gherkin was fretting about the summer festival, Jed had gone back to his nonspeaking ways, and Rodney and Rachel were officially dating again and seemed much happier.

Still, there were some things that took getting used to. For example, now that theirs was a permanent arrangement, Jeremy wasn't sure how much cuddling he was expected to do. While Lexie seemed content to cuddle constantly, Jeremy could think of other more gratifying forms of intimacy. Still, he wanted to keep her happy. Which meant . . . what? How much was enough? Did they have to cuddle every night? How long? And in what position? Was he supposed to nuzzle, too? He was doing his best to figure out all the intricacies of Lexie's desires, but it was confusing.

Then there was the temperature of the room when they were sleeping. While he was happiest with the air conditioner blasting and the overhead fan whirring, Lexie was always cold. When it was ninety degrees and humid outside, with the outer walls and windows warm to the touch, Jeremy might set the thermostat to sixty-eight degrees, crawl into bed with a thin sheen of sweat on his brow, dressed only in underwear, and lie completely uncovered. A moment later, Lexie would exit the bathroom, turn the thermostat up to seventy-four degrees, crawl under the sheet and two blankets, pull them up to her ears, and shiver as if she had just crossed the arctic tundra.

"Why's it so cold?" she'd ask, getting comfortable.

"Because I'm sweating," he'd answer.

"How can you be sweating? It's freezing in here."

At least they were on the same page when it came to making love, he thought. In the weeks immediately following the ceremony, Lexie seemed to be endlessly in the mood, which—in Jeremy's opinion, anyway—gave definition to what a honeymoon was supposed to be. The word *no* wasn't in her vocabulary, and Jeremy chalked it up to the fact that her inhibitions were loosened not only because they were officially a couple, but because he was, in fact, irresistible to her. He could do no wrong, and he was so intoxicated by the feeling that he would daydream about her while working around the house. He would visualize the soft contours of her body or remember the sensation of her touch against his naked skin; he'd draw a deep breath remembering the sweetness of her breath or the luscious feel of her hair as his combed his fingers through it. By the time she'd return from work, it would be all he could do to offer a friendly kiss, and he'd spend the dinner hour staring at her lips as she ate, waiting for the opportunity to make his move. He was never turned down. He might be reeking and dirty from working in the yard, and still it seemed as if they couldn't get their clothes off fast enough when they entered the bedroom.

Then, out of the blue, things changed. It was as if the sun rose one morning and by the time it set, the Lexie he knew had been replaced by a non-responsive twin. He remembered it clearly, since it was the first time he'd been rejected: It was June 17, and he'd spent the rest of the morning alternately convincing himself it was no big deal and wondering whether he'd done something wrong. Later that night, it happened again, and for the next eight days, that was the story of their relationship. He'd make his move, she'd say that she was tired or simply not in the mood, and he'd lie beside her sulking, wondering how on earth he'd come to be viewed as simply a roommate who was still required to cuddle before falling asleep in a room that felt like a furnace.

"You woke up on the wrong side of the bed this morning," she remarked the morning after the first rejection.

"Didn't sleep well."

"Bad dreams?" she asked, sounding concerned.

Despite hair that was askew and long pajamas, she was strangely seductive, and he didn't know whether to be angry or ashamed of himself for thinking about sex every time he saw her. This, he knew, was the danger of habits; where the previous weeks had become a pattern he welcomed, she was obviously of a different opinion. But if there was one thing he'd learned from his first marriage, it was never to complain about the frequency of sex. In this, men and women were different. Women sometimes wanted; men always needed. Big difference, one that in the best of circumstances reached a sort of reasonable compromise that fully satisfied neither but was somehow acceptable to both. But he knew he'd sound as if he were whining if he complained that he wished the honeymoon had lasted just a bit longer. Say, for instance, for the next fifty years.

"I'm not sure," he finally responded.

His confusion during those next few weeks was underscored by the fact that during the day she seemed the same as always. They read their newspaper, shared the appropriate tidbits; she asked him to follow her to the bathroom while she got ready in the mornings, so they could continue their conversation.

He spent every day trying not to dwell on it.

But every night he would crawl into bed and steel himself for yet another round of rejection, doing his best to convince himself that he wouldn't let it bother him. Of course, not before making the passive-aggressive move of turning the thermostat back to sixty-eight degrees. As the weeks passed, Jeremy grew increasingly frustrated and confused. One night they watched a bit of television, eventually turned off the lights, and Jeremy spooned with Lexie for a while before moving to the other side of the bed to cool off. In time, he felt her reach for his hand.

"Good night," she said, her voice soft, her thumb moving slowly over his skin.

He didn't bother to respond, but when he woke the following morning, Lexie seemed perturbed as she headed to the bathroom. He followed her in, and they brushed their teeth and gargled with mouthwash before she finally glared at him.

"So, what happened with you last night?" she asked.

"What do you mean?"

"I was in the mood and you just went to sleep."

"How was I supposed to know that?"

"I reached for your hand, didn't I?"

Jeremy blinked. This was how she made a pass at him?

"I'm sorry," he said, "I didn't realize."

"It's okay," she said, shaking her head, sounding as if it weren't okay at all.

As she headed to the kitchen, he made a mental note about the hand-holding-in-bed thing.

Two evenings later, while lying in bed, she reached for his hand again, and Jeremy spun toward her so fast, the sheets got tangled as he tried to kiss her.

"What are you doing?" she said, pulling back.

"You're holding my hand," he said.

"So?"

"Well, the last time that happened, it meant you were in the mood."

"That time I was," she said, "but I was sort of stroking your palm with my thumb, remember? This time I wasn't."

Jeremy tried his best to absorb that. "So you're not in the mood?"

"I'm just not feeling up to it. You don't mind if I just sleep, do you?"

He tried his best to avoid a sigh. "No, that's okay."

"Can we cuddle first?"

He paused before answering. "Why not?"

It wasn't until the following morning that

everything finally became clear. He woke to find her sitting on the couch—or rather looking as if she were trying to lie down and sit at exactly the same time—with her pajama top pulled up to her breasts. The lampshade was angled, casting light on her belly.

"What are you doing?" he asked, stretching his hands over his head.

"C'mere, quick," she said. "Sit next to me."

Jeremy took his place beside her on the couch as she pointed to her stomach.

"Just watch," she said. "Sit real still so you can see it."

Jeremy did as he was told, and all of a sudden a small spot on her belly seemed to bulge involuntarily. It happened so quickly, however, he wasn't sure what it was.

"Did you see it?" she exclaimed.

"I think I saw something. What is it?"

"That's the baby. She's kicking. In the past few weeks, I thought I felt her moving a little, but this morning was the first time I knew for sure."

The spot bulged again.

"There! I saw it!" Jeremy exclaimed. "That's the baby?"

Lexie nodded, her expression rapt. "She's been active all morning, but I didn't want to wake you, so I snuck out here where I could see it better. Isn't it incredible?"

"Amazing," Jeremy said, continuing to watch for it.

"Give me your hand," she said.

When Jeremy reached out, she took it and placed

it on her belly. A few seconds later, he felt it bulge and he grinned.

"Does it hurt?"

"No," she said, "it's more like pressure or something. It's hard to describe, except that it's wonderful."

In the soft yellow glow of the lamp, Jeremy thought she was beautiful. When she looked up at him, her eyes were shining. "Doesn't this make it all worthwhile?"

"It's always been worthwhile."

She put her hand over his. "I'm sorry we haven't fooled around lately, but I've been feeling nauseous again the past couple of weeks. It kind of surprised me, since I didn't really get morning sickness. But my stomach's been so woozy, I was afraid I might throw up if we made love, but at least I know why now."

"That's okay," he said, "I hadn't really noticed."

"Yeah, sure. I can tell when you're sulking."

"You can?"

She nodded. "You toss and turn. And sometimes you sigh. It's pretty obvious. But I'm not feeling queasy now."

"You're not?"

"In fact, I'm kind of feeling like I did right after our marriage."

"You do?"

She nodded again, her expression seductive.

If there was one other downside to their first couple of months together, it related to work. Just as he'd done in May and June, in late July Jeremy sent another of his prewritten columns up to his editor in New York. It was the last one. From this point on, he knew, the clock would be ticking. He had four weeks to come up with something new.

Still, when he sat at the computer, there was nothing.

With August came a type of heat that Jeremy had heard about but had never before experienced in such an unrelenting fashion. Though New York was humid in the summer and had more than its share of miserable, sweat-inducing days, he realized that he'd dealt with them by staying indoors with the air conditioner blasting. Boone Creek, on the other hand, was an outdoor town, with a river and summer festival that lured people out of their homes.

As Gherkin had predicted, the festival drew thousands from all over the eastern part of the state. The streets, crammed with people, were lined on either side with dozens of kiosks that sold everything from barbecue sandwiches to shrimp on a stick. Near the water, the traveling carnival had set up rides, and kids waited in lines to ride the mini-roller coaster and a creaky Ferris wheel. The paper mill across the way had donated thousands of pieces of lumber— two-by-fours, squares, circles, triangles, blocks of various sizes—and kids spent hours constructing imaginary buildings.

The astronaut was a big hit with the crowds and ended up signing autographs for hours. Gherkin, meanwhile, had displayed an uncanny knack for playing up the theme of space. In addition to face painting—instead of animals, the offerings were of space shuttles, meteors, planets, and satellites—he'd somehow convinced the Lego Company to donate a thousand kits so kids could assemble their own space shuttles. This activity, spread out beneath a giant canopy, was a huge hit even among the parents, as it was in the only shady spot around.

Jeremy soaked through his shirt within minutes, but Lexie, now a little more than six months along, was even more miserable. Though she wasn't large yet, she was definitely showing, and more than one of the older women in town who hadn't known of her pregnancy until the festival didn't bother to hide their surprise. Still, the general reaction after the obligatory raising of eyebrows was one of excitement for them.

Lexie gamely pretended to be far less miserable at the festival than she actually was, offering to stay as long as Jeremy wanted. Observing her flushed cheeks, Jeremy shook his head and told her that he'd seen enough and suggested they spend the rest of the weekend away from the crowds. After packing an overnight bag, they went to the cottage in Buxton. While it wasn't noticeably cooler, the steady breeze off the ocean and the temperature of the water offered a refreshing break. By the time they returned to Boone Creek, they learned that Rodney and Rachel were engaged. Somehow they'd been able to work through their problems, and two days later, Rachel asked Lexie to be her matron of honor.

Even the house was coming along; the major renovations were completed, the kitchen and bathrooms were as good as new, and all that was still required were the finishing touches that would turn the place from a work in progress to a home. They were scheduled to move in at the end of the month. Perfect timing, as it turned out, since they had just received an offer on the bungalow from a nice retired couple from Virginia who wanted to take possession as soon as possible.

Aside from the continuing writer's block, life was good for Jeremy. Though he sometimes reflected on the trials he and Lexie had gone through before marriage, he knew they'd emerged from them stronger as a couple. When he looked at Lexie now, he knew he had never cared for anyone as deeply. What he didn't know, what he couldn't know, was that the hardest days were yet to come.

Sixteen

.... ❖ ....

"We still haven't decided on a name for the baby," Lexie said.

It was an early evening in the second week of August; Lexie and Jeremy were sitting on the porch of their new home. Though they hadn't moved in yet, the workers had left for the day, and they were watching the water. Without a breeze, the water was flat and still, so mirrorlike that the whitewashed cypress trees on the far bank looked as if they were growing in opposite directions.

"I've decided to leave that up to you," Jeremy said. He was fanning himself with a copy of *Sports Illustrated* that he'd intended to read before realizing it had a better purpose on a hot summer night.

"You can't just leave it up to me. It's our baby. I want to hear what you think."

"I've told you what I think," Jeremy said. "You just didn't like it."

"I am not going to name our daughter Misty."

"Misty Marsh? How can you not like that?"

He'd suggested the name the week before as a

joke. Lexie was so dismissive that he'd been pressing it ever since, if only to tease her.

"Well, I don't." Wearing shorts and a baggy T-shirt, she was flushed from the heat. Because her feet had begun to swell, Jeremy had dragged over an old bucket so she could prop them up.

"You don't think it has a nice ring to it?"

"No more than other plays on your last name. You might as well want to name her Smelly Marsh or Creepy Marsh."

"I was saving those for her brothers."

She laughed. "I'm sure they'd be forever grateful. But seriously, you don't have any ideas?"

"No. Like I told you, whatever you decide is fine."

"That's the problem. I haven't decided."

"You know what the problem is, right? You bought every baby name book out there. You gave yourself too many choices."

"I just want something that fits who she is."

"But that's the thing. No matter what we choose, it won't fit right away. No baby looks like Cindy or Jennifer; all babies look like Elmer Fudd."

"No, they don't. Babies are cute."

"But they look the same."

"No, they don't. And I'll warn you right up front that I'm going to be extremely disappointed in you if you can't pick our daughter out in the nursery."

"No reason to worry. They have name cards."

"Ha, ha," she said. "You're going to know what she looks like."

"Of course I will. She'll be the most beautiful baby in the history of North Carolina, with photographers from around the world snapping pictures and saying things like 'She's so lucky that she got her father's ears.' "

She laughed again. "And dimple."

"Right. Don't let me forget that."

She reached for his hand. "What about tomorrow? Are you excited?"

"I can't wait. I mean, the first sonogram was exciting, but this one . . . well, now we'll really get to see her."

"I'm glad you're going."

"Are you kidding? I wouldn't miss it. Sonograms are the best part about all this. I hope they print me a picture so I can show it off while bragging to my buddies."

"What buddies?"

"Didn't I tell you? Jed? Man, he just won't leave me alone, calling all the time, talking my ear off, going on and on."

"I think the heat's getting to you. Last I heard, Jed still hasn't said a word to you."

"Oh, that's right. But it doesn't matter. I still want a picture for me, so I can see how beautiful she is."

She raised an eyebrow. "So you're sure it's a girl now, too?"

"I think you've convinced me."

"What does that say about Doris?"

"It says that in a fifty-fifty proposition, she picked correctly. As would fifty percent of the population."

"Still a nonbeliever, huh?"

"I prefer the word *skeptic*."

"My dream man."

"That's right." Jeremy nodded. "Just keep telling yourself that, so I don't have to prove it."

Lexie shifted in the chair, suddenly uncomfortable. She winced before settling back into place. "What do you think about Rodney and Rachel getting married?"

"I'm in favor of marriage. I think it's a fine institution."

"You know what I mean. Do you think they're rushing into it?"

"Who are we to ask that question? I proposed after a few weeks; he's known her since he was a little kid. I'd say they should be asking that about us, not the other way around."

"I'm sure they still are, but that's not the point . . ."

"Wait," Jeremy said, "you think they're talking about us?"

"I'm sure they are. Lots of people talk about us."

"Really?"

"Duh," Lexie said, as if the answer were obvious. "It's a small town. That's what we do here. We sit around and talk about other people. We find out what's going on in their lives, share what we think, debate whether other folks are right or wrong, and solve their problems if we have to in the privacy of our own home. Of course, no one would ever admit to it, but we all do it. It's pretty much a way of life."

Jeremy considered what she was saying. "Do you think people are talking about us right now?"

"Absolutely." She shrugged. "Some are probably saying we got married because I was pregnant, others are saying you'll never last in this town, still others wonder how we could afford the house and surmise that we're probably in debt up to our eyeballs, unlike their frugal selves. Oh, they're talking all right and probably having a grand old time, too."

"This doesn't bother you?"

"Of course not," she said. "Why should I care? They wouldn't think of telling us they did, and they'll be nice as punch the next time we see them, so we'll never know. And besides, we're doing it, too. Which brings me back to Rodney and Rachel. Don't you think they're rushing it just a bit?"

In bed that night, Jeremy and Lexie were both reading. Jeremy had finally gotten to *Sports Illustrated* and was in the middle of a story on female volleyball players when Lexie set aside her book.

"Do you ever think about the future?" she asked.

"Sure," Jeremy answered, lowering the magazine. "Doesn't everyone?"

"What do you think it's going to be like?"

"For us? Or for the world?"

"I'm serious."

"So am I," Jeremy answered. "It's a different question entirely, one that opens up all sorts of different subjects. We could talk about global warming, or the lack thereof, in regard to the fate of mankind. Or whether or not God truly exists, and how people are judged when it comes to being admitted to heaven, which renders life on earth somewhat meaningless. You could be referring to the economy and how it will affect our own future, or even politics and how the next president might be the one who leads us to doom or prosperity. Or—"

She put her hand on his arm, cutting him off. "Are you always going to be like this?"

"Like what?"

"This. What you're doing. Being Mr. Precise. Or Mr. Literal. I wasn't asking so we could get into a deep philosophical discussion. I was just asking."

"I think we'll be happy," he ventured. "I couldn't imagine living the rest of my life without you."

She squeezed his arm, as if satisfied. "I think that, too," she said. "But sometimes . . ."

Jeremy looked at her. "What?"

"I just wonder how we're going to do as parents. I worry about that sometimes."

"We'll be great," he said. "You'll be great."

"You say that, but how do we know? What if she ends up being one of those angry teenagers who dresses in black and does drugs and sleeps around?"

"She won't."

"You can't say that."

"I can," Jeremy said. "She's going to be a wonderful girl. How can she not, with you as her mother?"

"You think it's simple, but it's not. Kids are people, too, and once they start getting older, they make their own decisions. There's only so much you can do."

"It all goes back to the upbringing . . ."

"Yes, but sometimes it doesn't matter what you do. We can put her in piano lessons and soccer, we can bring her to church every Sunday, we can send her to cotillion to learn her manners, and we can shower her with lots of love. But once she becomes a teenager . . . well, sometimes there's nothing you can do. With or without you, in the end, children grow up to become the people they were meant to be."

Jeremy thought about what she'd said, then pulled

her closer. "Are you really worried about this?"

"No. But I think about it. Don't you?"

"Actually, I don't. Kids are supposed to become who they were meant to be. All parents can do is to do their best to lead them in the right direction."

"But what if that isn't enough? Doesn't that worry you?"

"No," he said. "She's going to be fine."

"How can you be so sure?"

"Because she will," Jeremy said. "I know you and believe in you, and you're going to be a fantastic mother. And don't forget, I have written articles about the subject of nature and nurture. Both are important, but in the vast majority of cases, environment is a greater indicator of future behavior than anything genetic."

"But—"

"We'll do the best we can. And I'm sure she'll turn out okay."

Lexie thought about what he said. "You really wrote articles on the subject?"

"Not only that, I did in-depth research beforehand. I know what I'm talking about."

She smiled. "You're pretty smart," she said.

"Well . . ."

"Not about your conclusions, but what you just said. I don't care whether it's true or not, but it was exactly what I wanted to hear."

"That's the baby's heart, right there," the doctor said the next day, pointing at the fuzzy image on the computer monitor. "And those are the lungs and the spine."

Jeremy reached over and squeezed Lexie's hand on the examination table. They were at the OB-GYN's office in Washington, which Jeremy had to admit wasn't his favorite place. Granted, he was looking forward to seeing the baby again—the first grainy pictures from the sonogram were still hanging on the refrigerator—but the earlier sight of Lexie on the table with her legs in stirrups . . . well, it made him feel as if he were interrupting something better done in private.

Of course, Dr. Andrew Sommers—tall and trim, with wavy dark hair—did his best to make both Lexie and Jeremy feel as if he were doing nothing more extraordinary than taking her pulse, and Lexie seemed more than content to play along. While Dr. Sommers was checking and poking, they talked about the recent spate of hot weather, a story on the news concerning forest fires in Wyoming, and the fact that the doctor still wanted to drive out to Boone Creek to eat at Herbs, a place that more than one of his patients had raved about. Every now and then he would work more typical questions into the conversation, inquiring about her Braxton-Hicks contractions, for example, or whether she ever felt dizzy or light-headed. Lexie responded as easily as if they were discussing these issues over lunch.

To Jeremy, who was sitting near Lexie's head, the scene seemed surreal. Yes, the man was a doctor, and Jeremy had no doubt the doctor saw dozens of patients a day, but still, when the doctor tried to engage him in conversation, he did his best to meet the doctor's eyes as he answered, while ignoring what was being done to his wife. He supposed Lexie had grown used to all this, but it was the sort of thing that made him glad to be male.

After the doctor left, Jeremy and Lexie were left alone for a few minutes while they waited for the sonogram technician; when she entered, she asked Lexie to pull up her shirt. Gel was squirted on the expanding drum of her belly, drawing a quick gasp from Lexie.

"Sorry, I should have warned you it was cold. But let's see how your baby's doing, okay?"

The technician led Jeremy and Lexie through the sonogram, moving the hand piece, pressing harder and softer on her belly as she pointed out what she was seeing.

"And you're sure it's a girl?" Jeremy said. Though he'd been assured the last time he was here, he'd had trouble making sense of the image but had been too embarrassed to say anything.

"I'm sure," she said, moving the hand piece again. Pausing, she pointed at the screen. "Oh, here's a good shot . . . look for yourself."

Jeremy squinted. "I'm not sure what I'm seeing."

"This is the butt," she clarified, pointing to the screen, "and these are the legs here. Like she's sitting on the camera . . ."

"I don't see anything."

"Exactly," she said. "That's how we know it's a girl."

Lexie laughed, and Jeremy leaned toward her. "Say hello to Misty," he whispered.

"Hush! I'm trying to enjoy this," she said, squeezing his hand.

"Okay, let me get a few measurements here, to make sure the baby's developing on schedule, okay?"

The technician moved the hand piece again, hit one button and then another. Jeremy remembered her doing the same thing the last time they were here. "She's right on schedule," the technician added. "It says here she's due October 19."

"So she's growing okay?" he asked.

"Seems to be," said the technician. She moved the hand piece again to measure the heart and femur, then suddenly froze. Instead of pushing the button, she moved the hand piece away from the leg, zeroing in on what seemed to be a white line stretching toward the baby, something that looked almost like static or a flaw in the screen. She frowned slightly as she zeroed in on it. All at once, she began moving the hand piece more quickly, pausing frequently to examine the new image. She seemed to be checking the baby from every angle.

"What are you doing?" Jeremy asked.

The technician seemed lost in concentration. "Just checking something," she murmured. She continued trying to zero in on the image before shaking her head. She raced through the rest of the measurements, then went back to what she'd been doing before. Images of the baby from every angle appeared and disappeared. Again, the technician zeroed in on the wavy line.

"Is everything okay?" Jeremy pressed.

Her eyes were still focused on the screen as she drew a long breath. Her voice was surprisingly steady.

"I see something that the doctor might want to have a look at."

"What does that mean?"

"Let me get the doctor," she said, rising. "He'll probably be able to tell you more than I can. Stay where you are and I'll be right back."

Perhaps it was the measured sound of her words that made the blood drain from Lexie's face. Jeremy suddenly felt her squeeze his hand again, this time hard. A series of dizzying images flashed through his mind, for he knew exactly what the technician had meant. She'd seen something unusual, something different . . . something *bad*. And in that instant, time stopped as his mind raced through possibilities. The room seemed to close in as he tried to make sense of the fuzzy line he'd seen.

"What's going on?" Lexie whispered. "What happened?"

"I don't know," Jeremy said.

"Is something wrong with the baby?"

"She didn't say that," Jeremy said as much to steady himself as her. He swallowed through the sudden dryness in his throat. "I'm sure it's nothing."

Lexie seemed on the verge of tears. "Then why's she getting the doctor?"

"She probably has to if she sees something."

"What did she see?" she asked, almost pleading.

"I didn't see anything."

He thought about it again. "I don't know."

"Then what is it?"

Not knowing what else to do or even what to say, he scooted his chair closer. "I'm not sure. But the baby's heartbeat was fine, and she's growing. She would have said something earlier if something was wrong with the baby."

"Did you see her face? She seemed . . . scared."

This time, Jeremy couldn't respond. Instead, he stared at the far wall. Despite the fact that he and Lexie were together, Jeremy suddenly felt very much alone.

A moment later, the physician and the technician entered the room, forced smiles on their faces. The technician took her seat as the doctor stood behind her. Neither Jeremy nor Lexie could think of anything to say. In the silence, Jeremy could hear his own breathing.

"Let's take a look," Dr. Sommers said.

The technician added a bit more gel; when she placed the hand piece on Lexie's stomach, the baby came into view once more. When the technician pointed to the screen, however, it wasn't toward the baby.

"Can you see it?" she said.

The doctor leaned forward; so did Jeremy. Again, he saw the wavy white line. This time, he noticed that it seemed to be coming from the walls encircling the baby in the surrounding dark space.

"Right there."

The doctor nodded. "Has it attached?"

The technician moved the hand piece, and various images of the baby came into view. She shook her head as she spoke. "When I was looking earlier, I didn't see that it had attached anywhere. I think I checked everywhere."

"Let's make sure," the doctor said. "Let me take over for a minute." The technician rose, and the doctor took her place.

The doctor was silent as he moved the hand piece

again; he seemed less adept at the machine, and the images appeared more slowly. Like the technician, he leaned toward the screen. For a long time, no one said anything.

"What is it?" Lexie's voice trembled. "What are you looking for?"

The doctor glanced at the technician, who quietly left the room. When they were alone, the doctor brought the white line into view. "Do you see this?" he asked. "This is what is known as an amniotic band," he said. "What I've been doing is checking to see if it's attached to the baby anywhere. If it does attach, it's usually on the extremities, like the arms and legs. So far, though, it seems that it hasn't attached, and that's good."

"Why? I don't understand," Jeremy said. "What do you mean by band? What can it do?"

The doctor exhaled slowly. "Okay, this band is made up of the same fibrous material as the amnion—the sack that holds the baby. See it here?" He ran his finger in a roughly circular manner over the sack, then to the band. "As you can see, one end of the band is attached here to the sack, the other end is floating free. This free-floating end can attach to the fetus. If that happens, the baby will be born with amniotic band syndrome, or ABS."

When the doctor spoke again, his tone was deliberately neutral. "I'll be perfectly frank: If that happens, it greatly increases the odds of congenital abnormalities. I know how hard this is to hear, but that's why we really took our time examining the images. We wanted to be sure that the band hasn't attached."

Jeremy could barely breathe. From the corner of his eye, Jeremy saw Lexie bite her lip.

"Will it attach?" Jeremy asked.

"There's no way to know. Right now, the other end of the band is floating in the amniotic fluid. The fetus is still small right now. As it grows, the likelihood of attachment increases, but true amniotic band syndrome is rare."

"What kinds of abnormalities?" Lexie whispered.

It wasn't a question the doctor wanted to answer, and it showed. "Again, it depends on where it attaches, but if it's true ABS, it could be serious."

"How serious?" Jeremy said.

He sighed. "If it attaches to the extremities, the baby could be born without a limb, or with a clubfoot, or with syndactyly, which is webbing between the fingers. If it attaches elsewhere, it could even be worse."

As the doctor answered, Jeremy found himself growing dizzy. "What do we do?" he forced out. "Is Lexie going to be okay?"

"Lexie will be fine," he said. "ABS doesn't affect the mother in any way. And as for what to do, there's really nothing we can do except wait. There's no reason for bed rest or anything like that. I will recommend that we get a level two ultrasound, which will create a clearer image, but again, all we'll be looking for is to see whether the band has attached to the fetus. And again, I don't think it has. After that, we'll do serial ultrasounds—probably one every two or three weeks, but that's all we can do for now."

"How did it happen?"

"It wasn't anything you did or didn't do. And keep in mind that so far it doesn't look like it's attached. I know I've said that before, but that's important to understand. So far, there's nothing wrong with your baby at all. Her growth is fine, her heartbeat is strong, and her brain is developing normally. So far, so good."

In the silence, Jeremy could hear the steady, mechanical hum of the ultrasound machine.

"You said it could get even worse if it attaches elsewhere," he said.

The doctor shifted in his seat. "Yes," he admitted. "It's unlikely that it will, though."

"How much worse?"

Dr. Sommers slid his file off to the side, as if deciding how much to say. "If it attaches to the cord," he said at last, "you could lose the baby."

Seventeen

.... ❖ ....

They could lose the baby.

As soon as the doctor left, Lexie broke down, and it was all Jeremy could do to keep his own tears in check. He was drained and speaking on autopilot, reminding her again and again that so far the baby was fine and she would probably stay that way. Instead of calming her, his words seemed to make her feel worse. Her shoulders heaved and her hands trembled as he held her; by the time she finally pulled back, Jeremy's shirt was soaked with her tears.

She said nothing as she dressed; instead, the only sound in the room was the raspy intake of her breath, as if she were trying not to cry. The room felt unbearably close, as if all the oxygen were being sucked away; Jeremy was unsteady on his feet. When he saw Lexie buttoning her blouse over the rounded bulge of her belly, he had to lock his knees to keep from falling over.

The fear was suffocating and overwhelming; the sterility of the room struck him as surreal. This couldn't be happening. None of it made sense. The earlier ultrasounds had picked up nothing. Lexie hadn't had so much as a cup of coffee since she'd found out she was pregnant. She was healthy and strong, she got enough sleep. But something was wrong. As he stared, he could imagine the band floating in the amniotic fluid like the tentacles of a poisonous jellyfish. Waiting, drifting, ready to attack.

He wanted Lexie to lie down, to cease all movement, so the tentacle wouldn't find its way to the baby. At the same time, he wanted her to walk around, to keep doing what she had been doing, since the tentacle was still floating free. He wanted to know what to do to increase the chances that their baby would be okay. The air in the room was almost gone now, and his mind was going white with fear.

Their baby might die. Their little girl might die. Their little girl, the only one they might ever have.

He wanted to leave this place and never come back; he wanted to stay here and talk to the doctor again to make sure he understood everything that was happening. He wanted to tell his mother, his brothers, his father, so he could cry on their shoulders; he wanted to say nothing, to carry the burden with stoicism. He wanted his baby to be okay. He repeated the words over and over in his mind, as if willing her to stay away from the tentacle. When Lexie reached for her purse, he caught sight of her red-rimmed eyes and the image almost broke his heart. None of this was supposed to have happened. It was supposed to be a good day, a happy day.

But the joyous anticipation was gone now, and tomorrow would be worse. The baby would be bigger, and the tentacle would get closer. And every passing day would increase the danger.

In the hallway, the technician immersed herself in paperwork as they passed on their way to the doctor's private office. As they sat across the desk from the doctor, he showed them the printouts from the sonogram. He walked them through the same descriptions, told them the same things about the amniotic band. He liked to go over things a second time, he said. Most people didn't really hear him the first time around because of the shock. He emphasized again that the baby was doing well and that he didn't think the band had attached. This, he said again, was good news. But all Jeremy could think about was the tentacle floating inside his wife, drifting, moving close to the baby, and then veering away. Danger and safety, playing a deadly game of tag. The baby growing, getting larger, crowding the sack. Could the band float freely then?

"I know how hard this is to hear," the doctor said again.

No, Jeremy thought, he didn't. It wasn't his baby, his little girl. His little girl in pigtails and kneeling by a soccer ball was smiling in a picture frame atop the doctor's desk. His daughter was fine. No, he didn't know. He couldn't know.

Outside the office, Lexie broke down again and he held her tightly. They said almost nothing to each other on the ride home, and later Jeremy barely remembered the drive. At home, he went straight to the Internet and searched for information on amniotic band syndrome. He saw pictures of webbed fingers, stunted limbs, missing feet. He was prepared for those; he wasn't prepared for the facial deformities, abnormalities that made the baby look barely human. He read about spinal and intestinal deformities in those instances where the tentacle attached to the body. He closed the screen, went to the bathroom, and ran cold water over his face. He decided to say nothing to Lexie about what he'd seen.

Lexie had called Doris the moment they got home, and the two of them were now sitting in the living room. Lexie had cried when Doris came to the door, and she cried again later as she sat on the couch. Doris began crying as well, even as she assured Lexie that she was sure the baby would be okay, that there was a reason the Lord had blessed them, that Lexie should continue to have faith. Lexie asked Doris not to tell anyone, and she promised not to. Nor did Jeremy tell his family. He knew how his mother would react, how she would sound on the phone, the regular calls that would follow. But even if his mother believed she'd be supporting Jeremy, to him it would feel the other way around. He couldn't handle that, couldn't imagine having to support someone else right now, even his mother. Especially his mother. It was hard enough to support Lexie and keep his own emotions in check. But he had to be strong, for both of them.

Later that night, as he lay in bed with Lexie beside him, he tried to think of anything but the tentacle that was waiting to ensnare the baby.

*　　　*　　　*

Three days later, they went in for the level II ultrasound at East Carolina University Medical Center, in Greenville. There was no excitement when they checked in or filled out the forms; in the waiting room, Lexie moved her purse from the end table to her lap and back again. She walked toward the magazine rack and picked one out but didn't open it once she returned to her seat. She tucked a strand of hair behind her ear and glanced around the waiting room. She tucked another strand behind her other ear and looked at the clock.

In the preceding days, Jeremy had learned everything he could about amniotic band syndrome, hoping that by understanding it, he would no longer fear it. But the more he learned, the more anxious he felt. At night he tossed and turned, sick not only at the thought that the baby was in danger, but at the knowledge that more than likely this would be the only pregnancy Lexie would ever experience. This pregnancy wasn't supposed to have happened, and sometimes, in his blackest moods, he found himself wondering whether it was the universe's way of paying him back for breaking the rules in the first place. He wasn't meant to have a child. He'd never been meant to have a child.

He said nothing about any of this to Lexie. Nor did he tell her the complete truth about ABS.

"What did you find out on the computer?" she'd asked the night before.

"Not much more than the doctor told us," Jeremy said.

She nodded. Unlike him, she was under no illusion that knowledge would lessen her fears.

"Every time I move, I wonder if I'm doing something I shouldn't."

"I'm not sure that's how it works," he said.

She nodded again. "I'm scared," she whispered.

Jeremy slipped his arm around her. "I am, too."

They were led into the room, and Lexie pulled up her shirt when the technician entered. Though the technician smiled, she could sense the tension in the room and went straight to work.

The baby appeared on the screen, and the image was much clearer. They could see the baby's features: her nose and chin, her eyelids and fingers. When Jeremy peeked at Lexie, she squeezed his hand with painful intensity.

The amniotic band, the tentacle, hadn't attached yet. There were ten weeks to go.

"I hate waiting like this," Lexie said. "Waiting and hoping and not knowing what's going to happen."

She said exactly what Jeremy was thinking, the words he refused to utter in her presence. A week had gone by since they had received the news, and although they were surviving, that's all it seemed they could do. Survive and hope and wait. Another ultrasound was scheduled in less than two weeks.

"It's going to be okay," Jeremy said. "Just because the band is there doesn't mean it's going to attach."

"Why me, though? Why us?"

"I don't know. But it's going to work out. Everything's going to be fine."

"How do you know that? You can't know that. You can't promise me that."

No, I can't, Jeremy thought. "You're doing everything right," he said instead. "You're healthy and you eat right and you take care of yourself. I just tell myself that as long as you keep doing those things, the baby will be fine."

"It's just not fair," she cried. "I mean, I know it's petty, but when I read the papers, I always come across stories about girls who have babies when they didn't even know they were pregnant. Or have perfectly healthy babies and abandon them. Or smoke and drink and everything turns out okay. It's not fair. And now I can't even enjoy the rest of the pregnancy. It's like I wake up every day and even if I'm not thinking about it specifically, I walk around with this sense of anxiety, and then *boom!* It hits me all at once and I remember and I find myself thinking that something inside me might kill the baby. Me! I'm doing this. My body is doing this, and no matter how hard I want to stop it, I can't and there's nothing I can do."

"It's not your fault," Jeremy said.

"Then whose is it? The baby's?" she snapped. "What did I do wrong?"

It was the first time Jeremy realized that Lexie wasn't simply frightened, but felt guilty as well. The realization made him ache.

"You didn't do anything wrong."

"But this thing inside me—"

"Hasn't done anything yet," he said gently. "And part of the reason, I'm sure, is that you've been doing everything right. The baby is fine. That's all we know for sure right now. The baby's doing great."

Lexie whispered so softly that Jeremy barely heard her. "Do you think she'll be okay?"

"I know she'll be okay."

Again, he was lying, but he couldn't tell her the truth. Sometimes, he knew, lying was the right thing to do.

Jeremy had little experience with death. But death had been Lexie's companion throughout her life. Not only had she lost her parents, but she'd also lost her grandfather a few years back. While Jeremy claimed to empathize, he knew he was incapable of fully understanding how hard it must have been for her. He hadn't known her then and had no idea how she'd reacted, but he had no doubt how she would react if their baby died.

What if they went through the next ultrasound and all was well? It wouldn't matter, he thought, for the amniotic band could still ensnare the umbilical cord. What if that happened when she went into labor? What if they were a few minutes too late? Yes, the baby would be lost, and that would be heartbreaking. But how would Lexie be? Would she blame herself? Would she blame him, since the odds of another pregnancy were basically nil? How would she feel when she walked by the baby's room in the new house? Would she keep the baby furniture or sell it? Would they adopt?

He didn't know, couldn't begin to fathom the answers.

What made him hurt, however, was something else.

Amniotic band syndrome was rarely fatal. But abnormalities and deformities were the rule, not the exception. It was the unspoken topic between Lexie and himself, something that neither wanted to discuss. When they talked about their worries for the baby, it was always couched in terms of possible death instead of the more realistic scenario. That their baby would look different; that their baby would have serious abnormalities; that their baby would face countless surgeries; that their baby might suffer.

He hated himself for thinking that it would matter, because when it came right down to it, he knew he would love the baby no matter what. He didn't care about missing limbs or webbing between her fingers; he would raise her and care for her as well as any father could. Still, when he thought about the baby, he couldn't deny that he envisioned her in almost clichéd snapshots: wearing an Easter dress while surrounded by tulips, or splashing through the sprinklers, or sitting in the high chair, smiling broadly through the chocolate cake smeared on her face. He never imagined her with deformities; he never saw her with a cleft palate or missing a nose, or with an ear the size of a penny. In his mind's eye, she was always perfect and bright eyed. And Lexie, he knew, imagined her exactly the same way.

He knew that everyone had his or her burdens, that no one's life was perfect. But some burdens were worse than others, and despite the terrible way it made him feel about himself, he wondered whether death would be easier than their daughter living with a severe abnormality—not a missing limb, but something far worse—one that would make her suffer for the rest of her life, no matter how long that might be. He couldn't imagine having a child for whom pain and suffering were as constant as breathing or the beating of her heart. But what if that was his child's destiny? It was too terrible to contemplate, and he tried to force the thought from his mind.

Still, the question haunted him.

Time moved slowly the following week. Lexie went off to work, but Jeremy didn't even attempt to write. He couldn't find the energy to concentrate, so instead he spent much of the time at the house. They were in the final stages of the renovations now, and Jeremy took it upon himself to begin cleaning. He washed the windows inside and out, he vacuumed the corners of the stairs, he scraped paint splatters from the counters in the kitchen. It was tedious, mind-numbing work, but it served to clear his mind, to keep his fears at bay. The painters were finishing up the rooms downstairs, and the wallpaper for the baby's room was already hung. Lexie had picked out most of the major pieces of furniture for the room, and when they arrived, Jeremy spent two afternoons putting everything together and finishing the room. After Lexie got off work, he brought her to the house. At the top of the stairs, he asked her to close her eyes and he led her to the doorway.

"Okay," he said, "you can open your eyes now."

For an instant, there were no worries about the future, no fears for their daughter. Instead, it was the Lexie of old, the Lexie who looked forward to motherhood, who smiled easily and found everything

261

about the experience memorable.

"You did this?" she asked, her voice soft.

"Most of it. I had to have the painters help me with the blinds and the curtains, but I did the rest."

"It's beautiful," she murmured, moving inside.

On the carpet was a throw rug decorated with ducks; in the corner, the crib—with a soft cotton sheet on the mattress and colorful bumpers already attached—sat beneath the mobile they'd purchased a lifetime ago. The curtains matched the rug and the small towels atop the chest of drawers. The changing table was fully stocked with diapers, ointments, and wipes. A small musical merry-go-round, playing quietly, sparkled in the soft yellow light from a decorative lamp.

"I figured that since we'll be moving soon, I should go ahead and get this room out of the way."

Lexie moved to the bureau and picked up a small porcelain duck. "Did you pick this?"

"It matched the rug and the curtains. If you don't like it—"

"No, I do. It's just that I'm surprised."

"Why?"

"When we went shopping, you didn't seem that into it."

"I guess I'm finally getting used to the idea. And besides, I couldn't let you have all the fun. Do you think she'll like it?"

She moved to the window, running her finger over the curtain. "She's going to love it. I love it."

"I'm glad."

Lexie let the curtain drop and moved to the crib.

She smiled when she saw the small stuffed animals, but all at once it faded. She crossed her arms, and Jeremy knew that the worries had returned.

"We should be able to move in this weekend," he said, wishing he knew what else to say. "In fact, the painters said we can begin moving our things in anytime. We might have to keep some furniture in the bedrooms while they finish painting the living room for a while, but the other rooms are ready. I was thinking about setting up my office next, then maybe the master bedroom. But either way, since you're working, I'll take care of it."

"Yeah," she said, nodding. "Okay."

Jeremy put his hands in his pockets. "I've been thinking about the baby's name," he said. "And don't worry, it's not Misty."

She glanced over at him, one eyebrow raised.

"I don't know why it didn't come to me earlier."

"What is it?"

He hesitated, remembering how it would look on a page in Doris's journal, remembering how it looked when he saw it on the headstone adjacent to Lexie's father's. He took a deep breath, strangely nervous.

"Claire," he said.

He couldn't read Lexie's expression, and for an instant he wondered whether he'd made a mistake. But when she started toward him, she had the trace of a smile on her lips. Up close, she put her arms around him and then leaned her head against his chest. Jeremy wrapped her in his arms, and they stood in the nursery together, still afraid but no longer alone.

"My mother," she whispered.

"Yes," he said. "I can't imagine our daughter with any other name."

That night, Jeremy found himself praying for the first time in years.

Though he'd been raised Catholic and had continued to attend both Christmas and Easter Mass with his family, he seldom felt any connection with either the service or his faith. It wasn't that he doubted God's existence; despite the skepticism upon which he'd based his career, he felt that belief in God was not only natural, but rational. How else could there be such order in the universe? How else could life have evolved the way it did? Years ago, he'd written a column expressing his doubts that life existed elsewhere in the universe, using mathematics to bolster his point, making the case that despite the millions of galaxies and trillions of stars, the odds of *any* advanced life in the universe were almost nonexistent.

It had been among his most popular columns, one that elicited a great deal of mail. While most people wrote that they agreed with his belief that God created the universe, there were those who differed and offered the big bang theory as an alternative. In a follow-up column, Jeremy wrote about the big bang in layman's terms, essentially laying out the point that, according to the theory, it meant that all matter in the universe had at one point been compressed into a dense sphere no larger than a tennis ball. It then exploded, creating the universe as we know it. He concluded the column with the question "On the surface, which seems more believable? The belief in God or the belief that at one point, all the matter in the entire universe—every atom and molecule— was condensed into a tiny ball?"

Still, the belief in God was essentially a question of faith. Even for those, like Jeremy, who believed in the big bang theory, it said nothing about the creation of the sphere in the first place. Atheists would say the sphere was always there, those with faith might say that God created it, and there was no way ever to prove which group was right. That's why, Jeremy figured, it was called faith.

Still, he wasn't ready to accept that God played an active role in human events. Despite his Catholic upbringing, he didn't believe in miracles, and he'd exposed more than one faith healer as a fraud. He didn't believe in a God who sifted through prayers, answering some and ignoring others, no matter how unworthy or worthy a person might be. Instead, he preferred to believe in a God who bestowed all people with gifts and abilities and placed them in an imperfect world; only then was faith tested, only then could faith be earned.

His beliefs didn't fit in with the beliefs of organized religion; when he went to Mass, he knew he did so for his mother's benefit. His mother sometimes sensed this about him and suggested that he pray; more often than not, he said he would give it a try, but he never did. Until now.

That night, after decorating the baby's room, Jeremy found himself on his knees, begging God to help keep his baby safe, to bless them with a healthy child. With his hands clenched together, he prayed in silence, promising to be the best father he could be. He promised to start attending Mass again, promised to make prayer a part of his daily life, promised to read the Bible from cover to cover. He asked for a sign to let him know his prayer had been heard, that his prayer would be answered. But there was nothing.

"Sometimes I don't know what I'm supposed to say or do," Jeremy admitted.

Doris was sitting across the table at Herbs the following day; because he hadn't told his family, she was the one person he could confide in.

"I know she needs me to be strong, and I'm trying. I try to be optimistic, I tell her that everything's going to turn out okay, and I do my best not to make her any more nervous than she already is. But . . ."

When he trailed off, Doris finished for him. "But it's hard, because you're just as frightened as she is."

"Yeah," he said. "I'm sorry. I didn't mean to drag you into this."

"I'm already in this," she said. "And all I can say is that I know it's tough, but you're doing the right thing. Right now, she needs your support. That's one of the reasons she married you. She knew you'd be there for her, and when we talk, she says that you've been a big help."

Beyond the windows, Jeremy saw people eating on the porch, having ordinary conversations, as if they hadn't a care in the world. But nothing was ordinary about his life anymore.

"I can't stop thinking about it. We have another ultrasound tomorrow, and I dread it. I just keep imagining that we'll see that the band has attached. It's like I can see the expression on the technician's face and I notice how quiet she gets, and I just know she's going to tell us that we should talk to the doctor again. It makes me sick to my stomach to even think about. I know Lexie's feeling the same way. She's been real quiet the last couple of days. It's like the closer the ultrasound gets, the more we worry."

"That's normal," Doris said.

"I've been praying about it," he admitted.

Doris sighed and looked up to the ceiling, then back to Jeremy again. "Me too."

The next day, his prayer was answered. The baby was growing, the heartbeat was strong and regular, and the band still hadn't attached. It was good news, the doctor announced, and while both Lexie and Jeremy felt a surge of relief, the worries returned again by the time they reached the car, when they realized they would have to be back in two more weeks. And there were still eight weeks to go.

They moved into the house a couple of days later: Mayor Gherkin, Jed, Rodney, and Jeremy helped load the furniture into the truck, while Rachel and Doris handled the boxes and Lexie directed them. Because the bungalow was small, the new house felt empty, even after the furniture had been put in place.

Lexie gave them the tour: Mayor Gherkin immediately suggested that the house be added to the Historic Homes Tour, while Jed repositioned the stuffed boar near the window of the living room, giving it prominent display.

As Jeremy watched Lexie and Rachel move into the kitchen, he noticed Rodney lagging behind. Rodney glanced at Jeremy.

"I wanted to apologize," he said.

"For what?"

"You know." He shuffled his feet. "But I also wanted to thank you for keeping Rachel in the wedding. I've wanted to tell you that for a while. It meant a lot to her."

"It meant a lot to Lexie that she was there, too."

Rodney flashed a quick grin, then grew serious again. "You've got a nice place here. I never imagined it could look like this. You two did a fine job."

"It was all Lexie's doing. I can't take any credit for it."

"Sure you can. And this place suits you. It'll be great for your family."

Jeremy swallowed. "I hope so."

"Congratulations on the baby. I hear it's a girl. Rachel's already picked out a bunch of outfits for her. Don't tell Lexie, but I think she's going to throw her a surprise baby shower."

"I'm sure she'd enjoy that. Oh, and congratulations on your engagement. Rachel's a prize."

Rodney glanced toward the kitchen as Rachel vanished from sight. "We're both pretty lucky, aren't we?"

Jeremy couldn't answer, for once at a loss for words.

*　　*　　*

Jeremy finally made the call to his editor, a call he'd been dreading and putting off for weeks. He told him that he wouldn't be submitting a column this month, the first he'd ever missed. While his editor was surprised and disappointed, Jeremy informed him of the complications with Lexie's pregnancy. His editor's tone softened immediately; he asked if Lexie was in danger or whether she was bedridden. Instead of answering directly, Jeremy said that he'd rather not go into details, and by the pause on the other end, he knew his editor was imagining the worst.

"No problem," he said. "We'll just recycle one of your old columns, something you did years ago. Odds are people either won't remember it or never saw it in the first place. Do you want to pick something out, or would you rather I do it?"

When Jeremy hesitated, his editor answered his own question. "No problem," he said, "I'll handle it. You take care of your wife. That's the most important thing right now."

"Thanks," Jeremy said. Despite his occasional battles with his editor, the man did indeed have a heart. "I appreciate it."

"Is there anything else I can do?"

"No. I just wanted to let you know."

He could hear a squeak and knew his editor was leaning back in his chair. "Let me know if you can't make the next one, either. If you can't, we'll just run another old one, okay?"

"I'll let you know," Jeremy said, "but I'm hoping that I'll have something for you before long."

"Keep your spirits up. It's tough, but I'm sure everything will turn out okay."

269

"Thanks," Jeremy said.

"Oh, and by the way, I can't wait to see what you've been working on. Whenever you're ready. No rush."

"What are you talking about?"

"Your next story. I haven't heard from you, so I figure you've got something big in the works. You always go into hiding when you're working on a doozy of a story. I know you've got other things on your mind, but I just wanted you to know that a lot of people were impressed with what you did with Clausen, and we'd like to have the chance to publish your next big article here rather than in the newspapers or somewhere else. I've been meaning to talk to you about it, and to reassure you that we'll be competitive when it comes to your fee. It might do the magazine some good, too. Who knows, we might even be open to making a big deal about it on the cover. I'm sorry for bringing this up now—there's no pressure. Just whenever you're ready."

Jeremy glanced at his computer, then sighed. "I'll keep that in mind."

Though he hadn't technically lied to his editor, he'd omitted the truth, and after hanging up the phone, he felt guilty. He hadn't realized that when he'd called him, Jeremy had subconsciously expected to be told to pack it in, that they'd find someone else to do his column or just cancel it outright. He'd been prepared for that; what he hadn't been prepared for was how understanding he'd been. Which made his guilt even more acute.

Part of him wanted to call the guy back and tell him everything, but common sense prevailed. His editor had been understanding, well, because he had to be. What else could he have said: *Oh, sorry to hear about your wife and baby, but you've got to understand, a deadline's a deadline, and you'll be canned if I don't have something in my hands in the next five minutes*? No, he wouldn't have said that—couldn't have said that—especially considering what he'd said afterward: that the magazine wanted a chance to publish his next big article. The one he'd supposedly been working on.

He didn't want to think about it. He couldn't think about it; the fact that he couldn't even write a column was bad enough. But he'd accomplished what he'd needed to do. He'd bought himself four weeks, maybe eight. If he didn't come up with something by then, he'd tell his editor the truth. He'd have to. He couldn't be a writer if he couldn't write, and there'd be no use pretending anymore.

But what was he going to do then? How would he pay the bills? How would he support his family?

He didn't know. Nor did he want to think about it. Right now, he had enough on his mind with Lexie and Claire. In the grand scheme of things, those were far more important than worries about his career, and Jeremy knew he would have put his concerns about them first even if he had been writing. But the simple fact was that right now he had no choice.

Eighteen

····❖····

How could he describe the next six weeks? How would he remember them when reflecting back on his past? Would he remember spending his weekends with Lexie as they browsed garage sales and antique shops, finding just the right pieces to finish decorating their house? That Lexie turned out not only to have exquisite taste, but an ability to see how everything would fit into their decorating scheme? That her instincts as a bargain shopper enabled them to spend far less than he'd imagined they would? That by the end even Jed's gift looked as if it belonged in the house?

Or would he remember finally making the call to his parents about the pregnancy—a call in which he ended up crying uncontrollably, as if he'd bottled up his fears for far too long and only now had a chance to let his emotions flow freely, without worrying Lexie?

Or perhaps he would remember the endless nights he'd spent at the computer, trying and failing to write, alternately despairing and angry, as he felt the clock ticking toward the end of his career.

No, he thought, in the end he would remember it as a period of anxious transition—one divided into two-week increments between ultrasounds.

Though their fears remained the same, the initial shock had begun to wear off, and their worries no longer dominated their thoughts day and night. It was as if some survival mechanism kicked in to counter the unsustainable weight and turmoil of their emotions. It was a gradual, almost imperceptible process, and it wasn't until several days after the last ultrasound had passed that he realized he'd spent most of an afternoon without his worries paralyzing him. The same gradual change had come over Lexie as well. During that six-week period, they had more than one romantic dinner, laughed through a couple of comedies at the cinema, and lost themselves in the books they read before bedtime. Though the worries still arose unexpectedly and without warning—when seeing another baby at church, for example, or when a particularly painful Braxton-Hicks contraction occurred—it was as if they both accepted the fact that there was nothing they could do.

There were times, moreover, when Jeremy wondered whether he should even worry. Where once he had imagined only the worst possible outcomes, now he sometimes imagined that they might think back on the pregnancy with a sigh of relief. He could picture them telling the stories, emphasizing how awful the period had been, and voicing simple gratitude that everything turned out well.

Still, as the date for another ultrasound approached, both would find themselves growing quieter; in the ride to the doctor's office, they might not say anything. Instead, Lexie would hold his hand in silence as she stared out the passenger window.

The next ultrasound, on September 8, showed no change in the amniotic band. Six weeks to go.

They celebrated that night with chilled apple juice. As they sat on the couch, Jeremy surprised Lexie with a small wrapped gift. Inside was lotion. As she eyed it curiously, he instructed her to lean back on the couch and get comfortable. After taking the lotion from her hand, he slipped off her socks and began to rub her feet. He'd noticed that her feet had begun to swell again, but when she said as much, he denied noticing.

"I just thought you'd enjoy it," he claimed.

She grinned at him skeptically. "You can't tell they're swollen?"

"Not at all," he said, rubbing between her toes.

"How about my tummy? Can you tell that's bigger?"

"Now that you mention it. But trust me, you look a lot better than a lot of pregnant women."

"I'm huge. I look like I'm trying to smuggle a basketball."

He laughed. "You look great. From behind, you can't even tell you're pregnant. It's only when you turn to the side that I'm afraid you'll accidentally knock over the lamp."

She laughed. "Watch it," she teased. "I'm a pregnant woman on the edge."

"That's why I'm rubbing your feet. I know I'm getting off easy. It's not like I'm the one carrying Claire."

She leaned her head back and reached over to dim the lamp. "There, that's better," she said, getting comfortable again. "More relaxing."

He rubbed her feet in silence, listening as she murmured in pleasure every now and then. Jeremy could feel her feet warming as he ran his hands over them.

"Do we have any chocolate-covered cherries?" she whispered.

"I don't think so," he said. "Did you buy any yesterday?"

"No, but I was just wondering if you did."

"Why would I buy those?"

"No reason," she said. "It's just that I've kind of got a craving for them. Don't they sound good?"

He stopped rubbing. "Do you want me to run to the store to get some for you?"

"No, of course not," she said. "It's been a long day. And besides, we're celebrating. You shouldn't have to run out to the store just because I've got a silly craving."

"Okay," he said. He reached for the bottle of lotion and continued the massage.

"But don't you think those sound good right now?"

He laughed. "Okay, okay. I'll go get some."

She looked up at him. "You sure? I'd hate to put you out."

"It's no problem, sweetheart."

"Will you still rub my feet when you get back?"

"I'll rub them as long as you want me to."

She smiled. "Have I told you how glad I am that we're married? And how lucky I am to have you in my life?"

He kissed her softly on the forehead. "Every day."

For her birthday, Jeremy surprised Lexie with an elegant black maternity dress and tickets to the theater in Raleigh. He'd rented a limousine, and they shared a romantic dinner beforehand; for later, he'd arranged for a stay at a luxury hotel.

He decided it was exactly what she needed: a chance to get out of town, space to escape from her worries, time to spend as a couple. But as the evening wore on, he realized that it was what he needed as well. During the performance, he watched Lexie, relishing the play of emotions across her face, her utter absorption in the moment. More than once, she leaned toward him; at other times, they turned toward each other simultaneously, as if by unspoken agreement. On the way out, he caught others staring as well. Despite her obvious pregnancy, she was beautiful, and more than one man turned his head when she passed. That she didn't seem to notice how others saw her filled him with pride; despite their marriage, it still felt like a dream, and he almost shivered when she slipped her arm through his as they exited the theater. When the driver opened the door, he wore a look that let Jeremy know he thought Jeremy was a lucky man.

It's been said that romance in the latter stages of pregnancy is impossible, but Jeremy learned how wrong that was. Though Lexie had reached the point in her pregnancy where making love was uncomfortable, they lay close together in bed, sharing memories of their respective childhoods. They talked for hours, laughing at some of the things they did and wincing at others, and when at last they turned out the lights, Jeremy found himself wishing the night would never end. In the darkness, he wrapped his arms around her, still amazed at the thought that he could do this forever; and just when he was beginning to doze off, he felt her gently move his hands to her belly. In the stillness, the baby was awake, moving and kicking, each sensation making him believe that all was right and would turn out well. When they finally fell asleep, he wanted nothing more than to spend another ten thousand evenings like the one they'd just shared.

The next morning, they ate breakfast in bed, feeding each other fruit and feeling like a honeymooning couple again. He must have kissed her a dozen times that morning. But on the drive home, they grew quiet, the spell of the past hours broken, both of them dreading whatever lay ahead.

The following week, knowing another seven days wouldn't help, Jeremy called his editor again; again, his editor said there was no problem and that he understood the pressures Jeremy was facing. But an almost imperceptible edge of impatience in his voice reminded Jeremy that he couldn't postpone the inevitable forever. That knowledge increased the pressure—and kept him awake for two nights—but it seemed inconsequential compared with the anxiety he and Lexie felt as they waited for their next ultrasound.

The room was the same, the machine was the same, the technician was the same, but somehow everything felt different. They weren't here to learn how the baby was doing, they were here to learn if she was going to be deformed or die.

The gel was smoothed over Lexie's tummy, and the hand piece was placed upon it. Both of them immediately heard the heartbeat: strong, fast, and steady. Lexie and Jeremy exhaled at the same time.

They'd learned by now what to look for, and Jeremy found his eyes drawn to the amniotic band and its proximity to the baby. He watched to see whether it had attached, could anticipate where the technician would move the hand piece next, knew exactly what the technician was thinking. He saw the shadows, forcing himself to keep quiet when he wanted to tell her to move the hand piece and then zeroing in when she did exactly that. He watched as the technician watched, knew what she was seeing, knew what she knew.

The baby was getting larger, the technician noted as if speaking to no one in particular, and she said the baby's size made it difficult to read accurately. She continued to take her time, bringing up one image after the other. Jeremy knew what she would say, knew she would tell them the baby was okay, but the words she spoke were unexpected. The technician explained that the physician had asked her to go ahead and tell them if things were going well and that she felt comfortable in saying that the band hadn't attached. Still, she wanted to get the doctor to make sure. She rose and went to get the physician. Jeremy and Lexie waited in the room for what seemed like forever. The doctor finally appeared, looking tense and tired; perhaps he'd delivered a baby the night before. But he was patient and methodical. After watching the technician, he ran his examination before agreeing with the technician's conclusion.

"The baby is fine," he said. "She's doing well, better than I expected. But I'm pretty sure the band is getting slightly larger. It seems to be growing along with the baby, but I can't be sure."

"What about a C-section?" Jeremy asked.

The doctor nodded, as if he'd anticipated the question. "We could, but C-sections come with their own risks. It's major surgery, and even though the baby is viable, she would be at risk for other problems. Considering that the band hasn't attached and the baby's doing fine, I think that would actually entail more risk for both Lexie and the baby. But we'll keep that possibility open, okay? Let's just keep going like we are for the time being."

Jeremy nodded, unable to speak. Four weeks to go.

Jeremy held Lexie's hand on the way back to the car; once inside, he saw the same concern on her face that he felt himself. They heard the baby was fine, but the news was a whisper compared with the deafening announcement that a C-section was out for the time being and that the band seemed to be growing. Even if the doctor wasn't sure.

Lexie turned toward him, her lips pressed

together, looking suddenly tired. "Let's go home," she said. Her hands rested instinctively on her belly, and her face was flushed.

"You sure?"

"Yeah," she said.

He was just about to start the engine when he saw her lower her head into her hands. "I hate this! I hate that just when you allow yourself to believe that everything's going to be okay, even for an instant, you find out that we were just being set up for something worse. I'm just so sick of this!"

I am, too, Jeremy wanted to say. "I know you are," he said soothingly. There was nothing else he could say; what he wanted was to somehow make the situation better, to fix it. What she wanted, he recognized, was for someone simply to listen.

"I'm sorry," she said. "I know this is just as hard on you as it's been on me. And I know you're just as worried. It's just that you seem so much better able to handle it than I am."

Despite it all, he laughed. "I doubt it. My stomach started doing flip-flops the instant the doctor walked in the room. I'm developing an aversion to doctors. They give me the heebie-jeebies. Whatever happens, Claire can't become a doctor. I'm going to have to put my foot down there."

"How can you joke at a time like this?"

"It's how I deal with stress."

She smiled. "You could throw a temper tantrum."

"I don't think so. That's more your style."

"I've been doing that enough for the both of us. I'm sorry."

"Don't be sorry. And besides, it was kind of good

news. So far, so good. That's what we were hoping for."

She reached for his hand. "You ready to go home?"

"Yeah," he said. "And let me tell you, I'm really looking forward to an apple juice on the rocks to steady the nerves."

"No, you have a beer. I'll have the apple juice and look on enviously."

"Hey," Lexie said the following week.

They'd just finished dinner, and Jeremy had gone into his office. He was sitting at the desk, staring at the computer screen. When he heard Lexie's voice, he turned to see her standing in the doorway, thinking again that despite the bulging belly, she was the most gorgeous woman he'd ever seen.

"How are you?"

"I'm fine. But I just thought I'd check to see how it's coming."

Since their marriage, he'd been telling her exactly what had been happening with his writing, but only when she asked. There was no use volunteering his own daily struggles when she got home from work. How many times could a person hear that her spouse is failing before she finally began to believe that he was a failure? Instead, he'd taken to retreating into his office, as if hoping for divine intervention and attempting to make the impossible possible.

"The same," he said, simultaneously evasive and descriptive. With his answer, he thought she might nod and turn to leave; that had been her response in the last couple of months, once she learned he'd already postponed his last two columns. Instead, she stepped into the room.

"Would you like some company?"

"I always love company," he said. "Especially when nothing seems to be working."

"Tough day?"

"Like I said, the same as always."

She entered his office, but instead of moving toward the chair in the corner, she walked toward him and put her hand on the armrest. Jeremy took the hint: He slid back the chair and she took a seat on his lap. She put her arm around his shoulder, ignoring his surprise.

"Sorry for squishing you," she said. "I know I'm getting heavy."

"It's no problem. Anytime you want to sit on my lap, feel free to do so."

She stared at him before finally letting out a long sigh. "I haven't been fair with you," she confessed.

"What are you talking about?"

"All of it," she said, tracing an invisible pattern on his shoulder. "I haven't been fair since the beginning."

"I don't understand what you're saying," he responded, ignoring her touch.

"All of it," she said again. "I've been thinking about all you've done in the last nine months, and I want you to know that I want to spend the rest of my life with you, no matter where that life brings us." She paused. "I know I'm not making any sense, so let me get to the point. I married a writer," she continued. "And that's what I want you to do."

"I'm trying," he said. "That's all I've been doing since I've been down here . . ."

"That's my point," she said. "Do you know why I love you? I love you because of the way you've been ever since we found out about Claire. Because you always sound like you're sure everything's going to be okay, because every time I get down, you seem to know what to say or what to do. But most of all, I love you for who you are, and I want you to know I'd do anything to help you."

She clasped her arms around his neck. "I've been doing a lot of thinking lately about what you've been going through. I don't know . . . maybe it was just too much. Look at all the changes you've made since January. Marriage, the house, the pregnancy . . . and on top of all that, you moved down here. Your job is different from mine. For the most part, I know what I'm going to do every day. Granted, there are times when it's tedious or frustrating, but it's not as if I think the library will close if I don't do my job. But your job . . . it's creative. I couldn't do what you do. I couldn't come up with columns every month or write articles like you do. They're amazing."

Jeremy didn't bother to hide his surprise as she ran a finger through his hair.

"That's what I've been doing at the library when I have a few extra minutes. I think I've read everything you've written, and, I don't know, I guess I just don't want you to stop. And if living here is what's stopping you, I can't ask you to make that sacrifice."

"It's not a sacrifice," he protested. "I wanted to come down here. You didn't force me."

"No, but you knew where I stood. You knew I never wanted to leave. And I don't, but I will." She met his gaze. "You're my husband, and I'll follow you, even if that means moving to New York if you think that will help."

He didn't know what to say. "You'd leave Boone Creek?"

"If that's what you think you need to write."

"What about Doris?"

"I'm not saying I won't visit. But Doris would understand. We've already discussed it."

She smiled, waiting for his response, and for an instant Jeremy considered it. He imagined the energy of the city, the lights of Times Square, the illuminated outline of the Manhattan skyline at night. He thought of his daily runs in Central Park and his favorite diner, the endless possibilities of new restaurants, plays, stores, and people . . .

But only for an instant. As he glanced through the window and saw the whitewashed bark of cypress trees standing on the banks of Boone Creek, with the water so still that it reflected the sky, he knew he wouldn't leave. Nor, he realized with an intensity that surprised him, did he want to.

"I'm happy here," he said. "And I don't think moving to New York is what I need to write."

"Just like that?" she said. "Don't you want some time to think about it?"

"No," he said. "I've got everything I need right here."

After she left, he started straightening up his desk and was just about to shut off the computer when he noticed Doris's journal near the mail. It had been on the desk since he'd moved in, and he realized he should return it. He opened it and saw the names on the pages. How many still lived in the area, he wondered, and what had become of the children? Did they go to college? Were they married? Did they know their mothers had gone to Doris before their births?

He wondered how many people would believe Doris if she appeared on television with her journal and told her story. He guessed half the audience, maybe even more. But why? Why would a person believe something so ridiculous?

Pulling up to the computer, he pondered the question, suggesting answers as they came to him. He made notes about how theory influences observation, how anecdotes differ from evidence, how bold statements are often perceived intuitively as truth, that rumors seldom have any basis in reality, that most people rarely require a burden of proof. He came up with fifteen observations and began citing examples to make his case. As he typed, he couldn't shake the feeling of giddiness, of amazement, that the words were flowing. He was afraid to stop, afraid to turn on the lamp, afraid to get a cup of coffee, lest the muse desert him. At first, he was afraid to delete anything, even when it was wrong, for the same reason; then instinct took over and he pressed his luck, and still the words came. An hour later, he found himself staring in satisfaction at what he knew would be his next column: "Why People Believe Anything."

He printed it and found himself reading the column once more. It wasn't done yet. It was rough, and he knew he needed to edit it. But the bones were there, and more ideas were coming, and he knew with sudden certainty that his block was over. Still, he jotted down several ideas on the page in front of him, just in case.

He left his office and found Lexie reading in the living room.

"Hey," she said, "I thought you were going to join me."

"I did, too," he said.

"What have you been doing?"

He held out the pages, not bothering to hide his grin. "Would you like to read my next column?"

It took a moment for her to process the words before she rose from the couch. Wearing an expression of disbelief—and joy—she took the pages. She scanned them quickly, then looked up at him with a smile. "You just wrote this?"

He nodded.

"That's wonderful!" she said. "Of course I'll read it. I can't wait to read it!"

She moved back to the couch, and for the next few minutes, Jeremy watched as she perused the column. Lost in concentration, she was twirling a strand of hair with her finger. It was while staring at her that he gleaned an inkling of what had been causing his writer's block. Perhaps it wasn't that he lived in Boone Creek; rather, it was that—subconsciously, at least—he felt he could never leave.

It was a ridiculous notion, one that he would have dismissed had anyone else suggested it, but he knew he was right, and he couldn't stop smiling. He wanted to celebrate by taking Lexie in his arms and holding her forever. He was looking forward to raising his daughter in a place where they could catch fireflies in the summer and watch the storms roll in from the shelter of their porch. This was home now, their home, and the realization led him to believe that the baby was going to be okay. They'd been through so much already that she had to be okay—and when they got the next ultrasound on October 6, the last they would have before delivery, Jeremy learned that he'd been right. So far, Claire was doing just fine.

So far.

Nineteen

······❖······

When he finally realized what was happening, everything seemed fuzzy and out of focus, but since he was dreaming, he supposed that could be excused. All he knew for sure was that the first word out of his mouth that morning was "Ouch."

"Wake up," Lexie said, poking him again.

Still groggy, he pulled the sheet higher. "Why are you elbowing me? It's the middle of the night."

"It's almost five, not the middle of the night. But I think it's time."

"Time for what?" he grumbled.

"To go to the hospital."

Once the words registered, he bolted upright, flinging back the sheet. He wiped the sleep from his eyes. "You're having contractions? When did they start? Why didn't you tell me? Are you sure?"

"I think so. I've been having Braxton-Hicks, but these feel different. And they're more regular."

He swallowed. "So this is it?"

"I'm not sure. But I think this is it."

"Okay," he said, taking a long breath. "Let's not panic."

"I'm not panicking."

"Good, because there's no reason to panic."

"I know."

For a long moment, they simply looked at each other.

"I need to take a shower," he finally said.

"A shower?"

"Yeah," he said, getting out of bed. "I'll be quick, and then we'll go."

He wasn't quick. He took a long shower, long enough to steam the mirrors to the point that he had to wipe them twice in order to shave. He brushed his teeth and flossed, then slapped on after-shave. He gargled twice. He took the time to open a new container of deodorant, turned the hair dryer on low, and added both mousse and gel before brushing his hair. His fingernails were a bit long, and he was cutting and filing them when he heard the door fling open behind him.

"What on earth are you doing?" she gasped. Holding her belly, she was hunched over. "What's taking so long?"

"I'm almost done," he protested.

"You've been in there almost half an hour!"

"Really?"

"Yeah, really!" Focusing through her pain, she blinked when she saw what he was doing. "Are you *clipping your fingernails?*"

Before he could answer, she turned and staggered out of view.

In rehearsing this day, Jeremy never imagined himself acting this way. Instead, he'd be the epitome of calm and collected. He would get ready with machinelike efficiency, keep an eye on his wife and alleviate her concerns, and grab the bags that Lexie had already packed before hustling to the hospital with hands that were steady on the wheel.

What he hadn't expected was how terrified he would be. He wasn't ready for this. How could he be a father? He had no idea what he was supposed to do. Diapers? Formula? How to hold the baby? He didn't have a clue. He needed another day or two to read a few of those books Lexie had been studying for months. But it was too late now. His subconscious attempt to delay had failed.

"No, we haven't left yet!" she said into the phone. "He's still *getting ready!*"

Talking to Doris, Jeremy knew. And sounding none too pleased.

Jeremy began to throw on his clothes and was pulling a shirt over his head when she hung up. Arching her back, she suffered through another contraction in silence, and he waited until it passed. Then, helping her to her feet, he began to lead her to the car, finally gaining some measure of control.

"Don't forget the bag," she said.

"I'll come back for it."

In a flash, they were in the car. By that time, another contraction had begun, and he began backing out in haste.

"The bag," she cried, wincing.

He slammed on the brakes and rushed back inside. He truly wasn't ready for this.

The roads were empty and black beneath the darkened sky, and Jeremy pressed the accelerator, speeding toward Greenville. Because of the possible complications, they'd decided to have the baby in Greenville, and Jeremy called the doctor's answering service to let him know they were on the way.

After another contraction passed, Lexie leaned back in her seat, looking pale. He pressed harder on the accelerator.

They sped along the deserted roads; in the rearview mirror, he could see the graying light of dawn on the horizon. Lexie was strangely quiet, but then again so was he. Neither had said a word since they got in the car.

"Are you doing okay?"

"Yeah," she said, not sounding okay. "You might want to drive faster, though."

His heart hammered in his chest. *Keep calm,* he told himself. *Whatever you do, just stay calm.* He could feel the pull of the car as they sped around a curve.

"Not that fast," she said. "I don't want to die before we get there."

He slowed the car, then found himself speeding up again every time she had a contraction. They seemed to be coming every eight minutes or so. What he didn't know was whether that meant he had plenty of time or not enough. He really should have read the book, any book. It didn't matter now.

Once in Greenville, the traffic picked up. Not too many cars, but enough to require him to stop at more than a few lights. At the second one, he turned toward Lexie. If anything, she seemed even more pregnant than she had when they'd begun the drive.

"You doing okay?" he asked again.

"Stop asking me that," she said. "Trust me, I'll let you know if I'm not."

"We're almost there."

"Good," she said.

Jeremy stared at the light, wondering why on earth it wouldn't turn green. Wasn't it obvious there was an emergency here? He glanced over at his wife, fighting the urge to ask again if she was doing okay.

He rolled to a stop at the emergency room entrance, and his frantic look and the loud announcement to all assembled that his wife was in labor brought an orderly to the car with a wheelchair. Jeremy helped Lexie from the car, and she moved to the wheelchair. He grabbed the bag from the backseat and followed them through the entrance. Despite the hour, the place was crowded and three people were waiting at the check-in window.

He figured they would head straight for the maternity ward, especially given the circumstances, but instead Lexie was wheeled toward the check-in window and he was forced to wait in line. No one behind the counter was rushing; the nurses seemed to be far more interested in sipping their coffee and chatting. Jeremy could barely contain his impatience, especially as he waited while those in front of him were checking in. None of them looked as if they were at death's door; most looked as if they wanted to get a prescription refilled. One even seemed to be attempting to flirt. Finally—*finally!*—it was his turn. Before he said a word, a nurse who seemed uninterested in his wife's plight thrust a clipboard toward him.

"Fill in the first three pages, sign the fourth, and I'll need to see your insurance card."

"Is this really necessary now? I mean, my wife's in labor. Shouldn't she go to the room first?"

The nurse turned her attention to Lexie. "How far apart are your contractions?"

"About eight minutes."

"How long have you been in labor?"

"I don't know. Maybe three hours?"

The nurse nodded and looked at Jeremy. "First three pages, sign the fourth. And don't forget the insurance card."

Jeremy took the clipboard and hurried toward a seat, feeling more than a little put out. Paperwork? They needed paperwork at a time like this? In an emergency? In his opinion, the world was drowning in paperwork already. The hospital had *reams* of paperwork, and he was about to set aside the clipboard so he could march up to the window and calmly explain the situation. The nurse just didn't seem to get it.

"Hello?"

Jeremy looked up at the sound of Lexie's voice. Her wheelchair was still stationed next to the check-in window, halfway across the room. "Are you just going to leave me sitting here?"

Jeremy could feel the eyes of strangers on him. More than one woman scowled.

"Sorry," he said, rising quickly. He scurried across the room to get her. Then, after wheeling her around, he started back toward his seat.

"Don't forget the bag."

"Right," he said. He went back to get it, ignoring the stares, and sat beside her.

"You doing okay?" he asked.

"I'm going to punch you if you ask me one more time. I'm serious."

"Yeah, okay. Sorry."

"Just get the paperwork ready, okay?"

He nodded and went to work on the forms, thinking again that he was wasting his time. They really should have given his wife a room first. He could have done the paperwork later.

It took a few minutes, and then he headed toward the check-in counter. As fate would have it, someone seemed to have exactly the same idea and got to the counter first, and he was forced to wait again. By the time it was his turn, he was stewing, and he handed over the clipboard without a word.

The nurse took her time again. She examined each page, made copies, and then grabbed a few wristbands from the drawer and began to write Lexie's name and identification number on them. Slowly. At a glacial pace. Jeremy tapped his foot while he waited. He was going to have to write a letter of complaint. This was ridiculous.

"Okay," the nurse finally said, "just take a seat and we'll call you when we're ready."

"We have to wait again?" Jeremy exclaimed.

The nurse eyed him over her glasses. "Let me guess. Your first baby?"

"As a matter of fact, it is."

The nurse shook her head. "Take a seat. Like I said, we'll call you. And put the wristbands on."

A couple of years later, Lexie's name was finally called.

Okay, it wasn't that long, but it seemed even longer. Lexie had already started another contraction, and she pressed her lips together, hands on her belly.

"Lexie Marsh?"

Jeremy stood up as if his pants were on fire and hopped behind the wheelchair. In a few quick steps, he was nearly at the swinging doors.

"Yeah, this is she," he said. "We're going to the room, right?"

"Yes," she said, oblivious to Jeremy's tone. "This way. We'll be going to the maternity ward. It's on the third floor. You doing okay, honey?"

"I'm fine," Lexie answered. "I just had another contraction. They're still about eight minutes apart."

"I think we should go," Jeremy said, and both Lexie and the nurse turned toward him. Granted, his tone might have been a little snappy, but this wasn't the time for chitchat.

"Is that your bag over there?" the nurse asked.

"I'll get it," Jeremy said, mentally kicking himself.

"We'll *wait*," the nurse said.

Jeremy wanted to say, *Gee, thanks* in his most sarcastic voice but thought better of it. For all he knew, this was the lady who would be assisting with the delivery, and the last thing he wanted was to get on her bad side.

He rushed back and grabbed the bag, and they headed through the maze of corridors. Up the elevator, down the hall, and into the room. Finally.

The room was empty, sterile, and functional in the way all hospital rooms were. Lexie got up from the wheelchair and slipped into a robe before climbing carefully into bed. For the next twenty minutes, nurses bustled in and out of the room. Lexie had her blood pressure and pulse taken, had her cervix measured, answered the same questions about the duration of her labor and the timing of the contractions, when she'd had her last meal, any complications with the pregnancy. Toward the end, she was hooked up to a monitor, and she and Jeremy stared at the speedy rhythm of the baby's heartbeat.

"Is it supposed to be that fast?" Jeremy asked.

"It's just right," the nurse reassured him. Then, turning to Lexie, she hooked the chart at the edge of the bed. "I'm Joanie, and I'll be checking on you as the morning progresses. Since your contractions haven't started getting closer, you might be here for a while. There's no way to tell how long labor will last. Sometimes it suddenly clicks and goes fast; other times it's more of a slow and steady progression. But don't feel you need to stay in bed. Some women find that walking around helps, others like to sit, and others find that going on all fours is helpful. You're not ready for the epidural you requested, so just do whatever you think you need to do to stay as comfortable as you can."

"Okay," she said.

"And . . . Mr. . . . ," she said, turning to Jeremy.

"Marsh," he said. "My name is Jeremy Marsh. And this is Lexie, my wife. We're going to have a baby."

The nurse looked amused by his response. "I can see that. But your role for the time being is to support her. Down the hall there's an ice machine, and feel free to bring her as many ice chips as she wants. There are some washcloths by the sink that you can use to wipe her forehead. If she does want to walk around, just be there to support her. Sometimes contractions hit just right and the legs get wobbly; you don't want her to fall."

"I can do that," he said, mentally going through the list.

"If you need a nurse, just press this button. Someone will get to you as soon as they can."

The nurse started toward the door.

"Wait . . . You're leaving?" Jeremy asked.

"I've got to check on another patient. And there's not really anything else I can do right now, except to put in the call to the anesthesiologist. I'll be back to check on you in a little while."

"What are we supposed to do in the meantime?"

The nurse thought about it. "I guess you could watch television if you like. The remote is by the bedstand."

"My wife's in labor. I don't think she's in the mood for television."

"Or not," the nurse said. "But like I said, you might be here a while. I once had a woman in labor for nearly thirty hours."

Jeremy paled, as did Lexie. Thirty hours? Before

they could dwell on it, another contraction started, and Jeremy's attention was diverted not only by Lexie's discomfort, but by the pain he felt when she dug her nails into his hand.

They turned on the television half an hour later.

It seemed wrong, but they couldn't think of anything else to do in between the contractions, which were still eight minutes apart. Jeremy had the sudden suspicion that the baby was going to take her own sweet time. Not even born yet and already mastering the skill of being fashionably late. Even had he not been told beforehand, he would have definitely made the assumption that he was having a girl.

Lexie was doing okay. He knew not only because he asked, but also because afterward she punched him in the arm.

Doris showed up about an hour later, dressed in her Sunday best, which seemed more than appropriate for this special day. Thinking back, he was glad he had showered. With no speedup in the contractions, they still had plenty of time.

Doris seemed to take over the room, arms flailing, looking as if she were swarming toward the bed. She'd had a child, she said, so she knew exactly what to expect, and Jeremy could tell Lexie was glad she'd arrived. When Doris asked if she was doing okay, Lexie didn't punch her. She simply answered the question.

He had to admit, that bothered him a bit. Actually, so did the fact that Doris was even around. He knew it was petty, that she'd raised

Lexie and wanted to share in this special day, but a part of Jeremy believed this was something that just the two of them should share. Afterward there would be plenty of time for bonding and sharing and feeling giddy. Still, as he moved to a chair in the corner of the room, he never considered saying anything. It was one of those instances where even the most delicate diplomacy might cause offense.

He spent the next forty-five minutes half listening to their conversation, half watching *Good Morning America*. A big chunk of it was devoted to the ongoing campaigns of Al Gore and George W. Bush, and Jeremy found himself tuning out whenever either of them opened his mouth. But it was easier than overhearing how selfish he'd been when she woke him earlier that morning.

"He was cutting his fingernails?" Doris said, eyeing him with mock outrage.

"They were getting kind of long," he said.

"And then he drove like a maniac," Lexie added. "The tires were actually squealing."

Doris shook her head in disappointment.

"I thought she was about to have the baby," Jeremy said defensively. "How was I to know that we had hours to spare?"

"Well, listen," Doris said, "I've been through this before, so I stopped at the drugstore on the way and picked you up a few magazines. Brainless stuff, but it'll help pass the time."

"Thanks, Doris," Lexie said. "I'm glad you're here."

"Me too," Doris said. "I've been waiting for this for a long time."

Lexie smiled.

"I'm going to pop downstairs and get a cup of coffee, okay?" Doris went on. "Would you mind?"

"No, go ahead."

"Would you like anything, Jeremy?"

"No, I'm doing okay," he said, ignoring the growling in his stomach. If Lexie couldn't eat, then neither would he. It seemed like the right thing to do.

"See you soon," Doris chirped. On her way out the door, she touched Jeremy's shoulder and leaned toward him. "Don't worry about this morning," she said. "My husband did the same thing. I found him cleaning his office. It's normal."

Jeremy nodded.

The contractions started coming faster. First every seven minutes, then every six. An hour later, they seem to have stabilized again at five minutes. Joanie and Iris—another nurse—seemed to be switching off, alternating their visits.

Doris was still downstairs, and Jeremy found himself wondering whether she'd been able to read his mind about wanting to be alone. The television was still on, though neither was paying much attention to it. With the contractions coming faster, Jeremy was wiping Lexie's forehead and giving her ice chips. She hadn't yet wanted to go for a walk; instead her eyes seemed glued to the monitor, where she watched the baby's heartbeat.

"Are you scared?" Lexie finally said.

He saw the worry in her face. With the time drawing nearer, it didn't surprise him.

"No," he said, "not really. It hasn't even been two weeks since the last ultrasound, and she was doing fine then. I think if the band were going to attach, it would have done so by then. And even if it did, the doctor said that she was far enough along that any problems would be minor."

"But what if it attaches to the cord at the last minute? What if it cuts off the blood flow?"

"It won't," Jeremy reassured her. "I'm sure that everything's going to be okay. If the doctor was worried, I'm sure you'd be hooked up to a lot more machines and talking to a lot of different doctors already."

She nodded, hoping he was right but unwilling to convince herself until she knew for sure. Until she could hold the baby and see for herself.

"I think she should have a brother or sister," Lexie said. "I don't want her to be an only child like me."

"You turned out okay."

"I know, but still, I remember growing up and wishing that I had what most of my friends had. Someone to play with on rainy days, someone to talk to at the dinner table. You grew up with five brothers. Didn't you think that was wonderful?"

"Sometimes," Jeremy admitted. "But other times it wasn't so great. Being the youngest, I got taken advantage of a lot, especially in the mornings. I used to tell people that being the youngest of six meant a lot of cold showers and soggy towels."

She smiled. "I still want more than one."

"So do I. But let's get this one out of the way first. Then we'll see what happens."

"Can we adopt?" she asked. "I mean . . . well, you know . . ."

"If I can't get you pregnant again?"

She nodded.

"Yeah," he said. "We can adopt. I've heard it can take a long time, though."

"Then maybe we should start the process."

"I don't think you're in any condition to start anything right now."

"No, I mean when the baby is a couple of months old or something like that. We can keep trying to have a baby the regular way, but that way, we're still going forward if nothing happens. I don't want them too far apart in age."

He wiped her forehead again. "You've been giving this a lot of thought."

"I've been thinking about it ever since we found out about the amniotic band. Once I found out that there was a chance we could lose the baby, I realized how much I wanted to be a mother. And no matter what happens, I still do."

"Nothing's going to happen," he said. "But I know what you mean."

She reached for his hand and kissed his fingers. "I love you, you know."

"Yeah," he said, "I know."

"You don't love me?"

"I love you more than there are fishes in the sea, and higher than the moon." She looked at him curiously, and he shrugged. "That's what my mom used to say to us when we were little."

She kissed his fingers again. "Will you say that to Claire, too?"

"Every day."

With that, another contraction started.

Doris returned a little while later, and as the hours rolled on, ever so gradually, the contractions started coming even more quickly. Five minutes, then four and a half. At four minutes, Lexie had her cervix checked again—not exactly the prettiest picture, Jeremy thought—but afterward Joanie stood up with a knowing look.

"I think it's time to get the anesthesiologist," she said. "You're already six centimeters dilated."

Jeremy wondered exactly how that had been calculated but decided now was not the time to ask.

"Are the contractions more intense?" Joanie asked, tossing her glove into the garbage.

When Lexie nodded, she motioned to the monitor. "So far, the baby is handling it well. But don't worry, once you get the epidural, there's no more pain."

"Good," Lexie said.

"You could still change your mind, if you'd like to do this naturally," Joanie suggested.

"I'll pass," Lexie said. "How much longer, do you think?"

"It's still hard to tell, but if you keep going like you are, maybe in the next hour or so."

Jeremy's heart pounded in his chest again. Though it could have been his imagination, he thought the baby's heartbeat did the same. He tried to steady his breathing.

A few minutes later, the anesthesiologist appeared, and Joanie asked Jeremy to leave the room.

Although he consented, as he stood in the hallway with Doris, he found the idea of privacy a bit ridiculous. There wasn't a chance that hooking up the epidural could be nearly as invasive as having her cervix checked.

"Lexie said you were writing again," Doris remarked.

"I am," Jeremy said. "I've actually written a few more columns in the last week."

"Any big story ideas yet?"

"A couple. But we'll have to see if I do them. With the new baby, I don't know how much Lexie will appreciate it if I take off for a few weeks. But there's another story that I think I can do from home. It won't be like the Clausen piece, but it's strong enough."

"Congratulations," Doris said. "I'm happy for you."

"Me too," he said, and she laughed.

"I hear you're going to name the baby Claire," she said.

"Yeah."

"I've always loved that name," Doris said, her voice quiet. In the silence that followed, Jeremy knew she was remembering her daughter.

"You should have seen her when she popped out. She had a full head of the blackest hair you've ever seen, and she was loud. I knew right away I was going to have to watch her. She was a wild thing even from the beginning."

"She was wild?" Jeremy asked. "I got the impression from Lexie that she was the perfect southern belle."

Doris laughed. "Are you kidding? She was a

good kid, I'll grant you that, but she could really test the limits. In the third grade, she got sent home from school for kissing all the boys on the playground at recess. She even made a couple of them cry. So she got in trouble, right? Grounded for the rest of the day, told to clean her room, and we talked her ear off, explaining how that just wasn't appropriate behavior. So the next day at school, she did the same thing again. When we picked her up, we were at our wits' end, but she just said that she liked kissing boys, even if she did get grounded later."

Jeremy laughed. "Does Lexie know that?"

"I'm not sure. I don't know why I even brought it up. But having children changes your life like nothing else. It'll be the hardest and best thing you've ever done."

"I can't wait," Jeremy said. "I'm ready."

"Really? Because you seem terrified."

"I'm not," Jeremy lied.

"Hmm," Doris said. "Can I hold your hand when you say that?"

The last time she'd done that, Jeremy had had the strange sensation that she'd read his mind. Even if he didn't believe it had really happened, because . . . well, it just wasn't possible.

"No, as a matter of fact, you can't," he said.

Doris smiled. "It's okay to be a little nervous. And scared, too. It's a big responsibility. But you're going to do fine."

Jeremy nodded, thinking that in less than forty minutes he would find out.

*   *   *

305

With the epidural in, Lexie was no longer in pain and had to watch the monitor to even realize she was having a contraction. Within twenty minutes, her cervix had dilated to eight centimeters. At ten, the party would begin. The baby's heartbeat was still perfectly normal.

Without the pain, her mood improved dramatically.

"I feel *good*," she said, almost singing the last word.

"You sound like you've had a couple of beers."

"Feel that way, too," Lexie said. "It's a lot better than the way I was feeling. I like this epidural. Why would anyone want to do this naturally? Labor pains *hurt*."

"So I've heard. Do you need any more ice chips?"

"Nope. Doing great now."

"You're looking better, too."

"You're not so bad yourself."

"Well, I showered this morning."

"I *know*," she said, singing out the word again. "I can't *believe* you did that."

"I wanted to look good for the pictures."

"I'm going to tell all my friends."

"Just show them the pictures."

"No, I mean about you taking your own sweet time while I was writhing in agony."

"You were on the phone with Doris. You weren't writhing."

"I was writhing on the *inside*," she said. "I'm just tough and don't show it."

"And beautiful, don't forget."

"Yeah, that too. You're a lucky man."

"Yes, I am," he said, reaching for her hand. "I love you."

"I love you, too," she said.

It was time.

The nurses went into a flurry of preparations in the delivery room. The doctor eventually appeared and, like the nurses, checked Lexie's cervix again. Then, leaning forward on his stool, he explained what was going to happen. How he would ask her to push once the contraction started, how it might take two or three pushes to get the baby out. That in between he should conserve her strength. Lexie and Jeremy hung on his every word.

"Now, there's still the issue of the amniotic band," he said. "The heartbeat has been good and steady, so I'm not expecting anything unusual in the birth. I don't think it's attached to the cord, and the baby doesn't seem to be in any distress. There is a chance, however, that it could still entwine the cord at the last minute, but by then there's nothing we can do except get the baby out as fast as we can, and I'm prepared for that. We'll have a pediatrician in the room, and he'll examine the baby, checking for amniotic band syndrome, but again, I think we got lucky."

Lexie and Jeremy nodded, looking nervous.

"You're going to do fine," he said. "Just do what I tell you, and in a few minutes you'll be parents, okay?"

Lexie drew a long breath. "Okay," she said, reaching for Jeremy's hand.

"Where do I go?" Jeremy said.

"Right where you are is fine."

As the doctor finished up with everything he needed to do, another nurse entered the room, along with the pediatrician, who introduced herself as Dr. Ryan. A sterilized tray of surgical tools was rolled toward the bed and uncovered. The doctor seemed completely at ease; Dr. Ryan chatted easily with the nurse.

When the next contraction started, the doctor told Lexie to grab her legs and push. Lexie grimaced with the effort, and the doctor checked the baby's heartbeat once more. Lexie strained, squeezing Jeremy's hand as hard as she could.

"Okay, good," he said, moving into a better position. He got comfortable on the rolling stool. "Now relax for a minute. Catch your breath and we'll try this again. Push a little harder if you can."

She nodded. Jeremy wondered whether it was possible to push harder, but Lexie seemed fine with it and began to push again.

The doctor was focused. "Good, good," he said. "Keep going."

Lexie kept pushing; Jeremy ignored the pain in his hand. The contraction ended.

"Relax again. You're doing fine," he assured her.

Lexie caught her breath as Jeremy wiped the perspiration from her brow. When the next contraction came, she went through the process once more. Her eyes were squeezed shut, her teeth clenched, her face flushed with effort. The nurses stood at the ready. Jeremy was still holding her hand, amazed at how fast things seemed to be moving now.

"Good, good," the doctor said. "Just one more big push and we're there . . ."

* * *

After that, everything went foggy, and he couldn't explain how it happened. Later, he would realize that he could remember only bits and pieces, and he sometimes felt guilty about that. His last clear memory of Lexie was one of her pulling up her legs as the next contraction started. Her face was shiny with perspiration, and she was breathing hard as the doctor told her to push one last time with everything she had. He thought he saw her smile.

And then? He wasn't sure, for his gaze was drawn toward Lexie's legs, toward the quick and fluid movements of the physician. Though he considered himself knowledgeable and worldly, it suddenly struck him that this was the first—and possibly only—time that he would witness the birth of his child, and at that point the room itself seemed to shrink. All at once, he was only dimly aware that Doris was still in the room; instead, he heard Lexie groan and watched as Claire began to emerge. First her head, and then with a quick shift of the physician's hands, the shoulders slid free, followed almost immediately by the rest of her body. In an instant, Jeremy had become a father, and he stared in amazement at the new life before him.

Covered in amniotic fluid and still attached to the umbilical cord, Claire was a slippery mass of gray and red and brown and seemed at first to be gasping; in an instant, Dr. Ryan placed her on a table, a suction tube was inserted in her mouth, and her throat was cleared. Only then did Claire begin to cry. The pediatrician began to examine her. From his spot, Jeremy couldn't tell whether the baby was doing okay. The world was still closing in. Vaguely, he heard Lexie gasp.

"I don't see any signs that the amniotic band attached," Dr. Ryan said. "She's got all her fingers and toes, and she's a cute little thing. Good color, and she's breathing fine. Apgar is an eight."

Claire continued to wail, and Jeremy finally turned toward Lexie. At that point, everything moved so fast that he was still having trouble processing it.

"Did you hear that?" he asked.

It was then, while looking at her, that he heard the long, steady beep on the machine behind him. Lexie's eyes were closed and her head lay back on the pillow, almost as if she were asleep.

His first thought was that it was strange that she wasn't craning her neck in search of the baby. Then, all at once, the physician rose from his stool so quickly that it shot out toward the wall behind him. The nurse shouted something about code, and the doctor yelled to the other nurse to take Jeremy and Doris from the room immediately.

Jeremy felt a sudden contraction in his chest. "What's happened?" he shouted.

The nurse grabbed his arm and started dragging him from the room.

"What's going on? What's wrong with her? Wait . . ."

"Please!" the nurse shouted. "You've got to go now!"

His eyes widened in terror. He couldn't turn away from Lexie. Nor could Doris. As if from somewhere far away, he heard the nurse shouting for help from the orderlies. The doctor was over Lexie now, pushing on her chest . . .

Looking panicked. They were all panicked.

"Nooo!" Jeremy screamed. He tried to shake free from the nurse.

"Get him out of here!" the doctor shouted.

Jeremy felt someone else grab his arm. He was being pulled from the room. This couldn't be happening. What was wrong? Why wasn't she moving? Oh God, she's going to be okay. This can't be happening. Wake up, Lexie . . . oh, please, God, wake up . . .

"What's happening?" he screamed again. He was led to the hallway, barely hearing the voices telling him to calm down. From the corner of his eye, he saw a stretcher being rushed down the hall by two orderlies. They vanished into the room.

Jeremy was being held against the wall by two other orderlies. His breathing was shallow, his body as tense and cold as cable wire. He heard Doris sobbing but could barely process the sound. He was surrounded by rushing people and all alone at the same time. This was what true terror felt like. A minute later, Lexie was being rushed from the room on a gurney. The doctor was still on top of her, giving her CPR. There was a bag over her face.

Then, all at once, time seemed to slow. His body finally loosened once Lexie vanished through the swinging doors at the end of the corridor. Suddenly he felt weak, and he could barely stand. He was dizzy.

"What's wrong?" he asked again. "Where are they taking her? Why isn't she moving?"

Neither the orderlies nor the nurse could look at him.

*　　*　　*

311

He and Doris were led to a special room. Not a waiting room, not a hospital room, but someplace else. Blue vinyl padded chairs lined the two walls of the carpeted room. An end table was littered with magazines, a garish mess beneath cold fluorescent lights. A wooden cross hung on the far wall. An empty room but for the two of them.

Doris sat pale and trembling, staring without seeming to focus on anything. Jeremy sat beside her, then rose to pace the room, then sat again. He'd asked her what happened, but Doris knew no more than Jeremy. She brought her hands to her face and began to cry.

Jeremy couldn't swallow. He couldn't think. He tried to remember what happened, tried to piece it all together, but he couldn't concentrate. Time slowed.

Seconds, minutes, hours . . . He didn't know how much time passed, didn't know what was happening, didn't know if she would be okay, wasn't sure what to do. He wanted to rush back into the corridor to find the answers. More than that, he needed to see Lexie to know that she was okay. Doris continued to cry beside him, her trembling hands clasped in a desperate prayer.

Strangely, he would always remember everything about the waiting room, but as much as he tried, he couldn't picture the face of the hospital counselor who eventually came to find him, and even the physician looked different from the way he'd appeared in the delivery room or during any of their previous appointments. All he would really remember was the cold terror he suddenly felt when he saw them appear. He stood, as did Doris, and though he thought he wanted answers, all at once he didn't want them to say anything at all. Doris held his arm, as if hoping he were strong enough to support them both.

"How is she?" Jeremy asked.

The doctor seemed exhausted. "I'm so sorry to have to tell you this," he began, "but we think your wife had what's called an amniotic fluid embolism . . ."

Again, Jeremy felt dizzy. Trying to steady himself, he focused on the specks of blood and fluid that had splattered on the doctor's gown during the delivery. The words echoed as if from a great distance as the doctor went on.

"We don't think the amniotic band had anything to do with it . . . they were completely separate events . . . Amniotic fluid somehow must have entered one of the vessels in the uterus. There was no way we could have predicted it . . . There was nothing we could do . . ."

The room closed in around him, and Doris sagged against him, her voice going ragged. "Oh . . . no . . . ," she said. "No . . . no . . ."

He strained to draw breath. Numbly, he heard the doctor going on.

"It's very rare, but somehow, once the fluid entered the vessel, it must have traveled to her heart. I'm sorry, but she didn't make it. The baby's fine, though . . ."

Doris staggered, but Jeremy was able to hold her upright. How, he wasn't sure. None of this was making any sense. Lexie couldn't be gone. She was fine. She was healthy. They were talking a few minutes ago. She'd delivered the baby. She'd pushed.

This couldn't be happening. It couldn't be real.

But it was.

The doctor seemed to be in shock himself as he continued to attempt an explanation. Jeremy stared through his tears, light-headed and nauseated.

"Can I see her?" he suddenly croaked out.

"She's in the nursery, under the lights," the doctor said, as if glad to finally have a question he could answer. He was a good man, and this was obviously hard for him. "Like I said, she's doing fine."

"No," Jeremy said in a strangled voice. He struggled to form the words. "My wife. Can I see my wife?"

Twenty

.... ❖ ....

Jeremy was numb as he made his way down the
corridor. The doctor walked half a step behind him,
saying nothing.

He didn't want to believe it, couldn't force himself to process the doctor's words. He had made a
mistake, Jeremy thought; Lexie wasn't really gone.
While the doctor had been talking, someone had
noticed something, brain activity or a faint heartbeat, and they'd sprung into action. Right now, they
were working on her and she was somehow getting
better. It was like nothing they'd ever seen, even
miraculous, but Jeremy knew she would make it. She
was young and strong. She'd just turned thirty-two
and she couldn't be gone. She couldn't be.

The doctor stopped outside a room near the
intensive care unit, and Jeremy felt his heart leap
in his chest at the thought that he might be right.

"I had her moved here, so you could have some
privacy," the doctor said. His face was grim, and
he placed a hand on Jeremy's shoulder. "Take all
the time you need. I'm so very sorry."

Jeremy ignored the doctor's words. His hand trembled as he reached for the door. It weighed a ton, ten tons, a hundred, but somehow he was able to open it. His eyes were drawn to the figure in the bed. She lay unmoving, with no equipment hooked up, no monitors, no IVs. She'd looked this way a hundred times in the mornings. She was sleeping, her hair spread over the pillow . . . but strangely, her arms were at her sides. Straight, as if they'd been placed in that position by someone who didn't know her.

His throat clenched and his vision became a tunnel, everything black except her. She was the only thing he could see, but he didn't want to see her like this. Not this way. Not with her arms like that. She had to be okay. She was only thirty-two. She was healthy and strong and a fighter. She loved him. She was his *life*.

But those arms . . . those arms were wrong . . . they should have been bent at the elbows, one hand over her head or on her belly . . .

He couldn't breathe.

His wife was gone . . .

His *wife* . . .

It wasn't a dream. He knew that now, and he let the tears flow unchecked, sure they would never stop.

Sometime later, Doris came in to say good-bye as well, and Jeremy left her alone with her grand-daughter. He moved through the hallway in a trance, only vaguely noticing the nurses he passed in the hallway and the volunteer who was pushing a cart past him. They seemed to ignore him completely, and he didn't know whether they avoided looking his way because they knew what happened or because they didn't.

He returned to the room where he'd met the doctor, feeling drained and weak. He couldn't cry anymore. There was nothing left, and he simply didn't have the energy. It was all he could do not to collapse. He replayed the images from the delivery room countless times, trying to figure out the exact instant the embolism had been triggered, thinking he might have seen something to warn him of what was coming. Had it been when she gasped? Had it happened a moment later? He couldn't shake the feeling of guilt, as if he should have convinced her to have a cesarean section, or at least not to strain as much as she had, as if her strenuous efforts had triggered it. He was angry with himself, angry with God, angry with the doctor. And he was angry with the baby.

He didn't even want to see the baby, believing that somehow, in the act of receiving life, the baby had taken one in exchange. If it weren't for the baby, Lexie would still be with him. If it weren't for the baby, their last months together would have been devoid of stress. If it weren't for the baby, he might have been able to make love to his wife. But all that was gone now. The baby had taken all of it. Because of the baby, his wife was dead. And Jeremy felt dead as well.

How could he ever love her? How could he ever forgive her? How could he see her or hold her and forget that she'd taken Lexie's life in exchange for her own? How was he not supposed to hate her for what she had done to the woman he loved?

He recognized the irrationality of his feelings and

sensed their insidious, evil character. It was wrong, it went against everything a parent was supposed to feel, but how could he silence his heart? How could he possibly say good-bye to Lexie in one moment and say hello to the baby in the next? And how was he supposed to act? Was he supposed to scoop her in his arms and coo sweetly, as other fathers would be doing? As if nothing at all had happened to Lexie?

And then what? After she came home from the hospital? At the moment, he couldn't imagine having to take care of someone else; it was everything he could do not to curl up on the floor right now. He knew nothing about infants, and the only thing he was certain about was that they were supposed to be with their mothers. It was Lexie who had read all the books; it was Lexie who'd baby-sat as a child. Throughout the pregnancy, he'd been comfortable in his ignorance, assured that Lexie would show him what to do. But the baby had other plans . . .

The baby who had killed his wife.

Instead of heading to the nursery, he collapsed into one of the chairs in the waiting room again. He didn't want to feel this way about the baby, knew he shouldn't feel this way, but . . . Lexie had died in childbirth. In the modern world, in a hospital, that just didn't happen. Where were the miracle cures? The made-for-television moments? Where in God's name was any semblance of reality in all this? He closed his eyes, convincing himself that if he concentrated hard enough, he could wake from the nightmare that his life had suddenly become.

Doris eventually found Jeremy. He hadn't heard her enter the room, but at the touch of her hand on his shoulder, his eyes flew open, taking in the swollen, tear-streaked wreck of her face. Like Jeremy, she seemed to be on the verge of breaking apart.

"Have you called your parents?" she said, her voice ragged.

Jeremy shook his head. "I can't. I know I should, but I just can't do it right now."

Her shoulders began to shudder. "Oh, Jeremy," she gasped.

Jeremy rose and wrapped his arms around her. They cried together, holding on, as if trying to save each other. In time, Doris pulled back and swiped at her tears.

"Have you seen Claire?" she whispered.

The name brought all his feelings rushing back.

"No," Jeremy said. "Not since I was in the delivery room."

Doris gave a sad smile, one that nearly crushed what was left of his heart. "She looks exactly like Lexie."

Jeremy turned away. He didn't want to hear that, didn't want to hear anything about the baby. Was he supposed to be happy about that? Would he ever be happy again?

He couldn't imagine it. What was supposed to be the most joyous day of his life had suddenly become the worst, and nothing in life could prepare someone for that. And now? Not only was he supposed to survive the unimaginable, but he was supposed to take care of someone else? The little one who had killed his wife?

"She's beautiful," Doris said into the silence. "You should go see her."

"I . . . uh . . . I can't," Jeremy mumbled. "Not yet. I don't want to see her."

He felt Doris watching him, as if reading him through the fog of her pain.

"She's your daughter," Doris said.

"I know," Jeremy responded, but all he could feel was the dull anger pulsing beneath his skin.

"Lexie would want you to take care of her." Doris reached out to take his hand. "If you can't do it for yourself, then do it for your wife. She would want you to see your child, to hold your child. Yes, it's hard, but you can't say no. You can't say no to Lexie, you can't say no to me, and you can't say no to Claire. Now come with me."

Where Doris found the strength and composure to deal with him, he was never certain, but with that, she took his arm and marched him down the corridor toward the nursery. He was moving on autopilot, but with each step he felt his anxiety growing. He was frightened at the thought of meeting his daughter. While he knew that the anger he felt toward her was wrong, he was also afraid that he wouldn't be angry when the time came, and that seemed wrong as well—as if somehow that meant he could forgive her for what happened to Lexie. All he knew for certain was that he wasn't ready for either possibility.

But Doris wouldn't be dissuaded. She pushed through a set of swinging doors, and in the rooms on either side, Jeremy saw pregnant women and new mothers, surrounded by their families. The hospital

320

buzzed with activity, nurses moving purposefully around them. He passed the room where the embolism had occurred and had to put a hand to the wall to keep from falling.

They passed the nurses' station and rounded the corner, toward the nursery. The gray-speckled tile was disorienting, and he felt dizzy. He wanted to break free from Doris's grasp and escape; he wanted to call his mother and tell her what happened. He wanted to cry into the phone, to have an excuse to let go, to be released from this duty . . .

Up ahead, a group of people clustered in the hallway, peering through the glass wall of the nursery. They were pointing and smiling, and he could hear their murmurs: *She's got his nose*, or, *I think she'll have blue eyes*. He knew none of them, but suddenly he hated them, for they were experiencing the joy and excitement that should have been his. He couldn't imagine having to stand next to them, to have them ask which child he had come to see, to listen to them as they would inevitably praise her sweetness or beauty. Beyond them, heading toward the offices, he saw the nurse who had been in the room when Lexie had died, going about her business as if the day had been utterly ordinary.

He was stricken by the sight of her, and as if knowing what he was feeling, Doris squeezed his arm and paused in midstep.

"That's where you go in," she said, motioning toward the door.

"You're not coming with me?"

"No," she said, "I'll wait out here."

"Please," he pleaded, "come with me."

321

"No," she said. "This is something you have to do on your own."

Jeremy stared at her. "Please," he whispered.

Doris's expression softened. "You're going to love her," she said. "As soon as you see her, you'll love her."

Is love at first sight truly possible?

He couldn't fathom the possibility. He entered the nursery with tentative steps. The nurse's expression changed as soon as she saw him; although she hadn't been in the delivery room, the story had made the rounds. That Lexie, a healthy and vibrant young woman, had suddenly died, leaving behind a husband in shock and a motherless newborn. It would have been easy to offer sympathy or even turn away, but the nurse did neither. Instead, she forced a smile and pointed toward one of the cribs near the window.

"Your daughter is on the left," she said. Her expression faltered, and it was enough to remind him of how wrong this scene was. Lexie should have been here, too. Lexie. He gasped, feeling suddenly short of breath. From somewhere far away, he heard her murmur, "She's beautiful."

Jeremy moved automatically toward the crib, wanting to turn back but wanting to see her, too. It seemed as if he were watching the process through someone else's eyes. He wasn't here. It wasn't really him. This wasn't his baby.

He hesitated when he saw Claire's name written on the sheathed plastic band around her ankle, and his throat clenched again when he saw Lexie's name. He blinked away his tears and stared down at his daughter. Tiny and vulnerable beneath the warming lights, she was wrapped in a blanket and wearing a hat, her soft skin a healthy pink. He could still see the ointment that had been applied to her eyes, and she had the strange mannerisms of all newborns: The movements of her arms were occasionally jerky, as if she were working hard to get used to breathing air as opposed to receiving oxygen from her mother. Her chest rose and fell quickly, and Jeremy hovered over her, fascinated by how oddly uncontrolled her movements seemed. Yet even as a newborn she resembled Lexie, in the shape of her ears, the slight point of her chin. The nurse appeared over his shoulder.

"She's a wonderful baby," she said. "She's been sleeping most of the time, but when she wakes, she barely utters a cry."

Jeremy said nothing. Felt nothing.

"You should be able to take her home tomorrow," she continued. "There haven't been any complications, and she's already able to suck. Sometimes that's a problem with little ones like her, but she took right to the bottle. Oh look, she's waking up."

"Good," Jeremy mumbled, barely hearing her. All he could do was stare.

The nurse laid a hand on Claire's tiny chest. "Hi, sweetie. Your daddy's here."

The baby's arms jerked again.

"What's that?"

"That's normal," the nurse said, adjusting the blanket. "Hi, sweetie," she said again.

Beyond the window, Jeremy could feel Doris staring at him.

"Do you want to hold her?"

Jeremy swallowed, thinking she seemed so fragile that any movement would break her. He didn't want to touch her, but the words came out before he could stop them. "Can I?"

"Of course," the nurse replied. She scooped Claire into her arms, leaving Jeremy to wonder how babies could be handled with such matter-of-fact efficiency.

"I don't know what to do," he whispered. "I've never done this before."

"It's easy," the nurse replied, her voice soft. She was older than Jeremy but younger than Doris, and Jeremy suddenly wondered if she had children of her own. "Have a seat in the rocker and I'll hand her to you. All you do is hold her with one arm under her back, and make sure you support her head. And then, most importantly, love her for the rest of her life."

Jeremy took his seat, terrified and battling an urge to break into tears. He wasn't ready for this. He needed Lexie, he needed to grieve, and he needed time. He saw Doris's face again just beyond the glass; he thought he saw her smile ever so slightly. The nurse drew nearer, handling the baby with the ease and comfort of someone who had done this a thousand times.

Jeremy held up his hands and felt the gentle weight of Claire as she came down into them. A moment later, she was nestled in his arms.

A thousand emotions swept through Jeremy at that moment: the failure he'd felt in the physician's office with Maria, the shock and horror he'd experienced in the delivery room, the emptiness of the walk down the hallway, the anxiety he'd experienced only a minute before.

In his arms, Claire stared up at him, her silvery eyes seeming to focus on his face. All he could think was that she was all that was left of Lexie. Claire was Lexie's daughter, in features and spirit, and Jeremy found himself holding his breath. Visions of Lexie coursed through his mind: Lexie, who'd trusted him enough to have a child with him; Lexie, who had married him knowing that while he would never be perfect, he would be the kind of father Claire deserved. Lexie had sacrificed her life to give her to him, and all at once he was struck by the certainty that had there been a choice, she would have done it all over again. Doris was right: Lexie wanted him to love Claire in the same way that Lexie would have, and now Lexie needed him to be strong. Claire needed him to be strong. Despite the emotional upheaval of the past hour, he stared at his child and blinked, suddenly certain that what he was doing now was the sole reason he'd been placed on this earth. To love another. To care for someone else, to help another person, to carry her worries until she was strong enough to carry them on her own. To care for someone unconditionally, for in the end that was what gave life meaning. And Lexie had given her life, knowing that Jeremy could do that.

And in that instant, while staring at his daughter through a thousand tears, he fell in love and wanted nothing more than to hold Claire and keep her safe forever.

Epilogue

····❖····

February 2005

Jeremy's eyes fluttered open with the ringing of the phone. The house was still quiet, cocooned in a dense quilt of fog, and he forced himself to sit up, amazed that he'd slept at all. He hadn't slept the night before, nor had he slept more than a few hours a night for the last couple of weeks. His eyes felt swollen and red, his head pounded, and he knew he looked as exhausted as he felt. The phone sounded again; he reached for it and pressed the button to answer.

"Jeremy," his brother said, "what's up?"

"Nothing," Jeremy grunted.

"Were you sleeping?"

Jeremy instinctively checked the clock. "Only twenty minutes. Not enough to do any damage."

"I should let you go."

Spying his jacket and keys on the chair, Jeremy thought again about what he wanted to do tonight. It would be another night of little sleep, and he was suddenly grateful for his unexpected nap.

"No. I won't fall sleep again. It's good to hear

from you. How are you?" Glancing down the hall, he listened for Claire.

"I was calling because I got your message," his brother said, sounding guilty. "The one you left a couple of days ago. You sounded really out of it. Like you were a zombie or something."

"Sorry," Jeremy said. "I was up all night."

"Again?"

"What can I say?" Jeremy replied. "It happens."

"Don't you think it's been happening a little too often lately? Even Mom is worried about you. She thinks that if this keeps up, you're going to get seriously sick."

"I'll be fine," he said, stretching.

"You don't sound fine. You sound like you're half-dead."

"But I look like a million bucks."

"Yeah, I'll bet you do. Listen, Mom told me to tell you to get more sleep, and I'm going to second that motion. Now that I woke you up, I mean. So go back to bed."

Despite his exhaustion, Jeremy laughed. "I can't. Not now, anyway."

"Why not?"

"It wouldn't do any good. I'd just end up lying here all night long."

"Not all night," he said.

"Yes," Jeremy said, correcting him, "all night. That's what insomnia means."

He heard his brother hesitate on the other end. "I still don't get it," he said in a baffled voice. "Why can't you sleep?"

Jeremy glanced out the window. The sky was

impenetrable, silver fog everywhere, and he found himself thinking of Lexie.

"Nightmares," he said.

The nightmares had begun a month ago, just after Christmas, for no apparent reason.

The day had started out ordinary enough; Claire had helped Jeremy make scrambled eggs, and they'd eaten together at the table. Afterward, Jeremy brought Claire to the grocery store and then dropped her off with Doris for a couple of hours in the afternoon. She watched *Beauty and the Beast*, a movie she'd already seen dozens of times. They had turkey and macaroni and cheese for dinner, and after her bath, they read the same stories they always did. She was neither feverish nor upset when she went to bed, and when Jeremy checked on her twenty minutes later, she was sound asleep.

But just after midnight, Claire woke up screaming.

Jeremy raced into her bedroom and comforted her as she cried. Eventually she calmed, and he pulled up the covers before kissing her on the forehead.

An hour later, she woke up screaming again.

Then again.

It went on like this most of the night, but in the morning she seemed to have no memory of what had happened. Jeremy, glassy-eyed and exhausted, was just thankful it was over. Or so he thought. However, the same thing happened that night. And the next. And the night after that.

After a week, he brought Claire to the doctor

and was assured there was nothing physically wrong with her, but that night terrors were, if not common, not completely out of the ordinary, either. They would pass in time, the doctor said.

But they didn't. If anything, they seemed to be getting worse. Where once she would wake two or three times a night, now it was four or five, as if she were having a nightmare in every dream cycle, and the only thing that seemed to calm her was the soft words Jeremy would whisper as he rocked her afterward. He'd tried moving her to his bed, as well as sleeping in hers, and he held her for hours as she slept in his lap. He tried music, adding and removing night-lights, and changing her diet, adding warm milk before bedtime. He'd called his mother, he'd called Doris; when Claire had spent the night at her great-grandmother's, Claire woke up screaming there, too. Nothing seemed to help.

If the lack of sleep made him tense and anxious, Claire was tense and anxious as well. There had been more temper tantrums than usual, more unexpected tears, more sassiness. At four, she was unable to control her outbursts, but when Jeremy found himself snapping back, he couldn't use immaturity as an excuse. Exhaustion left him frustrated, always on edge. And the anxiety. That's what really got to him. The fear that something was wrong, that if she didn't start sleeping regularly again, something terrible would happen to her. He would survive, he could take care of himself, but Claire? He was responsible for her. She needed him, and somehow he was failing her.

He remembered how his father had been the day

329

his older brother David had been in an auto accident. Later that night, eight-year-old Jeremy had found his father sitting in the easy chair, staring ahead vacantly. Jeremy remembered thinking he didn't recognize his dad. He seemed smaller somehow, and for an instant, Jeremy thought that he'd misunderstood his parents earlier when they had explained that David was fine. Maybe his brother had died and they were afraid to tell him the truth. He remembered feeling suddenly short of breath, but just as he was about to burst into tears, his father emerged from the spell he seemed to be under. Jeremy crawled into his lap and felt the sandpaper of his father's whiskers. When he asked about David, his father shook his head.

"He'll be fine," his father said, "but that doesn't stop the worries. As a parent, you always worry."

"Do you worry about me?" Jeremy asked.

His father pulled him close. "I worry about all of you, all the time. It never ends. You think it will, that once they get to a certain age you can stop. But you never do."

Jeremy thought about that story as he peeked in on Claire, aching with the desire to hold her close, if only to keep the nightmares at bay. She'd been down for an hour, and he knew it was only a matter of time before she would wake up screaming again. Inside the bedroom, he watched the gentle rise and fall of her chest.

As always, he found himself wondering about the nightmares, wondering what images her mind was conjuring up. Like all children, she was developing at an extraordinary rate, mastering language and nonverbal communication, developing coordination, testing limits of behavior, and learning the rules of the world. Since she didn't understand enough about life to be obsessed with the fears that kept adults awake at night, he assumed her nightmares were either a product of her overactive imagination or her mind's attempt to make sense of the complexity of the world. But in what way did that manifest itself in her dreams? Did she see monsters? Was she being chased by something frightening? He didn't know, couldn't even fathom a guess. The mind of a child was a mystery.

Yet he sometimes wondered if he was somehow at fault. Did she realize that she was unlike other children? Did she recognize that when they went to the park, he was often the only other father in attendance? Did she wonder why everyone seemed to have a mother while she didn't? He knew that wasn't his fault; it was no one's fault. It was, as he reminded himself frequently, the result of a tragedy without blame, and one day he would tell Claire exactly what his own nightmare was about.

His nightmare always took place in a hospital, but for him it was never just a dream.

He left her side, tiptoed toward the closet, and opened the door quietly. Pulling a jacket from a hanger, he paused to look around the room, remembering Lexie's surprise when she realized he'd decorated the nursery.

Like Claire, the room had changed since then. Now it was painted in yellow and purple pastels;

halfway up the wall was a wallpaper border displaying angelic little girls dressed for church. Claire had helped him pick it out, and she'd sat cross-legged in the room as Jeremy papered the walls himself.

Above her bed hung two of the first items he would reach to save in the event of a fire. When Claire had been an infant, he'd arranged for a photographer to take dozens of close-up photos in black and white. A few shots were of Claire's feet, others of her hands, still others of her eyes and ears and nose. He'd mounted the photos in two large framed collages, and whenever Jeremy saw them, he remembered how small she'd felt when he held her in his arms.

In those weeks immediately following Claire's birth, Doris and his mother had worked in tandem to help Jeremy and Claire. Jeremy's mother, who changed her plans and came down to stay for an extended visit, helped him learn the rudiments of parenting: how to change a diaper, the proper temperature for formula, the best way to give medicine so Claire wouldn't spit it back up. For Doris, feeding the baby was therapeutic, and she would rock and hold Claire for hours afterward. Jeremy's mother seemed to feel a responsibility to help Doris as well, and sometimes in the late evenings, Jeremy would hear the two of them talking quietly in the kitchen. Every now and then, he would hear Doris crying as his mother murmured words of support.

They grew fond of each other, and though both were struggling, they refused to allow Jeremy to wallow in self-pity. They allowed him time alone and assumed some of the responsibility of caring for Claire, but they also insisted that Jeremy do his share no matter how much he was hurting. And both of them continually reminded him that he was the father and that Claire was his responsibility. In this, they were united.

Bit by bit, Jeremy was forced to learn how to care for the baby, and as time passed, the grief began slowly to lift. Where once it had overwhelmed him from the time he woke until the time he collapsed in bed, now he found it possible to forget his anguish at times, simply because he was absorbed in the task of caring for his daughter. But Jeremy had been operating on autopilot then, and when the time came for his mother to leave, he panicked at the thought of being on his own. His mother went over everything half a dozen times; she reassured him that all he had to do was call if he had any questions. She reminded him that Doris was just around the corner and that he could always talk with the pediatrician if he felt worried about anything.

He remembered the calm way his mother had explained everything, but even so, he had begged her to stay for just a little while longer.

"I can't," she said. "And besides, I think you need to do this. She's depending on you."

On his first night alone with Claire, he checked on her more than a dozen times. She was in the bassinet beside his bed; on his end table was a flashlight that he used to make sure she was breathing. When she woke with cries, he fed and burped her; in the morning, he gave her a bath and panicked again when he saw her shivering. It took far more time to get her dressed than he thought it would. He laid her on a blanket in the living room and watched her as he sipped his coffee. He thought he would work when she went down for a nap, but he didn't; he thought the same thing when she went down for a second nap, but again he ignored his work. In his first month, it was all he could do simply to keep his e-mail up-to-date.

As the weeks rolled into months, he eventually got the hang of it. His work was gradually organized around the changing of diapers, feeding, bathing, and doctor's visits. He brought Claire in for shots and called the pediatrician when her leg was still swollen and red hours later. He buckled her in her car seat and brought her to the grocery store when he went shopping or to church. Before he knew it, Claire had begun to smile and laugh; she often stretched her fingers toward his face, and he found that he could spend hours watching her in the same way she watched him. He took hundreds of pictures of Claire, and he grabbed the video camera and recorded the moment when she let go of the end table and took her first steps.

Gradually, ever so gradually, birthdays and holidays came and went. As Claire grew, her personality became more distinct. As a toddler, she wore only pink, then blue, and now, at age four, purple. She loved to color but hated to paint. Her favorite raincoat had a Dora the Explorer patch on the sleeve, and she wore it even when the sun was shining. She could choose her own clothes, dress herself except for tying her shoes, and was able to recognize most of the letters in the alphabet. Her collection of Disney movie DVDs occupied most of the rack near the television, and after her bath, Jeremy would read her three or four stories before kneeling beside her as they said their prayers.

If there was joy in his life, there was tedium as well, and time itself played funny tricks. It seemed to vanish whenever he tried to leave the house— he was always ten minutes behind schedule—yet he could sit on the floor playing with Barbie or coloring in the Blue's Clues notebook for what seemed like hours, only to realize that only eight or nine minutes had actually passed. There were times when he felt he should be doing something more with his life, yet when he thought about it, he would realize that he had no desire to change it at all.

As Lexie had predicted, Boone Creek was an ideal place for Claire to grow up, and he and Claire often headed for Herbs. Though Doris moved a bit more slowly these days, she delighted in spending time with Claire, and Jeremy couldn't help but smile whenever he saw a pregnant woman enter the restaurant, asking for Doris. He supposed it was to be expected now. Three years ago, Jeremy had finally decided to take Doris up on her offer about the journal and had made arrangements for an experiment under controlled settings. In all, Doris met with ninety-three women and made her pre-dictions, and when the records were unsealed a year later, Doris had been correct in each and every instance.

A year later, the short book he wrote about Doris

stayed on the best-seller list for five months; in his conclusion, Jeremy admitted that there was no scientific explanation.

Jeremy made his way back to the living room. After tossing Claire's jacket on the chair beside his, he moved to the window and pushed aside the curtains. Off to the side, nearly out of view, was the garden that he and Lexie had started after moving into the house.

He thought of Lexie often, especially on quiet nights like these. In the years since she'd passed away, he hadn't dated, nor had he felt any desire to do so. He knew that people were worried about him. One by one, his friends and family had talked to him about other women, but his answer was always the same: He was too busy taking care of Claire to even consider attempting another relationship. Although this was somewhat true, what he didn't tell them was that part of him had died along with Lexie. She would always be with him. When he imagined her, he never saw her lying in the hospital bed. Instead, he saw her smile as she'd gazed at the town from the top of Riker's Hill or her expression when they'd felt the baby kick for the first time. He heard the contagious joy of her laughter or saw the look of concentration as she read a book. She was alive, always alive, and he wondered who he would have been had Lexie never come into his life. Would he have ever married? Would he still live in the city? He didn't know, would never know, but when he thought back, it sometimes seemed as if his life had begun five years ago. He wondered whether in another few years he would remember anything at all about his life in New York or the person he used to be.

Yet he wasn't unhappy. He was pleased with the man he'd become, the father he'd become. Lexie had been right all along, for what gave his life meaning was love. He treasured those moments when Claire wandered down the stairs in the mornings, while Jeremy was reading the newspaper and sipping coffee. Half the time, her pajamas were askew, one sleeve up, her tummy showing, the pants slightly twisted, and her dark hair was poofed out in a messy halo. In the bright light of the kitchen, she would pause momentarily and squint before rubbing her eyes.

"Hi, Daddy," she would say, her voice almost inaudible.

"Hi, sweetheart," he would answer, and Claire would go into his arms. As he lifted her and leaned back, she would relax against him, head on his shoulder, her small arms twined around his neck.

"I love you so much," Jeremy would say, feeling the shallow movement of her chest as she breathed.

"I love you, too, Daddy."

At moments like those, he ached that she never knew her mother.

It was time. Jeremy slipped on his jacket and zipped it up. Then, heading down the hall with her jacket, hat, and mittens, he went into Claire's bedroom. He placed his hand on her back and felt the quick rhythm of her heartbeat.

"Claire, sweetie?" he whispered. "I need you to wake up."

He shook her slightly, and she rolled her head from one side to the other.

"C'mon, sweetie," he said, reaching for her. He slowly scooped her into his arms, thinking how light she seemed. In just a few years, he would no longer be able to do this.

She moaned slightly. "Daddy?" she whispered.

He smiled, thinking she was the most beautiful child in the world.

"It's time to go."

Her eyes were still closed as she answered, "Okay, Daddy."

He sat her on the bed, slipped her rubber boots over the thick pajamas she'd worn to bed, and draped her jacket around her shoulders, watching as she slipped her arms into the sleeves. He slid on her mittens, then her hat, and picked her up again.

"Daddy?"

"Yes?"

She yawned. "Where are we going?"

"We're going to take a ride," Jeremy said, carrying her through the living room. As he adjusted her in his arms, he patted his pocket, making sure he had the keys.

"In the car?"

"Yes," he said, "in the car."

She looked around, her face showing the youthful confusion that he'd come to adore. She turned toward the window.

"But it's dark," she said.

"Yes," Jeremy said again. "And it's foggy, too."

Outside, the air was crisp and moist, and the lonely

stretch of road that passed by his house looked as if a cloud had been dropped upon it. In the sky, neither the moon nor the stars were evident, as if the universe itself had been erased. He shifted Claire in his arms so that he could reach for his keys, then placed her in the booster seat.

"It's scary out here," she said. "Like on *Scooby-Doo*."

"Kind of," he admitted, buckling her in. "But we'll be safe."

"I know," she said.

"I love you," he added. "Do you know how much?"

She rolled her eyes as if she were an actress. "More than there are fishes in the sea and higher than the moon. I know."

"Ah," Jeremy said.

"It's cold," she added.

"I'll turn the heater on just as soon as I start the car."

"Are we going to Grandma's?"

"No," he said. "She's sleeping. We're going to a special place."

Beyond the window of the car, the streets of Boone Creek were quiet, and the town seemed to be asleep. With the exception of porch lights, most of the homes were dark. Jeremy drove slowly, navigating carefully through the fog-covered country hills.

After pulling to a stop in front of Cedar Creek Cemetery, he removed a flashlight from the glove compartment. He unbuckled Claire from her car seat and headed into the cemetery, Claire's hand wrapped in his own.

Checking his watch, Jeremy noted that it was past midnight, but he knew he still had a few minutes. Claire was holding the flashlight, and as he walked beside her, he could hear the rustle of leaves underfoot. The fog made it impossible to see more than a few steps in any direction, but it had taken Claire only an instant to realize where they were.

"Are we going to see Mommy?" she asked. "Because you forgot to bring flowers."

In the past, when he brought her here they always brought flowers. More than four years ago, Lexie had been buried next to her parents. It had required a special dispensation from the county commissioners to have her buried here, but Mayor Gherkin had forced it through at the request of Doris and Jeremy.

Jeremy paused. "You'll see," he promised.

"Then what are we doing here?"

He squeezed her hand. "You'll see," he repeated.

They walked a few steps in silence. "Can we see if the flowers are still there?"

He smiled, pleased that she cared and also that coming here in the middle of the night didn't frighten her. "Of course we can, sweetheart."

Ever since the funeral, Jeremy visited the cemetery at least once every couple of weeks, usually bringing Claire with him. It was here she learned about her mother; he told her of their visits to the top of Riker's Hill, told her that it was here he'd first known he loved Lexie, told her that he'd moved here because he couldn't imagine a life without her. He talked mainly as a way of keeping Lexie alive in his memory, doubting whether Claire was even listening. Yet even though she was not yet five, she could now recite his stories as if she'd lived them. The last time he'd brought her here, she'd listened quietly and seemed almost withdrawn by the time they'd left. "I wish she didn't die," she'd said on their way back to the car. That had happened a little after Thanksgiving, and he wondered whether it had anything to do with her nightmares. They hadn't started until a month later, but he couldn't be sure.

Trudging through the moist and chilly night, they finally reached the graves. Claire aimed the flashlight toward them. He could see the names James and Claire; beside them was the name Lexie Marsh and the flowers they'd placed in front of the grave on the day before Christmas.

After leading Claire to the spot where he and Lexie had first seen the lights, he sat down and pulled his daughter onto his lap. Jeremy remembered the story Lexie had told about her parents and the nightmares she'd had as a child, and Claire, sensing something special was about to happen, barely moved.

Claire was Lexie's daughter in more ways than he realized, for when the lights began their dance across the sky, he felt Claire leaning against him. Claire, whose great-grandmother assured her that ghosts were real, stared transfixed at the show taking place before her. It was only a feeling, but as he held her, he knew that Claire would have no more nightmares. Tonight they would end, and Claire would sleep peacefully. No, he couldn't explain it—and later he would be proven correct—

but in the last few years, he'd learned that science didn't have all the answers.

The lights, as always, were a celestial wonder, rising and falling in spectacular fashion, and Jeremy found himself mesmerized along with his daughter. Tonight the lights seemed to last a few seconds longer than normal, and in the brightness, he could see the expression of awe on his daughter's face.

"Is it Mama?" she finally asked. Her voice was no louder than the wind in the leaves above them.

He smiled, his throat tight. In the quiet of the night, it seemed as if they were the only two people in the world. Jeremy took a long breath, remembering Lexie, believing that she was here with them, and knowing that if he could see her now, she would be smiling with joy, content in the knowledge that her daughter and husband were going to be okay.

"Yes," he said, holding her tight. "I think she wanted to meet you."